"FLAME OF FLAMES, I SUMMON YE!"

"No! No! Stop! Stop! Or the Flame will kill you!"

"Yea, verily, verily," roared Drake, working his enemy's protest into his act. "Bring down the Flame!"

And Drake raised his arms to the heavens.

There was a crash of thunder. The sky went green. Blue lightning writhed across the heavens in patterns like those a thread of water makes as it scrawls down a crooked stick. Then the clouds were gashed open by a Flame. It descended slowly, a monstrous, whirling column of angry purple and crackling red. Down from the heights it came, until its base stood before Drake and its heights in the heavens.

Drake had unknowingly called forth the magic. Now he could only stand before it, praying it would not consume him. . . .

(0451)

WORLDS AT WAR

- ☐ **THE LOST REGIMENT #1: RALLY CRY by William Forstchen.** Storm-swept through a space-time warp, they were catapulted through Civil War America into a future world of horrifying conflict, where no human was free. (450078—$4.95)

- ☐ **THE LOST REGIMENT #2: THE UNION FOREVER by William R. Forstchen.** In this powerful military adventure, soldiers from the past are time-space-warped to a warring world of aliens. "Some of the best adventure writing in years!"—*Science Fiction Chronicle* (450604—$4.95)

- ☐ **DAWN'S UNCERTAIN LIGHT by Neal Barrett Jr.** In a devestated, post-holocaust future filled with Wild West savagery, civil war, and irradiated mutant humans, orphan Howie Ryder grows up fast while searching to rescue his sister from an inhuman doom inflicted by a government gone awry. (160746—$3.95)

- ☐ **JADE DARCY AND THE AFFAIR OF HONOR by Stephen Goldin and Mary Mason.** Book one in *The Rehumanization of Jade Darcy*. Darcy was rough, tough, computer-enhanced—and the only human mercenary among myriad alien races on the brink of battle. She sought to escape from her human past on a suicide assignment against the most violent alien conquerors space had ever known. (156137—$3.50)

- ☐ **STARCRUISER SHENANDOAH: SQUADRON ALERT by Roland J. Green.** The United Federation of Starworlds and its most powerful enemy, the Freeworld States Alliance, must prepare for a war they hoped would never start. (161564—$3.95)

Prices slightly higher in Canada.

Buy them at your local bookstore or use this convenient coupon for ordering.

NEW AMERICAN LIBRARY
P.O. Box 999, Bergenfield, New Jersey 07621

Please send me the books I have checked above. I am enclosing $_____ (please add $1.00 to this order to cover postage and handling). Send check or money order—no cash or C.O.D.'s. Prices and numbers are subject to change without notice.

Name_____

Address_____

City _____ State _____ Zip Code _____

Allow 4-6 weeks for delivery.
This offer, prices and numbers are subject to change without notice.

WIZARD WAR CHRONICLES

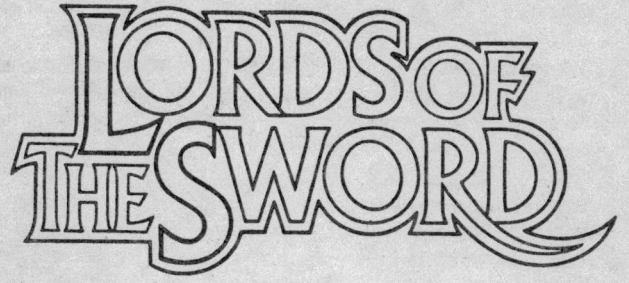

HUGH COOK

A ROC BOOK

ROC
Published by the Penguin Group
Penguin Books USA Inc., 375 Hudson Street,
New York, New York 10014, U.S.A.
Penguin Books Ltd, 27 Wrights Lane,
London W8 5TZ, England
Penguin Books Australia Ltd, Ringwood,
Victoria, Australia
Penguin Books Canada Ltd, 2801 John Street,
Markham, Ontario, Canada L3R 1B4
Penguin Books (N.Z.) Ltd, 182-190 Wairau Road,
Auckland 10, New Zealand

Penguin Books Ltd, Registered Offices:
Harmondsworth, Middlesex, England
Originally published in Great Britain by Colin Smythe Limited.

First Roc Printing, March, 1991
10 9 8 7 6 5 4 3 2 1

Copyright © Hugh Cook, 1988
All rights reserved

 ROC IS A TRADEMARK OF NEW AMERICAN LIBRARY, A DIVISION OF PENGUIN BOOKS USA INC.

Printed in the United States of America

Without limiting the rights under copyright reserved above, no part of this publication may be reproduced, stored in or introduced into a retrieval system, or transmitted, in any form, or by any means (electronic, mechanical, photocopying, recording, or otherwise), without the prior written permission of both the copyright owner and the above publisher of this book.

BOOKS ARE AVAILABLE AT QUANTITY DISCOUNTS WHEN USED TO PROMOTE PRODUCTS OR SERVICES. FOR INFORMATION PLEASE WRITE TO PREMIUM MARKETING DIVISION, PENGUIN BOOKS USA INC., 375 HUDSON STREET, NEW YORK, NEW YORK 10014.

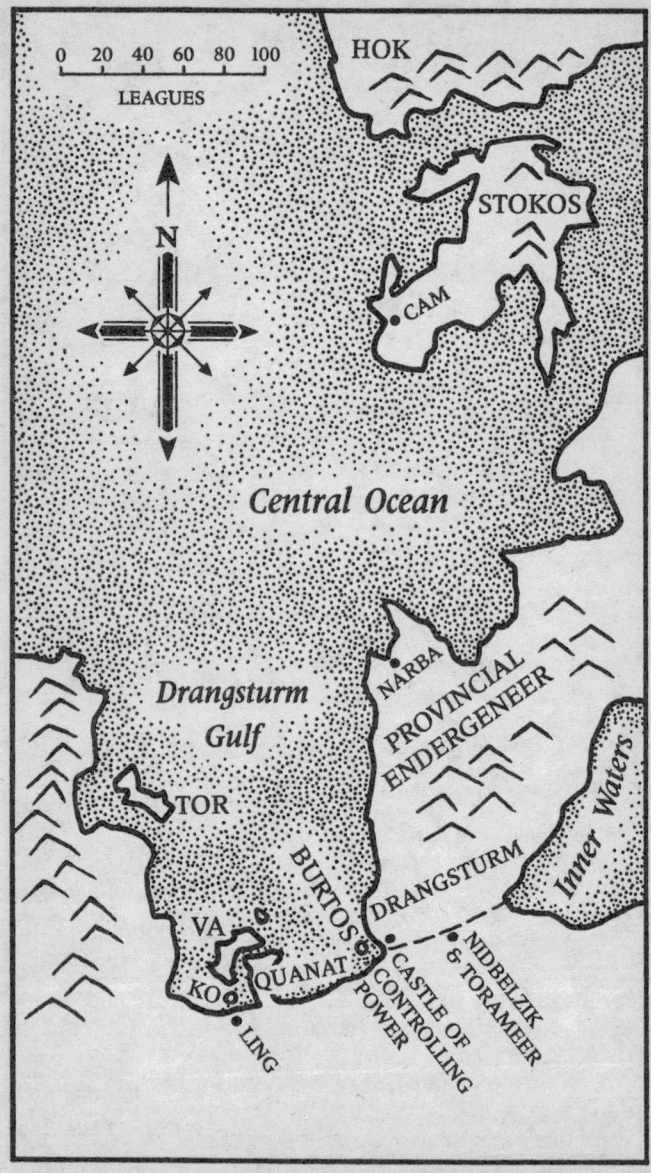

From the Memoirs of Miphon

My name is Miphon, and I am a wizard of Nin. We live in times of great turmoil in which the very fate of the world itself is uncertain. Perhaps the world we know will fall to ruin; perhaps the Confederation will meet with a final Destruction; perhaps the outlines of this most familiar world of mine will become blurred beyond recognition by the workings of legend and myth.

Accordingly, some prefatory remarks are in order. So let me note that this history opens on a time when the great continent of Argan was divided in two by the flame trench Drangsturm. South of Drangsturm dwelt the monsters of the Swarms, beasts of uncouth make distantly commanded by an occult entity known as the Skull of the Deep South.

Drangsturm was a gulf of fire built and maintained by the wizards of the Confederation. Thanks to the unrelenting vigilance of those wizards, the lands to the north of Drangsturm were able to enjoy peace and prosperity.

But Drangsturm was doomed in time to fall and fail; and the lands of peace and prosperity were doomed to be invaded by the monsters of the Swarms; and many things fair and precious were doomed to fall to ruin in the disasters of a great age of darkness.

In its time of peril, Argan would look to its heroes, and so it is fitting that I begin this account by telling something of the making and the shaping of one of the greatest of those heroes, the mighty Lord Dreldragon.

Now, the great Lord Dreldragon was destined to sue for the hand of a princess; and to court one of the most ravishing women of the ages, a queenly beauty from the far-fabled Ebrell Islands; and to dare his blade against the mightiest of dangers in the company of the mightiest of heroes; and to enter, in the fullness of his destiny, into the household of the great and magnanimous Arabin, the beneficent patron under whose protection these memoirs are being written and published.

Yet while Lord Dreldragon was born to a great destiny, his beginnings were humble. Even in his earliest years, Lord Dreldragon had intimations of the great destiny which awaited him, yet in the sturdiness of his youth he gladly bent his hand to the great labor of iron and of steel.

Know you the iron?

And know you the steel?

Iron is the strength of the rock, and steel is the rock made one with the tree. This at least is how the swordsmiths of Stokos describe the order of things. And certainly it is known that they get iron from the smelting of rock; and blend that iron with charcoal taken from the tree; though precisely how this charcoal is combined with this iron to make steel is a great secret, and one which the swordsmiths have never confessed to the world at large. Nor can I confess that secret here, for my own expertise lies with the exercise of my wizardry and the cure of the ills of the Flesh.

It was with iron and with steel that Lord Dreldragon worked in the early days of his youth, long years ago on the abovementioned island of Stokos. In those days, our hero-in-making gave expression to the dutiful humility of his youth by allowing himself to be called by a humble and familiar name, that name being Drake Douay.

Now, it happens that the young Lord Dreldragon was propelled toward his destiny by an unsought and entirely unexpected encounter with a disreputable gentleman-adventurer.

It happened as follows.

On the evening of his sixteenth birthday, the young

Lord Dreldragon celebrated in a restrained and dignified fashion which bespeaks an uncommon maturity. After exchanging one or two innocent kisses with a young woman with whom he was somewhat enamored, he abandoned that young maiden to the custody of her chaperone, then proceeded to enjoy a modest repast in the company of some other young gentlemen.

Unfortunately this quiet evening was soon disrupted by the hooliganism of some of the more disorderly elements of the lower socio-economic orders, and so Lord Dreldragon wisely decided to make an early night of it, and so said his good nights and withdrew to the forge, in which he was then serving as an apprentice swordsmith. But it appears that Lord Dreldragon's master of the moment had decided to make an early night of it, for Lord Dreldragon found the forge locked and barred against him, and so he sought and found modest accommodations by the waterfront. . . .

1

Iron: metal made on Stokos by smelting the local hematite, a blood-red ore containing 70 parts in 100 of iron.

Steel: iron alloyed with carbon. Made on Stokos by baking iron with charcoal in a sealed pot kept at red heat for eight days, then melting the "blister steel" thus produced in covered crucibles, skimming off the slag.

Firelight steel: fabric of the masterswords of Stokos; consists of interwoven layers of high carbon and low carbon steel; represents the height of the swordsmith's art.

Drake Douay had his sixteenth birthday two months before the start of the year Khmar 17. That night he celebrated by getting:
 (a) laid;
 (b) drunk;
 (c) into an enormous amount of trouble.

At midnight he was trapped in a cul-de-sac by four coal miners, two dogs and an angry butcher's boy, all of them out for his blood.

However, Drake was a practiced survivor. He escaped with nothing worse than bruised ribs, a broken toe, and a nick in his left ear where a dagger had scratched him in the skirmish.

Shortly afterward, he stood outside the temple of the

Demon Hagon, beating his fists against his naked chest and howling like a werewolf. Guards gave chase, but Drake lost them in the twisting back-streets of Cam. After that, he was so tired he decided it was time for bed. But, to his surprise, he found the door of Hardhammer Forge barred against him.

"Wake up, Muck, you grouty old octopus!" bawled Drake.

But got no response, which was scarcely surprising, since Gouda Much was nine-parts deaf and slept as soundly as a drunken crocodile quietly digesting a bellyful of plague-bloated rats.

Drake threw stones on the roof, then shouted, sang and howled, until one of the neighbors opened an attic window and threw a cat at him. Whereupon Drake decided on a tactical withdrawal.

Come dawn, he crawled out from underneath the boat where he had slept away the last of the night, yawned, grinned, stretched, hawked, then spat.

"Ahoy there!" called someone in very bad Galish.

Who was it?

A coal miner? The butcher's boy? The ruffian he had knocked out after last night's gambling quarrel?

It was none of the above, but a man rowing ashore from an evil-looking barque anchored out in the harbor of Cam. The ship's sails were furled, but, even so, Drake could see they were black.

"Ahoy yourself!" called Drake. "What ship are you from?"

"Never mind the ship," said the man, bringing the boat alongside some waterfront steps.

"Do you want a woman?" said Drake. "I can get you one cheap."

The stranger did not answer immediately, but secured the dinghy to a bollard with a painter, then came scrambling up the steps. He was an ill-favored fellow with coarse foreign features, a thick neck, a barrel chest, rough-cut black hair and a shaggy black beard.

"Who be you?" he said.

"Narda Narkin," said Drake Douay, answering at random.

Some mighty queer people came into Cam from time to time, so it was only common sense for Drake to reserve his true name.

"Pleased to meet you then, Narda Narkin," said the stranger. "I be Atsimo Andranovory. I search for three men. Rumor has them in Cam."

"Their names?" said Drake.

"Whale Mike, Ish Ulpin and Bucks Cat."

"I know them well," said Drake, who had never heard of them, but thought himself unlikely to profit by confessing ignorance. "I can direct you to their very door—for a price. What's it worth?"

"As much as the air between your lips," said Atsimo Andranovory, putting a hand to the hilt of the cutlass he wore at his belt.

Drake glanced around. The waterfront was deserted. His bargaining position was poor.

"Take the street which leads from the southern end of the waterfront," said Drake, pointing. "Take the third turning on the left then the second on the right, and it's the third house along."

"Thank you kindly," said Andranovory.

And, with perfect faith in these directions, set off. Whereupon Drake turned in the opposite direction, whistling a jaunty tune as he made for Hardhammer Forge.

It was going to be another fine day. The air was cool, calm and clean. The sky was an enormous ascension of blue, flaunting banners of white cloud. Drake was happy, despite fatigue and headache. He was young, he was strong—and everything was going his way.

On reaching the forge, Drake was dismayed by an enormous heap of dusty black coal which had been delivered the previous evening. It would have to be put in sacks then stacked in the cellar. That was apprentice work, hence Drake's work.

"Such is life," said Drake.

And slipped inside.

Hands in pockets, he leaned against a wall, looking around as if he owned the place. He breathed in heat and coal dust, and smirked. He was sixteen. He knew it all. He was ready for the world.

"What are you doing here?" yelled Gouda Muck.

"Why, I work here, don't I?" said Drake.

"Work!" screamed old man Muck. "That's a joke! You've never done a day's decent work in your life. You're such an ugly little runt you couldn't work if you wanted to!"

Drake was unhurt by the word "ugly." If there was such a thing as male beauty, then he, with his athlete's build and perfect muscle definition, was beautiful— and he knew it. But "runt"—now that stung. For Drake was fearfully close to being short, which was disastrous on Stokos, where the fashion was to be as tall as possible.

To annoy Muck, Drake made no answer, but simply whistled the lilting tune of that ditty which starts as follows:

Two whores and a sheepdog were tupping one day
When a cat and a virgin came dancing that way.

"Stop whistling!" shouted Muck. "You should be ashamed of yourself. You look like a walking rubbish heap."

Muck was exaggerating. But, in truth, Drake Douay was not a pretty sight. Or a pretty smell, either. Unwashed, largely unslept and decidedly dishevelled. Shirtless. Blood, dirt, paint, rust and tomato sauce splattered across his torso. Dried blood in his blond hair. Breath like a brewery.

"How did you get in such a state?" said Muck. "Look at yourself!"

"Can't," said Drake. "Got no mirror."

"Just as well," said Muck. "You'd frighten any self-respecting mirror to death."

"Mirrors can be frightened?" said Drake. "This sounds like experience speaking!"

At that, Muck picked up a beautiful chunk of specular iron with a hand which was old, gnarled, freckled with liver spots, and cunning with long experience. Muck heaved the rock at his apprentice. Drake ducked. The missile hit the wall, shattering into 376 pieces. Each fragment was made of crystallized hematite: for such is the nature of specular iron.

"Man, don't do that," said Drake. "This ducking business makes my head hurt."

"Then cease your cheek," said Muck, picking up a sword which he brandished so wildly that Drake feared for his head. "Tell me—what's this?"

Even inside the forge, the weapon glittered like an eagle's eye. It was a mastersword made of firelight steel. And not just any old mastersword, either, but the masterwork Muck had made many dusty years ago to win entry to the swordsmith's guild.

"That?" said Drake, sneering at the blade. "That's a giant's toothpick or a splinter of last month's moon, for all I know."

"It's a sword! And where should you be? At sword!"

"Oh? Is it Temple Day again?"

"Yes," said Muck, with satisfaction.

On these occasions, which happened every tenth day, everything at the temple of Hagon was half-price.

"What say," said Drake. "You set me free for the day. Just this once."

"No!" said Gouda Muck, who delighted in forcing his apprentices to labor extra hard on Temple Day.

"You're wrong to deny me religion," said Drake.

"I know you've got a sister in the temple," said Muck, putting down his mastersword. "I can't see you suffering too much denial. Why, I can smell a woman on you now!"

"That's not a woman," said Drake promptly. "That's a dog!"

"Then she's a dog with very poor taste," said Muck, not caring whether Drake's claim was literal or metaphorical.

"Graf begrik," muttered Drake.

"What was that?" said Muck sharply, suspecting— correctly—that Drake had just said something lewd.

"I said where's Dragon Tooth?" said Drake, scanning the sword rack, which held second-rate blades suitable for apprentice use.

"Yot's got it."

"Oh, but that's my favorite!"

"Don't worry, you've no monsters to kill today," said Muck, with a heavy attempt at sarcasm.

"No monsters?" said Drake. "Only because you're off-limits!"

Muck swung at him with a poker. But Drake, who had expected as much, ducked. And Muck's boot caught Drake hard near the base of his spine. The blow with the poker had been only a feint.

"Ow!" said Drake. "That hurt!"

"It was meant to," said Muck, picking up a strange sword which Drake had never seen before. "Here, take this. It's just come in. It's from Pribble's estate, in payment of a debt he owed me."

The strange sword was big and heavy, but Drake had the muscles to handle the weight. The blade balanced nicely.

"Mind you investigate it before use!" said Muck.

"That I will," said Drake, and, naked blade resting lightly on his shoulder, strolled out of the forge.

"Move yourself!" shouted Muck. "You haven't got all day!"

So Drake got the hustle on, at least until he was round the corner.

Drake swung his sword. Liberated from the gloom of the forge, it glittered in the daylight. He danced on the cobblestones between two rows of whitewashed buildings, stabbing at ghosts with his vorpal blade.

What should he call it?

"Warwolf," perhaps.

That was scarcely original, as many fabled swords and heroes bore that name. But Drake had the temperament of a craftsman rather than that of an artist; he preferred utility to originality any day of the year.

"I name thee Warwolf," he said. "Too long hast thou lingered amidst dust and debts. Thou shouldst have had ruler like me beforehand."

Then, whistling, he began to investigate the brave sword Warwolf.

By using it.

First he tried to lop the head off a stray cat—but it

was too quick for him. Then he slashed a branch off a stunted little tree trying to grow in a big streetside stone pot. That was reckless, since all potted trees in Cam were under the protection of King Tor. But it was still early morning, so few people were about in the streets to bear witness.

Rounding another corner, Drake was startled to be confronted by a watermelon stand. A massive, old, unpainted stand of weathered gray wood, heaped high with watermelons. This fearsome apparition made Drake entirely forget about his hangover.

"Not a watermelon stand!" he gasped. "Nay! Say not! But no! It is! My eyes fail! My blood turns to water!"

But, regardless of failing eyes and watery blood, Drake stood his ground. And challenged his fell foe.

"Stand aside!" he said. "Aside, I say! Or it shall go ill with you."

The watermelon stand, undaunted by this threat, made no effort to get out of his way. Drake knew his peril. For, truly, in all the annals of heroism and romance, there is no account of any man ever daring battle with a watermelon stand and living to tell the tale.

"Die, hell-fiend!" gritted Drake.

And hewed like a hero. *Thwap!* The nearest watermelon fell dead at his feet.

"Shalt fear the dreaded Drake Douay hereafter," snarled he, menacing a particularly big brute of a watermelon.

The monster's skin was a thick, tough, alien green, stippled with patterns of sunlight yellow. A challenge indeed! But Drake the Doughty stabbed with a strength against which even the strongest armor could not avail.

He wounded his enemy.

Ichor dripped from the wound.

Drake stabbed again—for, as is well known, the watermelon has neither heart nor liver, nor any other vital organ, and thus is seldom killed by a single stab wound.

"What's this?" said Drake. "It will not die! Could it be that I am face to face with an immortal?"

He drew his sword back, intending to strike the most awesome blow imaginable.

At that moment, the watermelon seller came roaring out of a nearby tavern, screaming threats and abuse. Drake snatched up half a watermelon and sprinted away with this trophy. He went flying up a side-street, which was steep, narrow and radically kinked.

Drake tore round one corner then whipped round another. The street steep, still rising. Another corner. He saw a fully laden coal cart waiting uphill. He dug in his heels for a final burst of speed. Gaining the coal cart, he kicked the chocks away from its wheels.

Panting harshly, Drake stood watching as the cart went rumbling downhill. Lumps of coal jumped for freedom as the cart jolted over the cobblestones. It was gaining speed.

"Look out below!" screamed Drake. "Runaway cart!"

Then the cart hit a kink in the street. It smashed into a wall. the wall shattered. The cart burst asunder. Coal dust exploded into the air. The wall collapsed. Until that moment, it had been supporting a roof. A landslide of skyblue tiles slithered from the roof and shattered in the street.

"Oh, great stuff, great stuff!" said Drake, trying to pant and laugh at the same time.

He would have clapped his hands for joy and delight—only that would have meant dropping both sword and watermelon.

"Zooma floragin!" screamed a manic figure, bursting out of the building which the cart had wrecked. "Thamana lok!"

"That's not polite," muttered Drake.

And, indeed, it was not polite at all—it was low and filthy gutter language.

As the demented figure gave chase, Drake fled.

Once he had lost his pursuer, Drake munched down the juicy pink flesh of the watermelon, then strolled along with a mouthful of pips, spitting them out one at a time. Which took skill, but he had been practicing for as long as he could remember (and stealing watermelons for that long, too).

Splip! Stlip!

Watermelon seeds flew, with considerable accuracy, through every open window he passed.

That was fun.

But, all too soon, he arrived at the sword field, which was not a field at all, but a dusty courtyard where, usually, three dozen apprentices would have been practicing sword.

"Bugger," said Drake.

The sun was getting up. The excitement of the coal cart crash had worn off. His legs were tired, his boots heavy. He was remembering his headache. It felt bad. How had he ever forgotten it? A wave of weariness rolled over him. He wanted to be in bed. But his bed was in the loft over the forge, so Muck would know exactly where to find him if he tried skiving off. Holding his sword by the pommel, Drake entered the sword field, letting the blade's point trail behind him in the dust.

Today there was nobody present but an instructor, and Sully Yot. All the other apprentices had been released by their masters so they could enjoy the delights of Temple Day.

"Ah, there you are, young Dreldragon!" said the instructor. Then, seeing what Drake was doing: "Get that sword out of the dust before I shove it up your arse! Get your arse over here! Get working!"

"Hey, man," said Drake. "Give us a break, why don't you? How about you come to the temple with us? I'll buy you a beer, man. A woman, even. Muck will never know different."

In reply, the instructor booted Drake in the backside, then set him to work with Yot, making the pair of them practice a two-man kata.

The swordsmiths' guild believed apprentices should learn weapon skills, the better to be able to make a decent killing blade. But they allowed no rough-and-tumble play with wasters.

As the instructor was fond of saying: "We are not teaching you how to brawl it out on a battlefield, but to learn how weight, length and balance dictate utility."

Nevertheless, sword training was deadly serious, done with bare blades and no protection. A single mistake could wound, mutilate or kill. However, though dangerous, it could almost have been mistaken for a kind of dance—for it was strictly a no-contact affair. Every thrust, fake, step, jump and counter was prearranged.

Drake, after years of this, was thoroughly bored with the rituals of the one-man, two-man and multiple-encounter katas. He longed to make steel chime with steel. But, when Yot struck and Drake parried, both halted their blades the instant before contact. For, if ever edge met edge, a sword might be notched, bent, or even broken.

"I need a drink," said Drake, after the first kata.

"Booze is the last thing you need," said the instructor.

"I didn't meant liquor, I mean water."

"Why would you be needing that? Because you've got the dry horrors, I suppose. And whose fault is that? You young kids! You shouldn't be allowed to drink."

"Liquor is holy," said Drake. "The High Priest says so."

"Steel is also holy."

"Who said that?" demanded Drake.

"I did!" said the instructor.

And kick-started his recalcitrant student.

Drake felt as if he was breathing a mixture of thorns and ashes. As the sun lifted itself above the wall of the sword field, his head began to throb. Yot—lanky, wart-faced, a vapid smile on his lips—was just dancing through the motions, holding his sword lightly, loosely, as if its hilt were a little girl's hand. How come Yot had all that height, when he had no decent use for it?

Round and round they went, their shadows scuffling

in the dust. And suddenly Drake could stand it no longer, and, with an almighty sweep, brought the flat of his blade crashing into the flat of Dragon's Tooth, knocking that sword right out of Yot's hand.

"Gaaa!" screamed Drake.

Hacking at his disarmed enemy.

He tried to halt his blade as it reached Yot's skin. But, despite all Drake's skill, Yot got a cut on the side of his neck. It was tiny—no more than a boy would get from scratching away a pimple. But Yot touched it, then, seeing blood on his fingers, fainted clean away. Yot had never liked the sight of blood—especially his own.

"Dogs, pox and buggeration!" said the instructor. "Get out of my sight!"

"As you wish," said Drake.

And strode toward the exit, weapon in hand.

"Hey!" said the instructor. "Come back! You've left something behind!"

"What, Yot? He'll come on his own two feet once he gets his wits back."

"No, ninny. This!"

And the instructor held up for Drake's inspection a strange little bit of hooked iron which he had fished out of the dust.

"What's that?" said Drake.

"It's a letter, you illiterate son of an octopus. The letter Açcøwæae, in fact."

"Well where did that come from?"

"Out of your sword, moron. Look!"

And, looking, Drake saw an indentation in the flat of his sword which precisely matched the shape of the bit of iron which the instructor alleged was the letter Açcøwæ.

"Look closely," said the instructor. "There's other iron letters in the steel. See? They spell out a word. A foreign word, yes, in one of the languages of Provincial Endergeneer. I won't tax your brain by making you learn it. But I'll tell you what it means. It means 'think before using!' "

And, having warned Drake that he would be taking

LORDS OF THE SWORD 21

the matter up with Gouda Muck, the instructor bid him good day.

Back at the forge, Muck was furious.

"Well, I wasn't to know," said Drake. "I didn't even know there were iron-bits there to start with."

"I told you to Investigate!" said Muck. "Haven't you learnt anything?"

"As much as I've been taught," said Drake.

Muck stared at him, speechless, face saying:

"¿¡!?"

Once Muck had recovered his voice, he used it to baste his apprentice nicely, then gave him a lecture on iron inlay.

"It sounds right fancy stuff," said Drake. "But how come we never do it here?"

"Because the best steel needs no adornment," said Muck. "Watch close. I'll show you how to replace this missing iron letter. We'll start from scratch."

And Muck showed Drake how to make a new letter by twisting bits or iron wire together. Then, with the blade white-hot, the cold iron was hammered into place.

"Now," said Muck. "We take the blade to welding heat and do just a little extra hammering to make sure the iron inlay stays there for a lifetime. What's welding heat, boy?"

"Don't know," said Drake.

"It's about a thousand degrees on the Saglag Scale, where zero is the temperature at which shlug freezes, and fifty is the temperature at which that thixotropic fluid known as dikle suddenly trembles into fluid. What does thixotropic mean, boy?"

"It means the heat at which tilps jiffle," said Drake.

Which was obscene, and uncalled for, and untrue to boot, and earned him a slap around the ears, that stung.

But it was a mere flea-bite compared to the beating he got the next day, after Gouda Muck had heard from the sword field instructor (whose truths conflicted somewhat with the tale Drake had brought back to the forge), from a man who sold watermelons, and from the Protector of the Royal Trees.

After the beating, Drake, somewhat tearful, confronted Muck.

"All you do is kick me and hit me," said Drake.

"Well, what else can I do?" said Muck. "You won't listen, you won't learn, you won't do as you're told."

"You could teach me how to make swords," said Drake. "That's what I'm here for. I've been here four years, and what have you taught me? Levil Norkin is only fifteen, and he made his first sword a year ago."

"Then maybe he'll finish up as a swordsmith," said Gouda Muck.

"You mean I won't?" said Drake in dismay.

"You don't get to be a swordsmith by spending your apprenticeship boozing, fighting, wenching and gambling," said Muck. "Have you never thought of that?"

Drake made no reply.

"Well?" said Muck.

"I never got much encouragement," said Drake.

"It's your life, not mine," said Muck. "You're not a child! Your life is what you make it."

"Do I—"

"Do you still have a chance? You may have. A slim chance, mind! But a chance, all the same. It really depends what you want out of life. Do you want to be a swordsmith? Or do you want to go back and live as your parents do?"

Drake thought of his parents and the life they lived, cutting coal out of the cliffs, gathering seaweed, fishing off the Wrecking Rocks. No, that was not what he wanted. Not at all.

"I . . . I love steel," said Drake, in a slow and sober voice. "There's . . . there's a special light about steel. It shines. I like—"

"Spare me the poetry!" said Muck. "I'll tell you what. If you promise to work hard, really hard, I'll let you start your first sword tomorrow."

"Really?" said Drake.

"When did I ever speak in jest?" said Muck.

"Done!" said Drake. "It's a bargain!"

"Right," said Muck. "Now hustle off, or you'll be late for your theory class."

As Drake sped away to his theory class, he exulted. So he was going to start on the real stuff at last! After all these years of sweeping, shovelling, pumping the bellows, grinding, sharpening and patching. He was going to be a real swordsmith, and make his own blade.

Wow!

"Great stuff!" said Drake. "Great stuff!"

And then, in two more years he would be a swordsmith himself, with apprentices of his own to beat about the ears.

Or so he thought.

In practice, it did not prove that easy.

For, half-way through his theory class, guards burst into the classroom.

"Dreldragon Drakedon Douay," said their leader. "Where are you?"

"Here," said Drake.

"You're under arrest."

"Arrest?" said Drake. "Whatever for?"

"Don't ask question. Come with us!"

And Drake was marched through the streets of Cam to the Iron Palace, where he was thrown into a cell, and told he would stand trial before King Tor in the morning.

"What have I done wrong?" wailed Drake.

"Boy, don't ask me," said his gaoler. "But unless you've been very, very good of late, you can expect to get your head chopped off tomorrow. The king's lately been in the worst of tempers imaginable."

Which was bad news indeed. For King Tor was an ogre—and the temper of an ogre is never the sweetest of things at the best of times.

2

Name: Parry Iklemass Tinklebeth Terrorjaw Tor. (NB: by law, none may address the king by any of his three first names, on pain of death.)

Birthplace: Cam.

Occupation: king.

Status: absolute ruler of Stokos.

Description: an ogre twice man-height; width almost equal to height; elephant-style ears; tusks jutting downward from upper jaw; age 54; hair black; eyes blue; six fingers on each hand; gray skin patterned like that of a crocodile.

Residence: the Iron Palace of Cam.

When night came, Drake hunched up in a corner of his cell and tried to get to sleep. It was almost impossible. The darkness echoed with the crash of great doors, the tramp of iron-shod boots, the garbled intercourse of coarse voices, occasional screams and the racket of hyena-flavored laughter.

Sitting in darkness, breathing an ineffable jail-stench in which the reek of blocked drains predominated, Drake imagined he heard rats moving in his cell on razor-clawed feet. He thought he heard them sharpening their teeth against the cold tombstone-sized slabs of the floor, At last he fell asleep and dreamed—

briefly—of the sword he would make with the help of Gouda Muck.

He woke to find things crawling over his face. He beat at them, knocking them into the dark. Spiders? Cockroaches? Something went whirling round his cell with a staccato clitter-clatter of wings.

"Grief," muttered Drake.

And found himself unable to regain the realms of sleep.

When morning came, the gaoler served breakfast, which was a jug of water and a bowl of fish chowder.

"What happens now?" said Drake.

"Now? Why, your trial starts shortly."

"Good," said Drake.

He was glad, for a prompt trial meant he would soon be out of here. Excellent! He was in a hurry to return to Hardhammer Forge. He wanted to get down to work, yes, to start on his first sword. Surely King Tor would let him go. What had he done wrong? Nothing serious.

Drake thought Tor might even give him some compensation for false arrest and wrongful imprisonment.

Yes.

"Rise and shine," said the gaoler, interrupting Drake's calculations of probable compensation. "We're going to the Iron Hall."

Shortly Drake was shown into the Iron Hall of the Iron Palace. He had never been in a building so large, or so full of noise and people. Once there, sitting on a hard wooden bench, watching King Tor administer justice, Drake swiftly began to change his mind about his prospects.

The ruler of Stokos seemed to take law and life very seriously indeed.

Again and again Tor cried:

"Off with his head!"

It seemed to be the king's favorite punishment.

Pleas for mercy did no good. Neither did grovelling. One particularly abject petitioner crawled to the throne and started licking the king's clawed feet. The snivelling fool was promptly kicked to death for his cowardice.

"Be bold," muttered Drake to Drake.

"What did you say?" demanded a guard.

"I said, funny how there's so much iron in this place," said Drake.

"Oh," said the guard. "That's easy enough explained. Things human-built tend to break when an ogre gets hold of them. The king's always complaining about how fragile everything is."

"Oh," said Drake, eyeing the king.

Who sat on a throne of black iron. Wearing leather trousers and a leather jacket, both studded with iron. Refreshments on an iron table beside him: live frogs in a huge bowl of cast iron. Blood in a chalice of wrought iron. A heap of mules' eyes on a plate of pig iron. At his feet, a gryphon.

"What," said Drake, "am I charged with?"

"You expect a bill of particulars?" said the guard, with a laugh. "We're not so stupid. If you knew what you were charged with, you'd be inventing lies and fantasizing alibis right now. Wouldn't you?"

"I'd be doing no such thing," said Drake, indignantly. "I'm a humble, law-abiding apprentice. And very religious into the bargain."

"We'll see about that," said the guard. "Your case is next."

Upon which King Tor pronounced sentence on his latest victim:

"Cut off the top of his head then feed him his own brains."

Drake shivered.

And an orderly shouted:

"Dreldragon Drakedon Douay! Be upstanding! Advance to receive justice!"

Drake got to his feet and strode forward with as much of a swagger as he could manage. His body was alive with frantic pulses. His heart was asking for out. His arsehole was quivering. His knees trembled.

He halted, ten paces in front of the king. Set his feet shoulder-width apart. And tensed the muscles in his legs, to keep them from shaking. He eyed the king's gryphon uneasily. The brute appeared to be asleep, its purple wings folded against its tawny lionskin body. On its great hooked eagle's beak was what looked suspiciously like dried blood.

"What have you been doing wrong?" said Tor, in a buffalo-built voice.

"Man," said Drake, in a loud voice which rang against stone and against iron, "you're real hot on wrong. How about some right for a change? If it pleases your majesty—and even if it doesn't—I've done a good bit right in my time. Yes. Good work at the forge. Good work with steel. Good work at sword, too."

King Tor snorted.

"Don't snort so quick!" said Drake. "It's logic, isn't it? Right should mean as much as wrong. But here you only talk of wrong, wrong, wrong, wrong. All about error. Well, I say this. Maybe I killed a couple of watermelons. Maybe I took a little twig off a tree—sorry about that, your ugliness, but it'll live. Anyway, those are only little wrongs. The great rights of my life should cancel them out altogether."

"You're talking nonsense," said King Tor.

"Not so!" exclaimed Drake. "Man, you should set up a court of rights as well as a court of wrongs. I volunteer for trial in such a court. I guarantee I'd walk away with reward rather than punishment. Stands to reason, doesn't it? If wrongs deserve punishment, rights deserve rewards. And in my case, rights outweigh wrongs by nine thousand to one."

Tor laughed. Even at ten paces, Drake was assailed by royal halitosis. Tor's breath stank like a heap of guts which has sat for twenty-four days in a midden pit. Drake did his best not to flinch.

"Let's see, little mannikin," said King Tor. "Let's see exactly what you're charged with. Bring in the witnesses!"

While Drake was still suppressing his indignation about being called a mannikin, the witnesses trouped in. And a long line they made. They began to give evidence.

There was the watermelon seller.

28   Hugh Cook

There was the Protector of the Royal Trees.

There was the owner of a certain coal cart.

There was the owner of a certain house which had been wrecked by a certain coal cart.

There was the father of a girl of fourteen whom Drake had deflowered on his birthday.

There was the owner of a certain boat which was somewhat the worse for wear as a consequence of Drake's birthday celebrations.

There was—

But why go on? It is a long list, and the recital of such a list would not increase the world's wisdom, and might well give the unwise certain ideas they would be better off not having.

Once the witnesses had finished, King Tor said:

"What have you got to say for yourself?"

"What have I got to say for myself?" said Drake. "Why, that I'd like to marry your daughter. For I'm just the man, as the witnesses have proved. Yea. For I am strong, brave, determined, resolute in decision, ruthless in action, swift, cunning, subtle as a serpent, fit, healthy, and the boldest cocksman who ever stalked the streets of Cam."

"Do your talents excuse you from obedience to the law?" said King Tor, in something which sounded fearfully like anger.

"Man," said Drake. "There's no excuse needed. Those petty little quibbling pranks hardly rate a slap on the hand, far less the greater punishments. Why, they're all but boyish larks of one kind or another.

"And I'll have you know this. That girl wasn't much of a virgin, she'd had her father and brother before me.

"As for the other things, why, most of them weren't my fault either. They were the fault of the way the world's built. It's a right flimsy place, your majesty, not built to take the strain of hard-living men like you and me. Why, if that cart had been built proper, it would never have ruptured when it hit that wall. That wall wasn't built well, either, or it would have stopped the cart. And that boat wasn't up to much, either.

"All in all, if you must talk punishment, I think you

LORDS OF THE SWORD 29

could let me get away with all this for no more than a slap on the hand."

King Tor sat in thought.

He drank a draught of blood. Good stuff! He burped, and wiped his lips. He plucked a frog from the snack-bowl and munched it down. Ah! Great eating!

"Well," said King Tor. "We were all young once."

Drake waited.

The king drank some more blood.

A little dripped from his lips to his leather trousers.

"You're right," said King Tor. "Those were but boyish pranks. So I'll let you off lightly. We'll have you birched in public today. You spend tonight buried to the neck in the public dungheap. Toward morning, we'll put you on a boat. Three leagues from shore, you'll be thrown overboard. That is my justice!"

Drake knew he had got a good deal. But he could not resist the impulse to push his luck.

"Man," said Drake, "my offer for your daughter still holds good."

Tor sat in silence, staring at Drake. Then:

"You have a very high opinion of yourself," said Tor.

"I'm a man's man, man," said Drake, wishing he had kept quiet.

Tor considered. There was, for once, something close to silence in the Iron Hall. Everyone assembled wanted to hear the king's judgment. Would this boy get to marry Hilda, the king's daughter? Or would he be torn to pieces on the spot for his impudence?

"You hold yourself nicely enough," said Tor, slowly. "But substance may differ from appearance. That three-league swim from sea to shore should tell us rather more about you. If . . . if you can make it back to my palace before sunset, then you're the man to marry my daughter."

"Why, that's right handsome of you," said Drake. "It's a deal."

And they shook on it. As Tor's six-fingered hand closed on Drake's, the ogre squeezed. Just slightly. Drake winced, and squeezed back.

"Good muscles there," said Tor, approvingly. "Good luck!"

"Thought of the fair visage of your daughter will sustain me, sire," said Drake gravely.

Tor laughed, released Drake and clapped his hands.

"Take him away!" said Tor.

So Drake was taken out and birched in public, getting the standard twenty lashes. And it's no good pretending it didn't hurt, because it did. Worse than the pain was the publicity—for, as Drake was well aware, Sully Yot was among those watching.

Then Drake was planted in the dung heap, naked, up to his neck in ordure. And it's no good pretending that was comfortable—it was the worst night he'd had in his life. But for a fresh breeze coming in off the sea, he would have perished that night by reason of the fumes from the dung.

Toward dawn, Drake experienced something very close to despair. He felt shattered. He doubted that he could swim even as far as a sick snail could crawl while a hungry man was gulping down a very small piece of bread and jam, let alone three leagues. Three leagues! That was six thousand paces!

Still, he had to try.

The sun was rising when Drake was dug out of the dung heap. First off, he was thrown into the harbor. The shock of the water revived him somewhat; he found he could swim, and swim quite well. Once he was clean—more or less—he was allowed to climb out of the harbor.

A considerable crowd had gathered to see the young man who had set himself up as a contender for the throne of Stokos. As someone threw a blanket over his shoulders, Drake gazed around at the mob. Why, he must be famous!

"Good morning, young Drake," said a familiar voice.

It was Gouda Muck.

"Hi," said Drake. "Come to watch the fun, have you? Why couldn't you stay back at the forge torturing rats with a red-hot poker?"

"Don't be like that," said Muck. "I've brought you a present."

And so he had—a pair of new trousers and a thick jersey of greasy wool. Drake was startled.

"Why," said Drake. "Why, this—I—"

"Thank me by surviving," said Muck, clapping a hard and horny hand onto his shoulder. "You're a good lad, really. I know that."

Such presents and such praise were the very last thing Drake had expected to get on that particular morning. His heart was gladdened; he felt almost human again.

"Morning, young sprogling," said a rough but cheery voice.

It was Drake's uncle, Oleg Douay. And what had he brought with him? Why, breakfast!

Bacon, yes, and devilled kidneys, and bread greasy with fat. Drake scrambled into his new clothes then ate with a will, feeding warmth, strength and energy into his belly. Three leagues? No problem! He could do it lying on his back.

"That breakfast will see you drowned with cramp," said an anonymous pessimist.

"Not me," said Drake, carelessly, and downed another kidney. "What's that other package? Something else for me?"

"Some new boots," said Oleg Douay. "But I won't hand them over yet. I'll be waiting when you make it back to shore. I expect you to dine with me this evening."

"With pleasure," said Drake.

"Five shangles says you can't swim the three leagues wearing the boots," said a voice.

It was Sully Yot, half-hidden among the crowd.

"Done!" said Drake. Then, to his uncle: "Give me the boots." Reluctantly, his uncle handed them over.

"This isn't wise," said Oleg. "Those boots will drown you."

"Not me," said Drake, determined to win five shangles off Sully Yot.

Five shangles! Why, that was a week's wages. With

five shangles, he could be drunk for two and a half days without a moment's sobriety.

Then Drake remembered that his days of boozing, gambling and wenching were over. He was a serious swordsmith now, soon to settle down to the job of making his first blade. Well . . . once he'd made that weapon, surely a little celebration would be in order.

Yes. Surely.

"I'll be here myself when you get to shore," said Yot, "to make sure you're still wearing the boots. So no cheating!"

"I'll be wearing the boots all right," said Drake. "I'll keep them on if only for the pleasure of kicking you."

Then Drake was shown to the canary-yellow dinghy in which he would be rowed out to sea. The boat, he was told, was the *Walrus*. Unbeknownst to Drake, her owner had named her thus because he had once sailed on a pirate ship captained by a water-thief of that name.

Drake was introduced to the crew.

There were three of them. Ish Ulpin (owner of the *Walrus*) and Bucks Cat wee both human. The third, Whale Mike, was mostly ogre; he was twice man-height. But, unlike King Tor, he was of fairly slim build—his shoulders were no wider than a man's outstretched arms. He wore tarpaulin overalls and a great big leather apron with a huge pocket in the front.

The rowing boat—a big wide strongbuilt thing which would usually have had a crew of ten—settled noticeably as Whale Mike stepped into it. Drake dreaded to think what he weighed.

"Well, gentlemen," said Drake. "It looks like a good day for it. Shall we be setting to sea?"

He stepped into the boat. Ish Ulpin took the tiller; Whale Mike and Bucks Cat began to row. Men on ships in the harbor cheered or jeered according to their nature.

Then, as the *Walrus* passed by the bow of an ill-favored barque with furled black sails, a man leaned over the railing and cried:

"Hey, boys! That's the pup I told you about! The one who gave me the wrong directions!"

Looking up, Drake saw the man on the ship was Atsimo Andranovory.

"Belt him round the earhole for me!" cried Andranovory.

Whereupon Ish Ulpin did just that.

"Hit him again!" said Andranovory.

"No, that not fair," said Whale Mike. Then, raising his voice so Andranovory could hear: "You want hit boy, you know where to find him! You swim out after us if that what you want!"

Andranovory answered in curses.

Soon, he was out of earshot. The dinghy left the protection of the harbor and began to rock uncomfortably on the swells. Drake started feeling uneasy.

Or, to be precise, queasy.

All that bacon fat in his belly was getting distinctly uneasy about this adventure.

"You not happy stomach?" said Whale Mike. "Here, you get this good, she put you right."

And Whale Mike handed Drake a small stone bottle. What was in it, Drake didn't ask. He simply swigged. It was bitter. It burnt. At first, he felt worse than ever. Then his stomach settled, and seasickness threatened no more as the *Walrus* rowed out into the open sea.

3

Ish Ulpin: a lean, pale man with a thin, mirthless mouth. He is given to great anger; he loves to kill. Once was a gladiator in Chi 'ash-lan; later, sailed with the Orfus pirates of the Greater Teeth. Now works for King Tor as executioner and torturer, but is not averse to a little private enterprise on the side. In anyone's language, this man is dangerous.

Bucks Cat: a tall man with a wrestler's build; black hair; ebony skin; a knife-scar grinning on his throat. Born on Island Talsh in Sponge Sea. After capture in slaving raid, worked for many years in a quarry in the Ashun Mountains. Led slave revolt which took three years to suppress; spent five years on Greater Teeth before settling on Stokos.

Whale Mike: an ogre built as tall as King Tor. Has a trace of human ancestry (ogres can breed with humans, as wolves can with dogs) as evidenced by a face showing what is almost a standard human configuration. Small eyes of incontrovertible imbecility; cheeks bulging as if a full-moon resides within each; sallow yellow skin. He has no ears, only holes in the side of his head where ears should be. (His hearing, even so, is acute.)
His past is unspeakable.

The day was bright; the sun glittered on the sea and glinted from the blue and green tiled rooves of Cam. The clouds were few, white and very high. Drake felt strangely tranquil as he watched the whitewashed buildings of Cam receding into the distance. Three leagues was a long way to swim. But he had every confidence of success. In fact, he felt he had energy to spare. By way of showing off, he offered to row.

"You not row, man," said Whale Mike. "You sleep."

"I don't need to sleep," said Drake. "I know what's best for me."

"You like kitten," said Whale Mike. "Eyes not open yet. You not know which way up."

"It doesn't matter what he knows," said Ish Ulpin, with a laugh which suggested no humor. "It'll all be over soon enough in any case."

"What?" said Drake. "You think I'm going to drown or something?"

"Shut up," said Bucks Cat.

"You make nice sleep," said Whale Mike. "That always good thing. Not much sleep in water. That not so?"

Drake hated to take advice from anything which looked so stupid, but, in the end, he made himself as comfortable as he could and closed his eyes. And slept, right enough. Dreaming of munched frogs and dripping blood. After a while, he woke to hear someone—Ish Ulpin, by the sound of it—talking about Andranovory.

"We should have taken old Andranovory's offer," said Ish Ulpin. "It's our chance to get back to the Greaters."

"Yes," said Bucks Cat.

"You really want go back there?" said Whale Mike. "I not like that. We happy here, that not so? In Greaters, nobody trust anybody. That not nice."

"Who cares about nice?" said Ish Ulpin. "I care about money."

And Drake thought: *Well, and so do we all.*

Then drifted off to sleep again. Waking considerably later. What had woken him? A gull, yes, the harsh cry of a gull. Lament of the ages. He sat up, blinked. His eyes hot, red, sore. Infected from the dung heap? Maybe. The boat rocked. His arse was sore. His back was sore. A boat was no place to sleep.

"Hey," said Drake. "Where are we?"

He looked for the shore. It was a fair way distant. Well, to be exact: an unfair way distant. The whitewashed buildings with their roofs of blue and green tiles were shrunk by distance to the size of flecks of paint.

"This is more than three leagues!" said Drake.

And promptly leaped overboard. The sea was so wet! So big! So dark! Drake was most unhappy about it. But he was even less happy when Ish Ulpin picked up a harpoon and threatened him.

"Back in the boat, boy," said Ish Ulpin. "Get in, or I spear you."

"What is this?" said Drake.

"Don't argue," said Ish Ulpin. "Get in!"

Drake paddled back to the boat. Whale Mike hauled him aboard, then took his turn at the tiller. Buck Cat and Ish Ulpin continued rowing.

"Hey, man," said Drake uneasily. "Three leagues is but six thousand paces. We're that far from shore already, I'll swear to it."

He got no answer. He felt stupid, sitting there dripping wet, so stripped himself naked, wrung out his clothes then put them back on. Leaving his boots off. Those lovely new boots had felt dangerously heavy when he had been swimming in the sea. He bitterly regretted making his bet with Sully Yot, because it was clear enough now that he was going to lose his five shangles. Yes, and Yot would never let him forget it.

"Hey, boys," said Drake, "row me most of the way back in and I'll let you have three shangles. That's one each. That's a lot of money."

Bucks Cat laughed, and pulled on his oars with a will.

"You're going too far!" said Drake.

"And we'll go further yet before you jump," said Ish Ulpin, sunlight glinting on his fine white teeth as he smiled.

Smiled without humor.

"What is this?" said Drake. "Vigilante justice or something?"

"Exactly," said Ish Ulpin.

"I'm a citizen!" shouted Drake. "A very religious boy! Just a boy, a tender-hearted boy. I want to work hard and worship, to learn obedience under the law, yes, learn my lessons, pay my taxes, reform, be good. Why are you doing this to me?"

"Certain merchants have paid us to," said Ish Ulpin. "Aye, and paid well, too. Nice work for easy money."

"Merchants?" said Drake. "Who? The guy with the watermelon stand? Or that man with the daughter?"

"None of those," said Ish Ulpin. "Nay. Men of more importance. Men who fear to see a fool named Dreldragon marry King Tor's daughter."

"What?" said Drake. "They're in lust with her?"

"Nay. But they fear a fool like you as king. You marry her tomorrow, the king could be dead the next day. He's old enough to die."

"He might last another thirty years," said Drake.

"And might not," said Ish Ulpin. "The people who pay us want no risks."

"You can't do this!" howled Drake.

But got no reaction. Until Whale Mike said:

"He only boy, you know. We long way out. He not get back. This far enough, yes?"

"You always were soft in the head," said Bucks Cat. "I've swum further than this myself. He might do the same himself."

"Unless we put a harpoon through him," said Ish Ulpin. "How about it?"

"Yes," said Bucks Cat.

"Oh no," said Whale Mike. "That cruel. We not do that. We give him maybe just little chance. That nice, give some joker chance."

"Was it you who gave Jon Arabin a chance?" said Ish Ulpin.

"What you talking about?" said Whale Mike.

"When Slagger Mulps had him thrown overboard with all that iron tied to his feet," said Ish Ulpin. "You did the knots for the iron, didn't you?"

Whale Mike's big foolish face split in a grin.

"Oh yes," he said. "Good knots, eh? Jon, he smart fellow. He get those knots undone real nice. I make knots so he have little chance. No much. But he come up all right. That good fun. Old Walrus, he real pissed off. Good stuff. Jon blow kiss, that cracked me up, that real funny."

"So that's why the Warwolf survived," said Bucks Cat. "Because Mike was in one of his funny moods."

"I had a sword called Warwolf," said Drake. "Who's the Warwolf you're talking about?"

"You shut up," said Ish Ulpin. "We've heard enough out of you."

"Yes," said Bucks Cat. "Keep your mouth shut, or we'll tie the anchor to your feet before we throw you over. I'll do the knots myself. They won't come undone if I do them!"

Drake, seeing the threat was serious, kept quiet thereafter. He counted what gulls he saw. There were not many of them. How far did gulls fly from shore? Some, he had heard, lived eternally at sea, never touching ground from one year to the next. He looked at his toes. Wriggled them. There were little ginger hairs growing on his toes. That was funny, that his head-hair should be blond yet his toe-hair ginger.

Knowing he might be close to death, he started to review his life.

What did he see?

Mostly, lost opportunities. Women never laid, foes never beaten, fruit never stolen. Well, if he got out of this, the world would see a change in Drake Douay. Yes. No more Mr. Nice Guy! He'd go for what he wanted, yes, ruthlessly, yielding to nothing. Life was short, so: grab while the grabbing's good.

While Drake was thinking thus, the crewmen rowed on. Bucks Cat put a line out and trolled for fish, with some success. As each fish was hauled aboard, it was cut up then eaten raw. Drake was horrified.

LORDS OF THE SWORD 39

"This good," said Whale Mike, throwing Drake a lump of fish. "Eat!"

"No," said Drake. "Raw fish is poison. Everyone knows that."

"I eat, I not hurt," said Whale Mike.

"You're not human," said Drake.

"Oh, I human enough," said Whale Mike complacently. "Come on, you try. That way find things out."

"So it is," said Drake, remembering what he had been taught in his theory classes about the experimental method.

But, even so, he was most reluctant to eat something which almost all of Stokos regarded as deadly poison. Finally, compelled by hunger, he tried some of the fish. It was not bad at all. And he got no harm from it.

"Well," said Drake, "they do say that travel broadens the mind."

He was starting to feel quite comfortable in the boat. He had managed to convince himself that the crewmen would never force him into the sea. No, they were just indulging in a rather cruel joke. Sooner or later, they would admit as much. Then everyone on the brave boat *Walrus* would have a good laugh, and they would turn and row for shore. Once there, the crewmen might buy Drake a beer by way of apology. A beer? Two beers, minimum! They might buy him a woman, as well. Then Drake would go home and get a good night's sleep. And, bright and early in the morning, he would start on his first sword.

With such thoughts, Drake comforted himself. Until, toward sunset, when only a line of distant clouds marked the position of the shore, Ish Ulpin gave an order:

"Ease oars!"

The *Walrus* wallowed in the greasy swells. What lay beneath the sea's surface? Immense depths of dark, of cold, of drifting seaweed and hunting sharks.

"Sorry about this," said Whale Mike.

"You mean . . ." said Drake. "You mean you're really—"

"Did you think we were joking?" said Ish Ulpin. "Jump!"

"Yes," said Bucks Cat. "Before we cut your lips off."

"This isn't fair!" said Drake. "I never did anything to hurt you."

"You lied to one of our friends," said Ish Ulpin. "You gave Atsimo Andranovory duff directions. Aye. You met him on the waterfront and—"

"But that's ridiculous!" said Drake. "You can't kill me just because of that!"

"Ish Ulpin joking," said Whale Mile. "We not kill you because of that. We kill you because that our job. You better leave now."

"Yes," said Bucks Cat, jabbing at Drake with a harpoon. "Leave now, if you want to leave with your liver."

Bucks jabbed again. And Drake jumped. The oarsmen turned the good boat *Walrus* around and started rowing for the shore.

"This is a joke," said Drake, swimming after them. "It is a joke, isn't it? It could be, you know. I'll hold no grudge. I'll swear to you. Everything I own. My flesh, my body."

"Keep your distance," said Ish Ulpin, snatching the harpoon from Bucks Cat.

Ish Ulpin was ready to kill. Yes. It was no joke.

Drake trod water, floundering around in the swell and the slop. He swore. He wailed in despair. Then he shouted:

"It's too late now!" he screamed. "Too late for me to get to the palace by sunset! So I'll never marry the king's daughter! Your merchants have got what they want! They're safe! You've earnt your money! I'll never be king! Pick me up, for love of your mother!"

"I've no love for my mother," called Ish Ulpin. "In fact, I strangled the bitch to celebrate my fourteenth birthday."

And on rowed the boat.

Bucks Cat, holding the tiller, reclined like a lady of leisure. He trailed his free hand over the side, so water played around his fingers. He was safe. He was earning good money for this murder. He was happy. And he was letting Drake know just how good he felt.

Whereupon Drake was filled with seething anger, with outrage, with implacable hatred. He would not drown! He would live! He would get to shore then murder those boatmen, one by one! Hang them! Jugulate them! Smash them to pulp then jump up and down on their splattered bowels!

Drake forced himself out of his trousers. He lay on his back, kicking his feet to keep himself afloat. He knotted each trouser-leg at the ankle. Then held the trousers by the waistband, so the legs dangled limply in the water. Then, treading water, he brought the trousers sweeping in a sudden arc toward the sea.

Air shot into the trouser-legs. The waistband, widened to a circle by the inrush of air, hit the sea. Drake forced it down. The trouser-legs stuck up into the air. Drake laid himself across the crotch of the trousers, trapping the waistband beneath him.

He was now afloat on his trousers. Bit by bit, the air would surely leak out, but by repeating his trick he could refill them. He looked a right daft lunatic, floating on his trousers with his naked arse shimmering in the seas of sunset. But he would live, unless he died of cold, or was eaten by sharks, or was set upon by giant seabirds, or—

Yes, probably he would die.

"But I'm not dead yet," said Drake.

And floated.

All grim determination.

Darkness came, bringing a night longer than all the wormholes that ever were, longer than every bit of spaghetti which has ever been made since the dawn of time.

Drake fell asleep often, experiencing just a flash of dreamtime hallucination before waking again to the cold everwash of the sea. The greasy wool which protected his torso helped keep him alive. But for the warmth of wool, Drake would have been dead long before dawn.

By the time dawn approached there was no determination left. Only a boy of sixteen, alone, lonely, exhausted almost beyond endurance, cold to the bone, nine parts dead, skin wrinkled by the sea.

"It's lighter," said Drake. "A new day . . ."

Life is hope.

The east was gray. Then sullen red. Then ginger. Then up came the sun, as bright and cheerful as ever. Blue shone the sky. Blue sky. White clouds.

"It is a good day to die," said Drake, since that was the kind of thing heroes were supposed to say.

Maybe heroes convinced heroes. But Drake failed to convince Drake. As far as he could tell, no day was a good day to die.

But it didn't look like he had much choice in the matter, for, by the bright happy sunlight, he saw a fin sliding through the sea. An evil fin. Sleek. Cold. Polished as a knife. Then out from the water came a sleek and polished head, which whistled at him in a high and alien language.

"I see," said Drake. "A whistling shark. Well, nice to be eaten by a novelty, I suppose."

The brute rolled on its side, then dived. Going under. Drake drew his knees to his belly. Where was it? Where was it?

"Show yourself, bugger-breath!" he snarled.

And the monster did. It came out of the sea. It leaped right out of the water, described a fantastic arc, then plunged beneath the waves again. Then surfaced. Grinning. Yes! Its vicious beak of a mouth was grinning at him! There was no mistaking that expression. What next? Laughing, no doubt.

The smiling shark began to circle. The swells lifted Drake up then dropped him down. His trousers were almost empty of air: he was getting lower and lower in the water.

"Come on, shark!" said Drake. "Make an end of it, you ugly bugger!"

But the shark just circled, chirruping now and then. Another joined it. Two of them, then. No, three!

"A dinner party, is it?" said Drake. "Man, sorry to show up for dinner with a bare arse."

It was time to fill the trousers again.

Or drown.

"Life is hope," said Drake.

And maneuvered himself off his trousers, meaning to slip them behind him to catch another load of air. But he was so weak that, as the last of that air-support left him, he slipped beneath the waves, losing his grip on the trousers. Which sank.

Drake sank.

Grabbing for the surface.

Something rose up beside him. He seized it. He found himself brought to the surface. By a shark. Too exhausted to scream, he lay there in the sea, lay with his cheek against the water-smooth flank of the shark, his arm over its great smooth back.

Then remembered that sharks are not smooth, for their skin has more teeth than their jaws. So this must be a dolphin, yes, he had heard of such, that accounted for the whistling and all, it was a dolphin, life answering to life just as the legends claimed. And Drake, unable to help himself, wept.

And heard someone hail him:

"Ahoy there! You with the fish!"

Now the dolphin is no fish, for its blood is warm, and, what's more, mother dolphins give birth to their young in a fashion close to human, then suckle their babies on milk. But Drake knew well enough that the voice was speaking to him.

"So it's true," he said. "The dead begin to speak to you as you die. Well, who'd have thought it?"

Then the voice called again. Turning his head, Drake saw a ship on the sea behind him. If he had looked around earlier, he would have seen it much sooner.

"Investigate," said Drake. "That's what I should have done."

Then the dolphin submerged, leaving him floundering in the swell. But hope gave him strength, and he kept himself afloat until the ship came alongside. It was a xebec with sails of the palest lilac, a hull painted gold and topsides of silver. It looked like something out of a dream.

Looking up, Drake saw a woman looking down. She was tall. She was luxurious. Her hair was red, her skin also; her mouth was broad, her breasts high-lofted.

"Are you all right?" she said anxiously, in Galish tinged with a foreign accent.

Drake floated there, gazing up at her. What a mouth! What a nose! What beautiful body-lines! Suddenly he remembered all the good resolutions he had made in the face of death: Go for what you want! Yield to nothing! Grab while the grabbing's good!"

Well, then . . .

"Will you marry me?" said Drake.

"What?" said the woman, her face showing alarm.

"Marry me! I'm in love!"

"You're crazy," she said.

Drake lacked the strength to protest. He floated, his hair—beautifully clean by now—floating around him in the easy seas. Then a capture net scooped him from the water, and he was hauled aboard like a bit of dead meat.

Shortly, he was lying on hard boards with a coarse woollen blanket draped over his nakedness. The tall red woman was bending over him, feeding him sips of water.

"Careful, now," she said, supporting his head. "Not all at once!"

He seized her hand, and kissed it.

"Marry me," he said.

"I'll learn you a rather hard lesson, if you talk on so foolish," she said, a note of warning in her voice.

She was, he judged, about four years older than him, and a good head taller. He was in lust with her. Strenuously in lust. Or, to be more exact: he liked what he saw, and his ego compelled him to imagine that he had strength enough for lust, even after the trauma of his deep-sea survival exercise. It was that same ego which compelled him to pursue his suit:

"Tell me," said Drake, "tell me at least your name."

"Zanya," she said. "Zanya Kliedervaust, lately of the temple of the Orgy God on the Ebrells."

"The Orgy God?" said Drake. "That sounds like my kind of deity."

"Mayhap," said Zanya. "But I have renounced the temple. Also the flesh it worships. I seek a higher calling. That I hope to find on Stokos."

At that moment, they were interrupted by a tall, well-built man with violet eyes and purple skin. He wore a purple robe; heavy golden ear-rings dangled beside his cheeks.

"Zanya," he said. *"Faa n'koto afa dree takaloka tee?"*

"Gaa n'moto seki seki," answered Zanya. *"Ka ta funofoonu ti."*

"Who are you?" said Drake, staring up at the big purple man.

"He speaks no Galish," said Zanya. "But his name is Oronoko. He's a prince from one of the provinces of Parengarenga."

"Yakoto," said Prince Oronoko, smiling as he put a hand to his heart. *"N'mo k'nozo Oronoko. Ka nafunafu."*

"Is this your boyfriend?" said Drake.

"He's a pilgrim," said Zanya. "He came to the Ebrells in a quest for purity. We've been questing together ever since."

"I see," said Drake. "Questing for long enough to share a language between you."

"Oh, I've known the speaking of Frangoni for years," said Zanya. "It's a language common enough on the Ebrells."

Drake wanted to question her further, but first he had to deal with the ship's captain, a lean, anxious man who came bustling along the deck, peered at Drake with some misgivings, then asked, in a high-pitched voice scarcely half a tone away from hysteria:

"How came you to be in the water? What evil put you there? Witchcraft, perhaps?"

"Nay, man," said Drake, improvising. "I was on my uncle's fishing boat. Then up came a kraken! Ah, a brute of a thing it was! Terrible with tentacles. It drowned the boat. Ate all but me."

His eyes were bright, his voice frenzied.

"Say no more," said the captain, his fears of the occult apparently appeased. "Leisure back, boy. Rest. Sleep. We'll land in Stokos soon enough. That will be time for you to make a settlement with your grief."

All the way back to Stokos, Drake's resolution hardened. His flesh, for the moment, was too weak to harden with his resolution. But there was no doubt about it. He could have, would have, must have this big beautiful red-skinned Ebrell bitch.

But he was to be disappointed.

For, on reaching Stokos, Zanya quit the ship swiftly, in company with Oronoko, without even bothering to learn Drake's name.

"Must follow," muttered Drake to Drake.

And he gave chase.

But he had scarce taken a dozen steps when the ground snatched itself from under his feet and a sheet of stifling black tar rolled across the surface of the sun.

When Drake recovered consciousness, he found himself lying on a truckle-bed in the room which housed the skull collection which was the pride and joy of his uncle, Oleg Douay. When Drake called out, his uncle came to his bedside.

"What happened?" said Drake.

"Why, the sea gods saved you, that's what happened," said Oleg. "I prayed to them mightily. My faith, as you see, is justified."

"No," said Drake. "I mean down at the waterfront. What happened there?"

"You fainted, or so report would have it. Nothing to be ashamed of. After what you've been through, it's a wonder you could walk from the ship on your own two legs. Rest."

"Man," said Drake, "a woman came off that ship. She—"

"Never you mind about women!" said Oleg. "There'll be plenty of time for that later."

Shortly, Drake had a visitor: it was Sully Yot.

"Five shangles," said Yot, sticking out his hand.

"Man!" said Drake. "That's a fine form of greeting!"

"Pay up!" said Yot, obviously delighting in his triumph.

It occurred to Drake that, if the mischances of fate ever reduced him to slavery, then Yot was the very last person he would want as a master.

"Man, I'll pay all right, but only if you can find a woman for me."

And Drake proceeded to name and describe Zanya Kliedervaust. By diligent inquiry, Yot found she had taken work in the leper colony on the outskirts of town. Drake paid over the five shangles, though the news gave him little joy.

He dared not venture to the leprosarium. For ordinary leprosy is terrible, but in that colony they had something worse still—blue lepers, who suffered outbreaks of blue sores, then great septic ulcers, then a black rot which consumed the eyes. Then a terrible variant of gangrene which broke out all over and finished them. They generally took two long, slow years to die, from the time the first blue sores erupted on their skin.

Love conquers all?

Maybe.

But Drake was not in love—he was in lust. And lust alone was not sufficient to compel him inside a leper colony.

"Woe is me!" cried Drake.

Then remembered that life did, after all, have some compensations. For he was about to start work on his first sword, was he not? That happy thought gave him the strength to rise from his bed after only three days of recuperation.

But, on proceeding to Hardhammer Forge, Drake found his hopes of making a sword of his own were not yet to be fulfilled. Gouda Muck had received a special order from King Tor for five blades of firelight steel. Muck was working flat out; he lacked the time to supervise apprentice work.

"But you promised!" said Drake.

"Wait till these blades are done," said Muck. "I'll be no use as a teacher if Tor chops my head off, will I?"

Drake had to concede the logic of that.

"How long before you're finished?" he asked.

"How long is a piece of string?" said Muck. "What have you done about those men who threw you overboard? Have you reported them?"

"Not yet," said Drake.

"Then I suggest you get on with it," said Muck, who loved justice as much as any other man. "Today. Off you go!"

"But I'm supposed to go to theory class this afternoon."

"Do you care?"

"I do," said Drake, with both truth and determination. "I've decided to go all out for what I want. And what I want is to be a swordsmith, yes, the very best swordsmith on Stokos."

"I'm impressed," said Muck, who wasn't, but thought such an attitude deserved encouragement. "Right. Go to theory class this afternoon, then tomorrow morning make your report."

That night, Drake dreamed of the horrifying tortures which would claim Ish Ulpin, Bucks Cat and Whale Mike once King Tor was persuaded to punish them. He woke early, and, after a quick breakfast, hurried off to the Iron Palace to make his report.

4

Place: Stokos, a deeply indented island in Gulf of Veda off western coast of continent of Argan.

Area: by Court Cartographer's reckoning, about 4,750 vlests (some 12,000 square leagues).

Population: 123,045 according to the taxcount of Tor 5.

Ruler: King Tor (an ogre of noble birth).

Capital: the seaport of Cam (pop. 53,000).

Religion: worship of the demon Hagon.

Language: Kerzen, Arham and Ligin (all native to Stokos); also Galish (lingua franca of Cam, where all three native tongues meet and compete).

Literacy: 27 percent.

Life expectancy: 53 years.

Economy: mining; fishing; banking, import-export; steel production: metalwork (particularly weapons).

Lust mixes but poorly with justice.

By the time Drake's pursuit of Zanya had been stalled by the discovery that his lover was working in a leper colony, the boatmen who had tried to murder Drake had fled Cam. Indeed, they had fled Stokos, for the wrath of King Tor would be terrible if he learned they had exceeded his instructions.

He did learn—for, obedient to Muck's instructions, Drake went and told him. And his wrath was indeed terrible.

"By royal decree," said King Tor, in a voice which woke the gryphon sleeping at his feet, "Bucks Cat, Ish Ulpin and Whale Mike are to be executed immediately if they ever again set foot on Stokos. Thus will justice be fulfilled."

"Well," said Drake, "now we've done with justice, how about marrying me off to your daughter?"

"You failed the challenge I set you," said King Tor. "You failed to get back to my palace by sunset."

"Be reasonable!" said Drake. "I never had a chance! Anyway, I survived perils worse than anything you had in mind—as you've heard. That proves I've got a lot going for me."

"This is true," said King Tor, munching on a frog. "But perhaps I was a little hasty to offer my daughter so casually. Come back in two years, when you finish your apprenticeship. We'll decide then."

Well. That was better than a poke in the eye with a blunt stick. Two years from now, he might be Prince Drake. No, probably the title would be more formal: Prince Dreldragon. Lord Dreldragon, maybe? Either way, it had a nice ring to it.

Meanwhile, there was still Zanya. Now was the time to chase her. If she became Drake's lover, she could still be his concubine when he married Tor's daughter. But Zanya was working with lepers! What if she got the disease herself? Drake thought about it. Lust confused his intellectual processes, such as they were: he decided Zanya was far, far too beautiful ever to get leprosy.

"She's too high-class for such a low-class disease," he declared.

Then dared himself as far as the rough-and-ready paling which marked the perimeter of the leper colony.

He did not see Zanya Kliedervaust, but, through generous gaps in the fence, he did see diseased corpses writhing on a huge pyre. A big purple-skinned man wearing nothing but a loin-cloth was heaping fresh wood on the fire. It was Prince Oronoko, who had been with Zanya on the xebec. Drake was so jealous he wanted to spit.

Imagine! A stinking foreigner enjoying the company of the fair Zanya Kliedervaust. Her company? Oh, she had been slick enough with her weird-rare talk about purity, but Drake could guess what pleasures she shared with her uitlander prince. Oronoko's muscles, oiled with sweat, glistened in the hot sun. Drake wondered how he would fare against Oronoko in a fight.

"Hey! You!" cried Drake. "Where are you keeping Zanya?"

Oronoko did not seem to hear. Belatedly, Drake remembered that the foreigner spoke no Galish. He spoke some kind of alien gibberish instead.

Purple-skinned Oronoko threw one last load of wood on the fire then went away, perhaps to get some more bodies. The flames hungered noisily. Stray bits of bamboo burst asunder in the heart of the blaze. Drake felt the heat of the fire amplifying the heat of the sun. A corpse, compelled by the inferno, sat up, its arms warping amidst the smoke in a parody of agony.

Then a shift of the wind sent smoke plunging in Drake's direction. Before he could flee, he was enveloped in thick choking smoke, in the stench of burning hair and charring flesh. He scrambled away, cursing, coughing, spluttering, eyes watering. He was stricken with terror. What if the smoke had contaminated him? What if he had caught leprosy from that filthy disposal fire?

He was no longer so sure that it would be safe to bed the fair Zanya Kliedervaust.

But he could not get her out of his mind.

Ten days after his ordeal at sea, Drake decided to discuss his problem with his sister.

"I'm in love," he said.

"Then demonstrate it," she said tartly. "Lean on your elbows! Stop dribbling!"

"I'm not in love with you, stupid," said Drake.

52 Hugh Cook

"Watch your language," said his sister, with danger in her voice, "or I'll spit in your eye!"

And Drake thought; *Women! They're so emotional!*

"Well," said his sister, shortly afterward, "who are you in love with?"

"A woman from Ebrell," said Drake, dreamily, staring up at the ceiling. "Red skin, red hair . . . she's gorgeous."

"Is she a good lay?"

"I haven't been able to find out," said Drake. And he explained.

"This is a hopeless case," said his sister. "You'd better see a pox doctor."

"For what?"

"For a cure for love. We've got a pox doctor working in the temple now. He's quite nice."

"Is he good in bed?" said Drake.

"He's a wizard, stupid. They don't go in for that kind of stuff."

"Oh," said Drake. "Somehow . . . somehow I don't think a pox doctor would help me."

But, that night, he endured grim dreams of blue leprosy. He dreamed of Zanya, of her body studded with blue sores, just as King Tor's leather clothing was studded with iron. He dreamed of Zanya suffering long, slow months of decay, eventually becoming ulcerated, blind, gangrenous. Then dead. He woke in a sweat.

And, that very morning, he fronted up to the temple for an interview with their pox doctor, who was a wizard of the order of Nin, one of the weakest of the eight orders of wizards. His name was Miphon. The temple of Hagon, hoping to end an unpleasant outbreak of gonorrhoea, had lately imported him to Stokos to advise on sexual hygiene. Miphon had given much valuable advice with respect to the use of condoms, and was almost ready to leave the island.

On being admitted to Miphon's presence, Drake saw the wizard was fairly old—maybe aged about thirty. He wore businesslike leathers and a broad-brimmed

LORDS OF THE SWORD 53

hat which sported a single feather. Being nervous, Drake started the interview by being rude.

"Why are your eyes green?" he said.

Miphon was unsurprised by this brusque demand for information. Guessing at Drake's unease, Miphon made allowances for it.

"My eyes are green," said he, "because I am descended from the elven folk. My great-grandfather was of the People."

So he spoke. But, as the Book of Wisdom puts it: "Much is spoken, but little is truthed." Drake, who knew as much, took Miphon's claim with a grain of salt.

"I see from your face that you disbelieve me," said Miphon. "But I can prove myself. Thanks to my elven ancestry, I am fay. I can read minds. I can tell who you are, what you are, and what you want."

"Tell, then," said Drake, disbelieving.

"You are Drake Douay, a swordsmith's apprentice," said Miphon. "You love the fair Zanya Kliedervaust, who resides in the leprosarium on the outskirts of this town of Cam."

Drake had never had his mind read before.

He was shocked. Startled. Stunned. Awed.

"My . . . my lord," said Drake. "I . . . I did not mean to be rude. I have never met an elven lord before. It was—the clothes confused me. I thought great people to dress greatly. Man, if you dressed with more style you'd get much more respect."

"The leathers serve," said Miphon. "Would you seek to embellish wisdom with gaudy silks and golden baubles? Do the postures of fashion improve veracity?"

"Embellish?" said Drake. "Veracity?"

He had learnt a great many very long words and complicated ideas in his theory classes, but there were still enormous gaps in his education.

"To embellish is to decorate," said Miphon patiently. "Veracity is another word for truth."

"Great is the wisdom of the elven lords!" said Drake.

"I did not say that I was an elf," said Miphon, "only that I am of elven descent. Not all of the powers of the People are mine. Only some."

Actually, there is less magic in the world than most folk think, and certainly less magic than Miphon claimed. For—regardless of the truth or otherwise of his claim to elven descent—the wizard Miphon was most certainly not fay. He was not telepathic. (Well, he could read the minds of rocks, stones and the lesser animals—such as the mole, phoenix, basilisk, badger, rat, mouse, dragon, gryphon, rabbit, cow and codfish—but such skill is of very little practical use.)

So how did he know about Drake?

Simple.

Drake's sister had already seen Miphon to brief him in depth regarding her brother's name, appearance and mission.

"Have no fear," said Miphon, "for I will do you no harm, even though I am mighty in power. Instead, I will tell you how to resolve your problem."

"You will cure me of love?" said Drake.

"Yes," said Miphon, handing Drake a little tablet. "Dissolve this in water to make a philtre which is a certain cure for love. Drink the philtre by the light of a full moon. Turn round widershins. Kneel down. Kiss the ground three times, each time saying the name of the woman you love. Then work as hard as you can for the next thirty days, doing every task your master sets you—or twice as much, if possible. That will cure you of love, for certain."

"Does the moon have to be full?" said Drake.

"Oh yes," said Miphon. "For this magic is animated by the power of the moon herself. Only by the full moon can such power be conjured."

Drake was very impressed.

This was great magic indeed!

In truth, the tablet contained nothing but a little salt and sugar. But Miphon, who was a great believer in the power of the placebo, had found he could cure a truly staggering range of conditions with such little tablets.

"Happy?" said Miphon.

"Well . . . if you can give me this kind of pill . . . why not a philtre to make the lady love me?"

"If you must have the lady," said Miphon, "then woo her. Pledge your love with poetry and flowers. Visit her daily. Let her know the sincerity of your devotions. Speak to her prettily, and persist. To destroy is easier than to create. Magic can destroy your love easily—but cannot create love for you in her."

"It's all very well to talk of wooing," said Drake. "But how can I? She's in the leper colony. It's death to enter—particularly with that blue leprosy on the loose."

"Leprosy is hard to catch," said Miphon. "As for blue leprosy—that's a different disease entirely. A kind of pox, only to be caught when man lies with woman. It's slow to develop, sometimes taking years to appear. That's why the nature of the disease is seldom properly understood."

"I see," said Drake.

"Trust me," said Miphon. "If you visit the leper colony, you'll likely come away unscathed. Yes, even if you visit a hundred times. Do you have any other questions?"

"Only this," said Drake. "Do wizards pork women? Or do they go for men?"

Miphon refused to be upset by this rudeness.

"We limit every indulgence," said Miphon gravely. "We must, because of the demands of the Balance."

"What is this Balance?" said Drake.

"Many have asked," said Miphon, "but few have been answered. You know your future now. You have magic to cure you of love, if you wish. If not—then woo the lady."

And with that, Drake had to be content.

That very evening, Miphon quit Stokos on a dirty, wallowing brig taking coal from Cam to Narba. The next morning, Drake was discussing the wizard with his sister, and saying what a marvelous mind-reading elf he was, when she broke into peals of laughter.

"He's no elf!" she said. "There's no such thing as elves."

"Then how did he know who I was?" said Drake. "How did he know what I wanted?"

"How do you think?" said she.

Drake put his mind to it.

And, since his mind had been rigorously trained in logic (and rhetoric, debate, analysis, and half a dozen other useless things besides) he soon came up with an answer which was claw-sharp and correct.

"Well," said Drake, "so that wizard was at least three-parts sham. So what about his tablet? What about his advice?"

"The answer to the tablet is easy," said his sister. "See what an alchemist makes of it."

So Drake went looking for an alchemist. He should have known better. After all, as part of his apprenticeship theory he had already learnt that there is no truth in alchemy, astrology, poetry, politics, paternity or weather forecasts. But Drake was young—and there is much the young can only learn the hard way.

Drake found an alchemist soon enough: a muttering, gnomish old man named Villet Vate, who had a dark narrow shop which he shared with moths, woodlice and a multitude of spiders.

"Come in, come in!" said Vate.

And Drake entered the shop; breathed its mysterious atmosphere of menthol, cajuput oil, cloves and camphor; breathed dust as well, and sneezed; gazed, open-mouthed, at mysterious stills, alembics and antique devices of unknown function.

"What's . . . what's this?" he said, touching a huge contraption of strangely-wrought metal.

"Ah, that," said Vate, rubbing his hands together. "That's a telescope. Very ancient, very ancient. All the best things are old."

"A telescope?"

"A device for looking on the faces of the stars," said Vate. "I can't quite make it work yet. But I'll get there, I'll get there."

(He was over-optimistic, for what he thought was a

telescope was in fact an electron microscope. And the device with which he hoped to transmute lead to gold was a zymometer. And his latest purchase—a curious metal sphere washed out of the sea by a storm—was not the magical treasure chest he imagined it was, but a bomb powerful enough to blow Stokos right off the map.)

"And what's . . . what's this?" said Drake, pointing to a very intricate device of interlocking wheels, arcs, crescents, levers and slides.

"That?" said Vate. "Ah, that's an astrolabe. It tells sun, moon, tide and time. It's elven work. Very ancient. Very rare. But for sale, if you've gold sufficient."

"No thanks," said Drake. "What I want is an assay."

"Of what?"

"This tablet. But—mind!—I want some left when you've finished with it."

"Break the tablet in half, then," said Vate. "Half is all I'll need."

Drake did as he was bid, then watched with intense interest as Vate dropped the sample into a mortar, ground it with a pestle, added seawater and sulphur and the urine of a rabbit, stirred the mixture with the feather of a white owl, decanted it, weighed it, adulterated it with snuff, stared at it through a magnifying glass, sniffed it, then pronounced:

"This tablet contains horn of unicorn, ground-up ginseng and essence of oyster, plus talcum powder, soap and a trace of cocaine."

"Will that cure me of love?" said Drake.

"Nay, man," said the alchemist. "It's an aphrodisiac!"

"Then what cure is there for love?" said Drake.

"This!" said Vate, holding up a sharp knife. "Come into the back room. I'll cure you for life in a moment."

"No thanks," said Drake.

And went away severely disillusioned with wizards and the world. But, since half the tablet remained, he took it. And, while that half a tablet contained no more than salt and sugar, Drake's faith in its qualities was such that he raged in lust for a week.

At this point it should probably be pointed out—in defense of the poor unicorn, which is increasingly rare these days—that there is no true aphrodisiac known to either man or woman (with the sole exception of propinquity, which does not come in tablet form).

In the end, Drake's lust diminished to normal levels (high, but not high enough to please him) and life itself returned to something close to normal.

Once more his main concern was his first sword. When was he going to get to make it? He dared not pester Gouda Muck, for fear the old man's temper would turn sour. But, in a frenzy of impatience, he watched Muck's slow but steady progress through his order list.

Just by watching, Drake began to learn a surprising amount. He was amazed at how much had escaped his notice in the last four years. Well, as the saying goes: "One can achieve either perfection of the religious life or perfection of the practical life."

Drake, till now, had always chosen religion over practicalities. But, if he had to go easy on religion in order to bring his apprenticeship to a successful conclusion, then he would make the necessary sacrifice.

"Come on, Muck," muttered Drake to Drake, morning and night. "Finish those swords! I want to get started on mine!"

5

Name: Gouda Muck.

Birthplace: Cam.

Occupation: swordsmith.

Status: taxpayer; senior citizen; second-best swordsmith on Stokos.

Description: old and ugly (Drake's opinion); wise and dignified (his own opinion); a waste of skin (his mother's opinion).

Residence: Hardhammer Forge, Ironbird Street, Cam, Stokos.

Gouda Muck was an atheist.
He was, quite possibly, the only atheist in the city of Cam. Most citizens enjoyed the practice of religion—indeed, for many devout souls, its consolations were all that made life worth living. But Gouda Muck was born to be a dissident. He refused to believe in the demon Hagon, far less to worship that formidable eater of souls.

He also avoided those sacred religious duties usually accepted even by unbelievers, viz:

† patronizing the temple casinos;
† copulating with the temple prostitutes;
† playing the temple numbers game;

60   Hugh Cook

† going to the temple cockfights;
† participating in the human sacrifices.

His main objection to all the above activities was that they cost an exorbitant amount of money.

"Religion," said Muck, "is a racket."

He could get away with talk like that, for he was the second-best swordsmith on Stokos, where metalworkers were valued highly.

Gouda Muck lived with three boys, but slept with none of them. One was a deaf mute who shovelled coal, worked the bellows, and exorcised the minor demons of puberty by raping chickens. The other two, Drake and Yot, were older, virgins no longer though beardless still.

The fair-haired Drake had, till now, been very religious: he loved to drink, gamble, fight and swear, and relished the privileges which came with having a sister in the temple. Unfortunately, there had been times when he had overdone things somewhat—and the people of Stokos, like people elsewhere, frowned on religious mania.

"Balance," said Drake to himself, "that's the thing. I've got to find a balance between the pleasures of religion and the demands of the world of work."

Yot, on the other hand, had no such problems to grapple with, for he was a spiritless fellow, a lank pale stripling with a runny nose (an allergy to coal dust made his life miserable with rhinitis) and warts.

And it was with Yot that the trouble began. It began only nine days after Drake saw the wizard Miphon—that is, just twenty days after Drake's ordeal at sea. It began when Yot, refusing to accept expense as excuse sufficient, demanded the real reason for Muck's dissent.

"I only believe in the Flame," said Muck, peering into the furnace.

"The Flame?" asked Yot.

"Aye, boy," said Muck, amused by Yot's wide-eyed attention. "The living presence of the High God of All Gods, which purifies as it witnesses."

LORDS OF THE SWORD 61

Drake, who was working in the forge at the time, heard that, but kept himself from sniggering. He wanted to hear more. So did Yot.

"How does it purify?" asked Yot.

"It burns, boy," said Muck. "Didn't your mother ever teach you that? Stick a hand in, if you doubt me—it'll do more than clean your fingernails. It burns, and I can see that it burns. Ocular proof, aye, that's the thing."

"But what's this business about gods?" asked Yot. "How did you find out about that?"

"The Flame spoke to me," said Gouda Muck. "And it speaks to me still."

And, seeing Yot's jaw drop, he continued the joke. At length.

Afterward, Drake teased Yot for believing in fairy tales. But Yot, stubborn in belief, refused to concede that Muck's dogma was a load of tripe and codswallop, conjured up for the whim of the moment. They fought. Drake, as usual, won—but Yot still made no intellectual concessions. He went on asking for tales of the Flame, and Muck went on telling them.

Well, all was fine at first. Then, after Muck had been telling these fairy tales for three days, the Flame did speak to him. It roared up out of the furnace, hung purple in the air, and shouted in a voice of drums and cymbals:

"Muck! Thou art who thou art!"

Then left, even as Muck fainted.

On recovery, Muck decided he had experienced a true religious revelation. Actually, the syphilis scrambling his brain had made him hallucinate. The syphilis, by the way, was a souvenir of his riotous youth—Muck had been solemnly celibate these past thirty-five years or more.

The Flame spoke often thereafter, bringing Faith to Gouda Muck; those gnawing spirochaetes had a lot to answer for. Muck listened to the Flame as he labored in the forge; he heard it as he ate his meals or walked by the dockside; the Flame gave him fresh revelations in his dreams.

How long does it take to create a religion?

Inspired by syphilis, Gouda Muck took precisely two days to lay down the foundations of his own faith.

The revelations of the Flame elevated Muck's personal quirks to the status of divine law: no drink, no gambling, no fighting and no loose women. What's more, thrift became an absolute virtue. Muck immediately began to help his apprentices be good by banking half their paltry wages into trust accounts managed by the Orsay Bank.

Drake had till then been happy enough as a swordsmith's devil, since all his hardships had been sweetened by the compensations of religion. With these denied to him—the confiscation of half his wages made certain of that—life went sour.

"Endure," said Drake to Drake.

He must live for the day when he was a master swordsmith, yes, with his own forge and apprentices.

"Muck," said Drake, one evening. "How about setting a definite date for me to start making my first sword?"

"Why should I do that?" said Muck.

"Because it will give me something to look forward to," said Drake.

"You've got nothing to look forward to," said Muck. "You're a filthy little scag-bag stuffed with iniquity. You pollute the forge by your very presence. All you're good for is slave labor."

"Oh, come now!" said Drake. "A joke's a joke, but—"

"I'm not joking!" roared Muck. "You'll never make a sword in this forge, no."

"But," said Drake, "I have to make swords. Lots of them. So I can finish my apprenticeship."

"Time will finish your apprenticeship nicely," said Muck. "But you won't be a swordsmith at the end of it, oh no. When I'm finished with you we'll kick you back to the filthy coal cliffs you came from."

Drake was staggered by this sudden turnaround. He really thought he'd finally come to terms with Gouda Muck. Now—what was he supposed to think? He could only suppose that he had grievously offended Muck in the last few days, though he couldn't for the life of him think of any really outrageous stunts he'd pulled.

Well, the situation was grim, that was for real. And . . . desperate situations called for desperate remedies. So . . .

"Man," said Drake, "I know we've cut each other up in the past, but that's over and done with. I respect you, man, I'll say that fair and square. You're the master. I'm but a child at your elbow. If I've done you wrong, I'm too much of a child to see what I can do to set things right. So—tell me, man. What have I done that's so terrible? What can I do to make amends?"

This display of humility really hurt him. He was intensely proud: he hated to grovel.

What was worse, his humility did him no good.

"You can't make amends," said Muck. "You went too far years ago. So you'll sweat death and dream buckles till your bones splinter."

"What?" said Drake, bewildered.

"The vizier of Galsh Ebrek calls," said Muck.

Then left the forge without further explanation.

The syphilis which had begun to destroy Muck's brain was, of course, invisible, so Drake had precious few clues to the reason for Muck's bizarre behavior. Was the man drunk? Worse: was he mad? Drake was reluctant to think so.

Was Muck serious?

That was a more important question. For if Muck was serious, then Drake's life was in ruins. Drake, turning things over in his mind, could only presume that his master was setting him a weird sort of test.

Yes.

A test to draw him out, to see how much initiative and determination he had. Maybe this was one of the secrets of the swordsmith's guild. Maybe every apprentice got set such a test, sooner or later, to see what he was really made of.

Accordingly, Drake set to work on a sword of his

own. Yot, who had been shovelling coal into sacks outside, came in and asked what he was doing.

"Never you mind," said Drake.

"It looks to me," said Yot, "as if you're starting work on a sword. You can't do that! Not till Muck gives you permission."

"I'll be the judge of what I can and can't do," said Drake.

And labored grimly until Muck returned at nightfall.

"What are you doing?" said Muck.

"Man, I'm making a sword," said Drake. "For I've got to start learning the real stuff sooner or later."

"I've told you already," said Muck, "your days of learning are finished. You're not human any longer, not as far as this forge is concerned. You're a piece of working meat, and nothing else."

"Man," said Drake, trying to keep himself from crying, "you're not being fair. You've got to teach me! That's why I'm here! To learn!"

"You're here to repent," said Muck. "To purify yourself."

"How do I do that?" said Drake.

"By working yourself to death."

"Right!" said Drake. "If you won't teach me, then I'll not stay here to sweat it out for starvation wages."

And, thirty days after his sixteenth birthday, Drake ran away. He fled to his parents' home in south-west Stokos. He was frightened, bitter, amazed at the sudden turn of events. A few days ago, everything had been going his way—and now? Disaster!

There was one bright spot on the horizon, of course: Drake's marriage prospects. But he could hardly rely too much on those, since King Tor might die any day, his demise destroying Drake's chances.

"Four years of my life!" sobbed Drake. "Four years of my life gone to this lousy apprenticeship! And what do I get out of it? I get kicked around like a cat."

The cat was the lowest form of life on the island of Stokos, for it was well known that the demon Hagon hated cats. They had it rough.

Drake had it rough, too, when he finally got home. He had only just finished explaining himself to his parents and to his brother Heth when agents from the swordsmith's guild arrived with a warrant, and whipped him back to Cam.

"We've a system for breaking people like you," said Muck, when Drake was brought back to the forge, whip-wounds bleeding. "We'll prove it out, if you try your nonsense a second time."

"Man," said Drake, "you've flipped! You're mad!"

"Don't answer back," said Muck. "You're just workmeat. A slave."

Well, there was no way Drake could take that in silence. So he did answer back, thus starting an argument, which Gouda Muck won by beating his apprentice into insensibility.

The next day, Drake went to complain to his uncle, Oleg Douay. He explained his problem.

"Muck says he won't teach me. He's going to work me like a piece of slave-rubbish till my apprenticeship runs out, then throw me on the slag heap."

"Come, boy," said Oleg, sure that Drake was exaggerating, "you had a little spat with your master, but that's no reason to act as if the world's coming to an end."

"He's serious!" said Drake.

"Oh, maybe he said a few words harder than he should have," said Oleg, "but don't take them to heart. I've known Gouda Muck for years. He's an honorable man. He'll do all right by you."

Unsatisfied by such reassurances, Drake promptly absconded a second time. And was hunted again, caught again, whipped again, and threatened with castration if he repeated his performance. The swordsmiths' guild was enormously powerful. There was no way Drake could fight it—not since his uncle refused to help.

"Maybe Muck will come to his senses," said Drake. "Maybe it's something he's eaten. I'll give him three months, yes, and see if he starts talking sense."

Meantime, Drake sought to console himself with

some of the pleasures of religion. He swiftly spent what savings he had. What now? He could hardly afford much on the half-wage Muck was doling out weekly.

"I need more money," said Drake.

He thought about robbing the Orsay Bank. Not a good idea! Many people had died that way, and nobody had yet succeeded. So he tried something more subtle—to borrow from the bank on the strength of the funds held in trust for him.

"We lend to nobody under twenty-five," said the Bankers. "And your funds are blocked till then, too."

"I hope you're paying me interest," said Drake smartly.

"Are you trying to squeeze us, boy? Get out, while you still have legs to get with!"

Fleeing the gaunt donjon of the Orsay Bank, he arrived back at the forge late, and got a beating which opened his whip-wounds. This was too much to bear, but worse was promised.

"The Flame has revealed Powers and Commands," said Muck grandly. "Any who resist Revealed Truth are worthy only of death. Thou shalt kneel down and worship—or die!"

Being the person he was, Drake acted boldly, and reported Muck's latest delusions to King Tor. He hoped to get Muck executed. For then, under the laws governing apprenticeships, the swordsmith's guild would be obliged to arrange for Drake to serve out the remainder of his apprenticeship under another master. With luck, that master would be Oleg Douay.

Unfortunately, Tor was busier than usual. Busy with what? With some weird and wonderful legislation his counsellors had lately proposed: a Bill to raise the minimum age for a mine worker to seven years, a Bill which would raise the age of consent to twelve, and a swag of Bills designed to limit the powers of a slavocrat over his human instruments.

"Let the Chamber of Commerce deal with it," said Tor.

"But this is serious!" said Drake. "There's not just heresy involved, either. Muck's refusing to teach—"

"Boy, I'm up to my ears in work," said Tor. "Go away! I don't want to see you until we consider you for marriage in two years' time."

So Drake got out while the getting was good.

He had scant faith in the Chamber of Commerce, so went and told Muck's mother instead. If she could knock some sense into her son, Muck might still come right, and prove himself as a decent master and a diligent teacher.

On learning the truth, Muck's mother was—to say the least—outraged. She had spent a lifetime in the temple, and was still working there at age ninety. Admittedly, these days she was a casino croupier, rather than the luxurious harlot she had been in the days when Muck was conceived.

She came hobbling down to the forge, leaning heavily on her swordstick, and told Muck just what she thought of him.

"You godless blaspheming heretic!" she said. "You're a waste of skin! I always thought so. Now I'm sure of it."

"Mother, dearest," said Muck. "Listen to me . . ."

And he began to preach. With eloquence. With a passion close to lust. With absolute conviction. And, slowly, his mother's expression began to change . . .

When Drake realized Muck's mother had been converted to her son's cult, he almost despaired.

"But," he said, "we can still try . . ."

And he denounced Muck to the Chamber of Commerce. That august body investigated, found the truth was worse than the report—the prophet of the Flame was starting to proselytize his neighbors—and promptly had Gouda Muck thrown into jail.

This happened on Midsummer's Day, two months after Drake's sixteenth birthday. By local reckoning, it was the middle of the year Tor 5; by the Collosnon dating which more of the world is familiar with, it was the start of Khmar 17. In any event, the date eventually became known as the Day of the Martyrdom of Muck;

its anniversary was ultimately enshrined as the most sacred event of the Holy Calendar of Goudanism.

Considering what some martyrs endure, Muck got off lightly. He was not beaten, flayed, singed, or starved, or exhibited in the stocks for the populace to throw stones at. His prison pallet had bedbugs, true, and his cell had rats—but his home had more of both. And, in any case, the terrible old man was soon released. All that money he had saved by never debauching himself in the temple had come in handy for bribes.

"How did you get out?" asked Yot.

"The Flame saved me," said Gouda Muck.

And, once said, it was impossible not to believe.

Muck spent long days brooding.

So did Drake.

Muck was showing no signs of coming to his senses. All attempts at getting rid of him had failed. So what now? Endure life as a virtual slave for the rest of his apprenticeship? Try again to run away? Or what? Drake decided that, as a point of honor, he would bring his apprenticeship to a successful conclusion despite anything and everything Muck might try.

"Living well is the best revenge," said Drake.

He imagined himself presenting a mastersword for the examination of the swordsmith's guild. Oh, that would give Muck a shock!

Accordingly, Drake went to see his uncle. He found Oleg painting some of his favorite skulls in patterns of red and green.

"What do you want?" said Oleg.

"I want to work at your forge in the evenings, after I finish work for Muck," said Drake. "I want you to teach me how swords are really made. I want you to give me all the learning so I can make my own mastersword."

"Oh, I can't do that!" said Oleg. "It wouldn't be ethical."

"But it's the only way!" said Drake, in tones of utter despair. "Muck still refuses to teach me!"

"Doubtless because you've been naughty," said

Oleg, dabbing a brushload of red paint into the nose-hole of one of his skulls. "Go back and apologize. You'll see. Things will soon come right."

Drake did apologize. Again. He grovelled.

It did him no good whatsoever.

"At least things can't get any worse," said Drake to himself.

He was wrong, of course.

Things can always get worse.

Shortly after Midsummer's Day, Drake's sister found a lump in her mouth. A friend examined it for her, and told her it was blue. The next day another lump sprouted. It could not be doubted: she had blue leprosy.

She cut her throat.

Drake mourned her for fifty days. In his grief, he no longer cared about his prospects for becoming a swordsmith. He also mourned for himself. For Miphon had made it clear that blue leprosy was spread by sex. Since Drake's sister had had the disease, it was even odds that he had it too.

"So what am I to do?" he said to himself.

He went and asked a priest for help.

"The answer is simple," said the priest. "As the wizard Miphon explained, there's no telling if you've got blue leprosy, for it may not show up for years. If you do get it, there's no cure, so don't bother looking for one. In the meantime, wear a condom every time you copulate with woman or man or dog or pig or whatever it is you fancy. That way, you won't spread the disease to anyone else."

Small comfort that was.

After another thirty days, however, Drake had got over his grief, fear and panic. Maybe he was infected. Maybe not. In any case, he was unlikely to find out for a year or two. Even if he had blue leprosy, a period of grace remained to him. He had better use that time wisely.

But how?

His sixteenth birthday was 150 days in the past. The end of his apprenticeship, which had once seemed to lie far away in the infinite future, would be upon him in little more than a year and a half. Oleg Douay still refused to believe Drake's account of his plight, or to give Drake the teaching he needed. Overtures to other swordsmiths brought blunt refusals.

It was clear he would never make a mastersword, or have his own forge, or have apprentices to kick around. He was getting old; his youth and hope were gone; he was finished. Sadly, Drake concluded that all that remained to him were the compensations of religion.

"I will devote what time remains to me," said Drake, "to the practical worship of the Gift."

The Gift? Sex! (And, technically, alcohol and drugs as well.)

Unfortunately, Muck had taken to banking his apprentices' wages with the Orsay Bank in toto. Drake was penniless. And, since his sister was dead, he no longer had special privileges at the temple.

"Right," he said. "I'll sell my body."

He had done it before, so he could do it again.

He cruised the docks, but found no buyers. For everyone knew why his sister had committed suicide, and none dared couple with someone who might be contaminated with blue leprosy. Thanks to the efforts of the temple of Hagon, knowledge of its etiology had spread throughout Cam. Priests boarded every incoming ship, preached doctrines of safe sex, advertised the temple prostitutes and warned against liaisons with dockside riff-raff.

"Right," said Drake. "I've got no sister. I've got no money. I can't sell my body. So how do I get a woman?"

Simple: he would have to make someone fall in love with him. Or at least in lust with him.

Since he might already be doomed to die of blue leprosy, the colony on the outskirts of town held little fear for him. He ventured there, and found Zanya Kliedervaust on her hands and knees scrubbing out bedpans.

"Remember me?" said Drake.

She looked up from her work.

LORDS OF THE SWORD 71

"Oh yes," she said. "I remember you. You're the crazy fisherman we hauled out of the sea a horizon away from Stokos."

"That's right," said Drake. "Only I'm a sword-smith, not a fisherman. Your body language tells me that you're looking for a relationship."

He had rehearsed that line—and many others besides—for a long time. It came out perfectly.

"What?" said Zanya, sounding both tired and puzzled.

"I'm seeking to make a treaty against the loneliness of flesh born into solitude," said Drake. "I aspire to harmonize our auras into one mutual faith."

"My Galish," said Zanya, "is not the best, though it improves steadily. You'll have to speak plain if you wish to be understood."

Oh! So there was a language problem! That was all right, then. For a moment, Drake had almost been afraid that his blond good looks were failing to make the right impression on the lady.

"Zanya," said Drake, "I like your looks, just as I'm sure you like mine. What say we get together tonight? We'd look right handsome together."

"What have you got in mind?" said Zanya.

"Some mutual moonlight, a dash of star-hunting, then a little lick of sweet honey."

Zanya entirely failed to recognize the import of these delicate euphemisms, which were part of the common language of courtship on Stokos.

"Speak plainly," she said. "What do you want?"

Drake, his eloquence thwarted by her linguistic ignorance, lost patience—and gave an answer which was, unfortunately, honest, clear, direct and straightforward.

"I'm in lust," he said. "I want to fornicate."

"I'm not meat," said Zanya coldly. "I'm a woman. There's a difference."

And she went back to her scrubbing.

"Sorry," said Drake. "I meant no offense. I didn't mean to be so blunt. But—"

"*Oronoko!*" bawled Zanya. "*Fana tufa n'fa n'maufi!*"

And out from a workshed came Prince Oronoko. The purple-skinned man was—as he had been when Drake last saw him—wearing only a loin-cloth. Perhaps he had been chopping wood: his body glistened with sweat, and he had an axe in his hands. Oronoko advanced, grinning. Drake fled.

Later, sullen and disconsolate, he brooded over his failure with Zanya. She hadn't even bothered to ask his name.

He thought—and thought hard—about the advice the wizard Miphon had given him. All that stuff about flowers, poetry, daily visits, sincerity, pretty speaking, persistence. Should he try it? No, it couldn't possibly work. It sounded too stupid for words. Anyway, there was Oronoko to think of. If Drake went back, the purple man would probably chop off his head.

Drake sulked.

Meanwhile, the Flame spoke long and hard to Gouda Muck. Until finally, on Midwinter's Day (the start of the year Tor 6, or the middle of Khmar 17, depending on one's calendar) Muck announced to the world that he was the incarnation of the Flame. And the Flame, by his account, was the High God of All Gods.

"Fall down and worship me," said Muck.

Some of his more credulous neighbors actually did. They fell to the ground, groaning. They licked his feet. They saw visions. They spoke in tongues.

"Good," said Muck. "You see? I am God!"

And Drake, dissenting, was severely kicked and beaten. He sought refuge with his uncle.

"Man," said Drake, "you've got to do something! Muck's mad, I'm sure of it."

"Endure," said Oleg Douay, who thought a little perdition would be good for the boy.

"But the man's mad, I tell you!" protested Drake.

"We're all mad," said Oleg Douay grimly, "or we'd have had more sense than to get ourselves born."

"We don't have a choice," said Drake.

"Of course we do!" said his uncle grimly. "Why,

only yesterday I was down by the shore in conversation with the sea gods, and they told me distinctly—"

Drake turned tail and fled.

By now, financial constraints made it virtually impossible for Drake to worship at the temple brothel. What's more, Gouda Muck forbid his apprentices even to go near the place. Of course, to forbid a thing is often to encourage a taste for it. Drake had always had a love for the Demon. Now, he became a true victim of religious mania, feeling he needed to practice religion at every possible moment just to keep himself sane.

But most forms of worship required money.

"What I need," said Drake, "is some kind of worship that will earn me money."

Gambling was the only religious practice which seemed to meet his requirements. So he took himself off to the casinos.

From the middle of winter to the beginning of spring, Drake tried his luck and his luck tried him. After that, the casinos cut off his credit. His gambling debts were huge, and the temple's enforcers were soon pressing him for payment.

Barred from the casinos, Drake chanced his fortunes privately, hazarding ill-lit backgammon saloons and murky dice-chess parlors. To finance his ventures, he borrowed where he could, signing notes to all and sundry with his thumbprint. He wagered ever more wildly, hoping to recoup his losses. But he drank while he gambled—never a good combination. He came home drunk one night, and, feeling reckless, spat into the fire in his master's sight.

"You have defiled my living flesh," said Gouda Muck—and began to beat him.

Drake fled. He was doing a lot of running away these days. He didn't like it. He wandered through the night, cursing, kicking cats, and working himself into a rage. This was all Zanya's fault! If that proud-faced bitch hadn't snubbed his offer, he'd never have got in this mess.

That suggested a way out.

If he porked her once, surely she'd see sense. One taste of Drake Douay, and she'd be eagering for more. Yes. She'd said no, but it was common knowledge that women often said no when they meant yes. How far was it to the leper colony? Not far at all: he was almost at the edge of town already.

Drake rolled up to the leper colony.

"Despatch for Zanya Kliedervaust," he said, brandishing a wallet (which was empty). "Urgent despatch. Immediate delivery required."

"You've been drinking," said the night porter.

"So I have," said Drake belligerently. "But I can still deliver a letter. If you don't want to let me through, wake your boss, and we'll talk it out with him."

The night porter saw sense, and gave Drake directions to Zanya's quarters. It was, after all, scarcely unusual for a courier to be drunk on duty. And they did work all hours of day and night.

Shortly, Drake entered Zanya's room—a mean little hut lit by a smoky oil lamp. The woman of his desires was sitting up in bed, reading a scroll of some kind.

"You!" she said.

"Me," said Drake.

"Get out!" she said.

"Hey," said Drake. "Don't be so hard on me. I don't mean any harm. What's with that scroll?"

"This?" said Zanya, mellowing ever so slightly. "This was lent to me by a friend. It's very interesting. It's all about Goudanism. That's the creed of Gouda Muck. I don't know if you've ever heard of him."

"I may have," said Drake cautiously. "What do you think of it?"

"Great!" said Zanya, her eyes shining. "Would you like to hear about it? Here, sit down on the floor and I'll read you some."

That was mighty accommodating of her, under the circumstances. But Zanya, as a priestess of the Orgy God on the Ebrells, had gained a vast experience of dealing with drunks. She thought Drake was not too dangerous. If she settled him down and spoke to him nicely, likely he would go to sleep. Then she could slip out and summon Oronoko.

"Why should I listen to something about Gouda Muck?" said Drake.

"Because of who he is," said Zanya, meaning no harm. "He's the High God of All Gods."

This was too much to bear. Drake had come to the woman who was the focus of all his desire—only to find Gouda Muck had come before him, in spirit if not in flesh.

With a scream of rage, Drake tore the scroll away from Zanya, and jumped on her.

She slapped a hand to his face and dug fingers into his eyes. Hard. He jerked his head back. Instantly her fingers slid to his throat and dug in. Viciously. Then she hooked an elbow into the side of his head. His world reeled. Agonizing pain exploded between his legs as she thumped him in the testicles.

Drake collapsed to the floor, a helpless heap of writhing misery. Zanya, who was indeed a well-built woman, picked him up and threw him outside.

"Don't come back!" she said. "Or I'll batter you dead!"

Drake crawled away into the darkness, groaned. But, after a while, the pain became manageable. He decided he had better go back and apologize, yes. Otherwise Zanya would be permanently soured against him. Manfully, Drake got to his feet. Someone was knocking at Zanya's door. Who? The door opened; a gleam of lamplight showed Prince Oronoko standing in the doorway.

If Drake's throat had not been so sore, he would have screamed his outrage. Instead, he stood silent as Oronoko entered. The door closed. Drake heard Zanya speak, then laugh. Well! So much for that! Drake's prospects for making his woman were—for tonight, at least—reduced to zero.

Drake was a long time getting back to the forge, since every step he took hurt him. Would the door be barred against him? It was not. Since Muck had discovered he was actually the High God of All Gods, he had lost all fear of mortal men. Everyone was asleep when Drake slipped inside, as quiet as could be.

Drake did not sleep that night. He brooded in the little attic where he was quartered, and while he brooded he drank from the crock of hard liquor he kept in his chest for emergencies.

He felt humiliated.

Rape was supposed to be easy, the perfect demonstration of a man's easy mastery over a woman. But Drake had failed. Everything he tried had gone sour. His whole life was a disaster. He was ready to kill himself.

But why should he? Why should he give Gouda Muck that satisfaction? No. He shouldn't kill himself. He should do something which would really piss Muck off in a big way. But what? Burn down the forge? No good—it was insured. Let's see. Another drink, yes, that was the story. First drink, then thought. Drink was good. It eased the pain in his balls and the pain in his eyes.

Toward dawn, sore, drunk, hurt and as reckless as ever, Drake crept downstairs and stole Muck's mastersword, the prize bit of steelwork which Muck had created years before to win admission to the swordsmiths' guild.

Sunrise found Drake on the docks of Cam, determined to sell that very same sword.

At that early hour, there was little life stirring. Drake, nothing daunted, went and knocked up Theyla Slonage, a merchant from Narba who had a certain reputation. Slonage, bleary and unbeautiful in the morning light, reluctantly invited Drake into his back room.

"What have you got for me?" asked Slonage. "And don't say yourself! You've spoilt your boyish beauty with those blacksmith's muscles. Look at your hands— Demon's grief, they're twice as tough a sharkskin. And you've been fighting. Have you looked at yourself? You've got two hideous-ugly black eyes."

Drake, in answer, revealed the sheathed sword which had been hidden down his trouser leg. Slonage without bothering to look at it, offered a thousandth of its value. Drake unsheathed the blade, slowly, fingerlength by fingerlength. Its naked beauty glimmered in the gloom. Drake, looking at it, felt almost sober.

Slonage sneered, but doubled his offer. However, Drake, who knew the price of steel, was hardly going to sell the masterwork for 0.2 percent of its value.

Drake eased open a shutter to let in the cool light of morning. Raising the blade to the light, he blew upon its surface. As his breath condensed upon the steel they both saw the patterns of the forging momentarily snake across the surface of the metal.

Theyla Slonage raised his offering to a hundredth of the sword's value. Drake replied by asking double, and they settled, at length, for a fiftieth.

Drake was not paid off in the shangles and jives minted by King Tor, but in Bankers' Money, the coinage issued everywhere by the Partnership Banks. He got five zeals—small rings of nine-carat gold, stamped on both inside and outside with banker's marks. He got a dozen bronze flothens, circular coins with threading holes in the middle. And he got, as well, a scattering of spings which he did not even bother to count.

There were nine Partnership Banks, each issuing the same identical coinage. And these banks—immensely rich, enormously powerful and intensely secretive—were:

† the Orsay Bank of Stokos;
† the Morgrim Bank of Chi 'ash-lan;
† the Safrak Bank of the Safrak Islands;
† the Monastic Treasury of Inner Adeer, located hard up against the Ashun Mountains in Voice, the retirement city of the rulers of the Rice Empire;
† the Flesh Trader's Financial Association of Galsh Ebrek;
† the Bondsman's Guild of Obooloo, capital city of Aldarch the Third, the Mutilator of Yestron;
† the Bralsh, of Dalar ken Halvar;

78   Hugh Cook

† the Singing Dove Pensions Trust of Tang;
† and the Taniwha Guarantee Corporation of Quilth.

How those far-flung organizations managed to coordinate their activities was one of the larger mysteries of the universe. However, most people—indeed, even most kings, princes, priests and emperors—were unaware that Bankers' Money was accepted in many far-flung places which were largely ignorant even of each other's existence.

The only person ever to ponder this conundrum seriously was the wizard Phyphor; that notable master of the Order of Arl was brooding about it yet again even as Drake emerged into the steadily strengthening sunlight of the dockside morning.

Drake, who was starting to feel a little anxious, settled his nerves with an early-morning beer. His newfound wealth made it hard for him to find the bottom of the beer mug, and it was mid-morning before he emerged again into the hot, raucous bustle of the docks.

He strolled along, hands dug deep in his pockets. He kicked a piece of shining sea-coal. Once. The sudden movement hurt his bruised, swollen testicles. He idled from stall to stall, scarcely listening to the babble of languages assaulting his ears as hoarse-voiced shills screamed the virtues of products as diverse as querns and keflo shell.

Then he saw a couple of big men prowling through the crowds. They wore long robes and carried iron-shod staves. Elsewhere, they might have been mistaken for wizards, but Drake recognized them on sight. They were two of the temple's enforcers. He knew they knew him well. He walked the other way, toward a man who was hawking passages to Androlmarphos.

". . .' Marphos today . . . noon sailing . . . 'Marphos today . . . one zeal for the beer-price passage . . ."

Drake made a drunken decision which he would never have made sober, and paid out for a passage to the foreign port, leaving at noon that same day.

6

Name: Dreldragon Drakedon Douay.

Alias: Drake (meaning, in the Ligin of Stokos, "pumpkin").

Occupation: swordsmith's apprentice.

Status: criminal on the run.

Description: a nuggety fair-haired beardless lad with hard hands and a blacksmith's muscles; he is shorter than fashion prefers, but not exactly stunted.

Prospects: if he survives to see his eighteenth birthday, he may be allowed to marry King Tor's daughter—which would bring him, in time, the throne of Stokos.

There was no nonsense about passengers on the good ship *Flying Fish*. They were battened down below decks for the passage to Androlmarphos, a run of about two hundred leagues as the aasvogel flies, but rather more as the ship tacks. The *Flying Fish*, which held several unofficial records for ultra-slow passages, generally made the voyage in six days.

Drake, being battened down below, was unable to hang over the stern rail waxing maudlin as the cliffs of Stokos receded into the distance. He hung over the side of his bunk instead, miserably seasick, and vomited into the pitching gloom. Fortunately, he was on the lowest bunk, with nobody below him. Unfortunately, there were three men in the tiers above, each as sick as he was . . .

By the time Drake had vomited up everything in his stomach, the anaesthetic effects of alcohol were beginning to wear off, and both his body and psyche were suffering. He tried to console himself by eating and drinking, but continued seasickness made both these enterprises counter-productive.

Bad weather stretched the voyage out. Once, the ship was almost wrecked on the shores of Hok, a mountainous coastal province of the Harvest Plains, lying due north of Stokos. Finally, nine full days after leaving Cam, the *Flying Fish* reached her destination.

It was a pale, unsteady youth who finally staggered down the gangplank to the dockside at Androlmarphos, the great trading city commanding the delta of the Velvet River. This was the first time Drake had set foot on the continent of Argan, fabled land of ruined cities, fallen empires, monsters, magic, sages, wizards and worse. He expected immediate amazements— but was swiftly disillusioned.

The bustling docks were much the same in 'Marphos as in Stokos. The ships looked no different; many, indeed, he had seen before at Cam. And, while the place was a polyglot babble of foreign languages, the dominant argot was the Galish Trading Tongue, which he knew well enough already.

Since Androlmarphos recognized Bankers' Money, Drake had no need to find a money-changer. Anywhere inland, he would have been less lucky: but in 'Marphos a full half-dozen currencies mingled promiscuously. He could even have spent the jives and shangles minted by his own King Tor, had he had any to his name.

Drake bought a fish sandwich and, eating it slowly, watched men lose money to a quick-talking rogue who hid a peanut under one of three little cups, shuffled these, then asked his victims to guess its hiding place. Drake was too canny to risk cold cash on a sucker's game like that, but nevertheless found the sight heartening—it suggested the Demon was worshipped here in Androlmarphos, if not in name then at least in deed.

He went to search for a bar.

Seventeen days later, when the last of his money was almost gone, someone tapped him on the shoulder and spoke his name. Turning, he saw it was Yot.

"Why, Sully Datelier Yot!" said Drake. "What brings you here? Come to enjoy yourself, perhaps?"

"No," said Yot, drawing a knife. "I've come to—"

But Drake, waiting to hear no more, threw half a mug of beer into the boy's face, then grabbed his knifehand. Their struggle precipitated a general bar brawl—it was that kind of drinking establishment, the only kind which would have tolerated Drake's seventeen-day binge. In the end, the Watch broke up the fight.

Yot escaped, but Drake was caught and hauled before a judge. He heard, as others have in his predicament, many fulsome phrases about the need for personal responsibility and the shortcomings of the younger generation. Then heard his sentence:

"Ship out or else."

"Or else what?" asked Drake incautiously.

"Or else we'll chop off both your feet and sell them to raise funds for charity!" roared the judge, who, having tried three dozen identical cases that day, was losing his sense of proportion.

"I've got no money," said Drake, who had been stripped of the last of his funds by the Watch.

"Then we'll help you earn some," said the judge with a pleasant smile, which suggested that something particularly nasty was coming. He had till then been speaking in Galish, but lapsed momentarily into Legal Churl. There was a pause before the translation came:

"Twenty days hard."

"Hard?" said Drake, in bewilderment.

It sounded thoroughly obscene to him.

"Hard labor, fool!"

Drake then spent twenty days chained to the oar of a galley, rowing up and down the long sweaty river-leagues inland from Androlmarphos. The work was tough, the rations poor, and the view monotonous. His galley once went upstream as far as Selzirk itself, but docked in the magnificent capital of the Harvest Plains by night, and was gone again before dawn. That irked Drake as much as anything else.

At least those twenty days gave him plenty of time to plan for his future. He would go back to Stokos. Yes. He would throw himself on the mercy of King Tor. Or would he? No: he would come not with a plea but with a sword. He would offer himself to Tor as an executioner. A Suppressor of Unorthodox Religions.

Once Drake's eloquence had persuaded Tor of the danger posed by Gouda Muck's cult, surely the king would be only too glad to have a vigorous young man like Drake in charge of the suppression of Muck's outlandish heresies.

Yes.

And once he had an official position, a fancy title, a sizeable income and a rainbow-colored uniform designed to show off his muscles, he'd make another assault on Zanya Kliedervaust. But he would refine his tactics first. He might even try some of the things the wizard Miphon had suggested. Would he pledge his love with poetry? No, never—he'd feel ridiculous. But he might take her flowers. Well, one flower, anyway. And maybe he shouldn't be so direct about demanding her body. Maybe he should give her some time to get used to him. How long? Three days? No, two should do it . . .

After twenty days on the galley, Drake expected liberty. But got no such thing. Instead, he was battened down in the hold of the *Gol-sa-danjerk,* a foreign ship which gave him less air, less space and less light than the *Flying Fish,* and kept him on shorter commons besides. Where he was bound, he knew not; the other exiles imprisoned with him knew as little as he.

"With luck," said Drake, "we're being deported to Stokos."

In fact, they had all been sold into slavery, and were

being carried north-west toward a slaving port in the Ravlish Lands.

At last, after what seemed an age—but was really only seven half-days and a fingerlength—an unfamiliar voice of command ordered them up on deck. They scrambled up through a recently unbattened hatch to find their ship still at sea. Another vessel was connected to the *Gol-sa-danjerk* by grappling hooks. Copious quantities of blood on the deck suggested that the connection had not been entirely welcomed. Indeed, Drake observed that most of the crew had become corpses. Strangers dressed in sealskins were busy stripping those corpses.

"Pirates," said Drake to himself.

This was a guess, but it was accurate.

"Which of you jerks can sail?" roared a pirate, in something approximating to Galish.

All except Drake proclaimed themselves to be sailors.

"You," said a pirate, pointing at him. "You know the sea, or don't you?"

"I know something better," said Drake, with a metalworkers' conceit which marked him as a true son of Stokos. "I know steel. Hammering, shaping, forging and sharpening. I'm a master craftsman, don't you know."

Gouda Muck would have laughed bitterly to have heard that joke—though Drake did know some of the basics.

"You're a landlubber, then," said a pirate, and knocked him to the deck.

Drake swiftly realized his mistake. The other prisoners swore themselves to be pirates, and were accepted into the fraternity of the sea-robbers. Drake, on the other hand, was looked on as near to useless.

A prize crew was left on the *Gol-sa-danjerk*, but Drake was dragged on board the pirate ship. Its sails, he saw, were black. It seemed strangely familiar. He was half-persuaded that this was the very same barque which he had seen anchored in the harbor of Cam the morning after his sixteenth birthday.

84 Hugh Cook

"What ship be this?" he said.

"The *Walrus*, friend," said a voice.

That voice sounded familiar. Indeed, it came from the mouth of Bucks Cat—one of the jeering boatmen who had forced Drake into the sea to drown a horizon away from Stokos. Even though that was more than half a year ago, the horrors of the occasion were, to say the least, vivid in Drake's memory.

"You!" said Drake.

"And me," said another man.

A lean, pale man. Ish Ulpin!

"Come along, darling," said Ish Ulpin. "We're going to introduce you to the captain. He might like a nice young boy like you."

So Drake was led along the deck of the *Walrus*. And an evil barque she was, too, a stinking tub of reeks and rats, with decks near as dirty as her bilges. Drake, however, had no time for detailed inspection, for he was shortly confronted with her captain, one Slagger Mulps. This man was nicknamed "the Walrus"—hence the name of his ship.

A weird sight he was.

Slagger Mulps was very tall and very thin, and had a very long very sharp nose. But what first impressed was his beard and his hair, both of which were green.

"On your knees!" said Ish Ulpin, "for you stand in the presence of our great captain, Slagger Mulps, the Walrus himself."

Drake held his ground. Ish Ulpin drove hard, bony thumbs into pressure points in Drake's shoulders, forcing him down to his knees.

"Who are you?" said Slagger Mulps.

His eyes, like his hair, were green—like those of the wizard Miphon. His arms were long, dangling right down to his knees. He had, Drake saw, two thumbs and three fingers on each hand.

"If you want me to talk," said Drake, "first find a human being for me to talk to."

Drake Douay had made a big mistake.

He had said the worst of all possible things.

For the Walrus was acutely conscious of his strangeness. He had led the worst of childhoods imaginable—teased, bullied and rejected on account of his green hair and his multiple thumbs. The experience had marked him for life.

The Walrus stared at Drake, envying his perfect conformity (height apart) to the human norm.

"I," said the Walrus, "am human. What's more, I'm likely the man who will kill you."

"Lucky you don't have a mirror," said Drake, "or you'd likely kill yourself."

The Walrus, who had seen himself mirrored in glass, metal and water often enough, was overcome with fury. Raising his voice, he shouted:

"Who wants to play with this thing before I kill it?"

"I do," said a rough, gruff voice.

And forward stepped a barrel-chested hairy brute in bloodstained sealskins, his coarse-featured face surrounded by shaggy black hair and a great big black beard. It was Andranovory.

The Walrus immediately regretted having spoken.

Andranovory was the worst of his men—a drunken, murderous, argumentative bully, an untrustworthy sadist hated by at least half the crew. In the past, he had treated prisoners in ways which gave Mulps nightmares.

"There are others more worthy," said the Walrus. "I give the pleasure of playing with this—with this thing to Ish Ulpin."

"And I," said Ish Ulpin, "yield that pleasure to my shipmate, Andranovory."

That personage grinned at Drake, showing broken rot-brown teeth.

"Atsimo Andranovory," he said, introducing himself. "I believe we've met."

"Oh, I don't think we have," said Drake.

"You don't remember me?" said Andranovory. "Well, you'll remember me hereafter. Give me a suck!"

And the raptor exposed his weapon to the cool sea breeze. His knob was crusted with festering sores.

"Suck!" said Andranovory.

"I'll not play woman," said Drake, in a voice shaking with tension.

Mulps sympathized with the boy who did not want to play woman—not, at least, with so many men watching.

"Lazy little bugger!" said Andranovory, giving him an idle slap. "But we can cure that. String him up by the ankles till he learns when he's well off."

While Mulps did not approve of such tortures, he could scarcely intervene. If his crew ever learned the true nature of his sensitive, infinitely tender soul, they would surely lose faith in him as a captain. Mulps was aware that he was not much of a sailor, or much of a fighter, either—it was his thrift and financial acumen, more than anything, which had brought him control of the ship.

So Mulps could only stand back and watch helplessly as Ish Ulpin and Bucks Cat, obedient to Andranovory's commands, tied Drake's hands behind his back then tied a rope to his ankles. The rope was slung over a yard-arm.

Drake lay on the hard deck, staring up at the blue sky. All around were unfriendly faces. He wished he had not given Andranovory those duff directions on the dockside of Cam, more than half a year ago. But, at the time, it had seemed such an innocent little trick.

"Mike!" yelled Ish Ulpin. "Come help us haul a rope!"

And something far too large to be human came trundling along the deck. It was twice the height of any man. It was as wide in the shoulders as a man's outstretched arms. It had no ears: only holes in the side of its head where ears should be.

It was Whale Mike.

"Oh, you," said Whale Mike, looking down at Drake in surprise.

"Yes, me," said Drake, staring up at the yellow-faced monster.

"What you down there for?" said Whale Mike.

"Because that toad-raping Atsimo Andranovory wants a suck," said Drake. "And I'll tell you this—he's not getting one from me!"

"Then you ask Walrus help you," said Whale Mike. "He our captain. He good joker."

"Our young friend here isn't exactly Slagger Mulps' favorite person," said Ish Ulpin. "He more or less said our beautiful green-haired captain wasn't human."

"Oh, that not very nice," said Whale Mike.

And pulled on the rope which ran up from Drake's feet and over the yard-arm. Drake was lifted clear of the deck. His hair flopped down. Blood rushed to his head.

"Heave ho!" said Bucks Cat.

And gave Drake a push which sent him swinging across the deck and out over the sea. He spun. He had a dizzy, giddy view of surging blue sea and dazzling sun. Then he was swinging back to where he had started from. Ish Ulpin was there to meet him. With a fist.

"That enough!" said Whale Mike, "You stop. This my friend!"

"Oh, man," said Bucks Cat, slapping Drake on the back. "You're in luck! Whale Mike's your friend!"

And he hooted with laughter.

It was such a good joke that even Ish Ulpin laughed. But Andranovory simply looked at Drake and said:

"If you get off this rope alive, I'll be waiting for you."

Drake, hanging upside down, dizzy, sore, sick, found it impossible to come up with a smart reply.

Whale Mike hauled Drake higher until their heads were level. Drake was well over twice his own height from the deck. A long way to fall. A lethal fall, if he landed on his head. Mike took a turn of rope around his fist, as if he meant to hold Drake there for some time.

"Great view," said Drake, starting to sway with the motion of the swells that rocked the ship.

But all he could see at that moment was Whale

Mike's swollen sallow yellow face and tiny imbecilic eyes. Mike hooked a couple of fingers into Drake's collar to stop him swaying.

"We no meet long time," said Mike.

"Too right," said Drake.

"You do good swim," said Mike. "You smart joker. Tough, eh? If not tough, then drown. You make good pirate maybe."

"Yeah, sure," said Drake. "Cut me down then I'll prove just how good."

"Not that easy, my friend. First you make An'vory happy. You suck, that not hurt you any. Then maybe some joker rough you up, but I make sure it not go too far. I say good word for you to Walrus. He not bad joker. He okay."

"No deal," said Drake. "I won't suck any filthy pirate cock. I'd rather die."

"That not so smart," said Whale Mike. "Not much good being you when you dead. That not so? You take care An'vory, I take care you. You say nice things to Walrus, then he happy, you happy. You my friend."

"My friend!?" shouted Drake. Stress, pain, nausea and disorientation suddenly yielded to an enormous outburst of hate, rage and anger. "My friend? How do you reckon? Man, you helped force me into the sea to drown! You tried to kill me!"

"That little thing between friends," said Whale Mike.

Drake was staggered by this bland assertion.

"You're twigged, man!" he screamed. "You've gone to rust! You can't make friends by drowning people!"

"That not so smart," said Whale Mike. "You need friend real bad. So you have long swim. So what? You not drowned. You not dead, so why worry?"

"You sound as if I should be grateful!" said Drake.

"You get good swim," said Whale Mike. "You get out of water, you feel real man. Real proud. You get good story, tell many times. Joker buy you beer, hear story. That not so? Not all bad, that swim. You get plenty beer."

That was true, up to a point. Drake had told the story of his deep-sea survival many times. He had got many beers out of it. But that was hardly the point.

"You're mad, you crazy bugger!" said Drake.

"No, you mad," said Whale Mike, sounding hurt. "You not right in head. I your friend. I try help. You not want help. Maybe you die, but that your problem, not mine."

And he unhooked his fingers from Drake's collar. Drake began to swing. And Mike hauled him up higher into the blue blue sky.

"Investigate," muttered Drake.

And did his very best to see how and where the rope was tied off. Whale Mike was fastening it to a cleat on the deck. Drake's life now depended on the safety of a knot tied by a moron. Grief!

He closed his eyes and tried to endure.

After a while, he found endurance impossible.

"All right!" he cried, with what voice was left to him. "I'll do it! I'll do it! Anything and everything! An'vory, sure. Even the captain, yes! Every man in the ship! Just let me down from here!"

But if anyone heard, nobody took any notice.

And Drake soon left off crying, for his throat was far too dry to continue.

All day he dangled, utterly helpless. He had no knife. Even if gymnastic flair and a touch of magic had allowed him to untie himself and get to the deck alive, he would have faced a shipload of pirates more than ready to hang him right up again—quite possibly by his testicles.

The wind got up.

The sea thickened.

It was, of course, sheer torture to be suspended there, swaying in sickening arcs as the ship rutted through the rolling seas. The weather worsened toward evening; by dayfall, they were in a regular storm. But Drake, by then, was only half-conscious.

When the ship struck, he heard the panic-stricken shouts of pirates only as another thread of violence in the nightmares of delirium. When the seas swirled up around him, he thought at first that his head was being shoved into a bucket of salt water.

Then realized he was afloat on the turbulent seas of night. Afloat? He was drowning! Feet tied together. Hands tied behind back. A wave wrecked him under. He tried to jack-knife to the surface. Failed. Then the seas slacked away. He was afloat upon liquid ebony, staring at blindness. He gasped darkness, found part of it breathable.

Something was pulling on his ankle-rope.

Moments later, Drake was hauled right up out of the water and seized by something huge: by a monster possessed of inexorable strength. Throat moistened by seawater, Drake screamed.

"Why you scream?" said a voice. "You safe now."

Who could that be?

Drake thought he could guess.

"You cuddle close," said the voice. "You shy? Not good be shy. Sea cold. Share heat."

"Can't cuddle," said Drake. "Can't anything. Hands tied."

"That no problem. Knife made for that."

And Whale Mike cut the water-swollen ropes which bound Drake's wrists. Drake's first thought was to seize the knife and kill his enemy. But he could not see the knife in the night. And, in any case, his hands were—for the moment—near enough to useless.

"Can't hold on," said Drake. "Too tired."

"Easy, man," said Whale Mike. "You not fall. I hold. You good friend, I not let you fall."

And Whale Mike cradled Drake in his arms. The night was full of sounds of seething sea, of wave-wreck and surf-shatter. But they could not drown out Mike's voice. He had started singing! He was crooning a song in some strange, strange foreign language which Drake did not understand. But, without understanding the words, Drake was fairly sure the song was a lullaby.

Whale Mike was still singing a lifetime later when the shroud-pale dawn illuminated the masts and rigging of the wrecked ship, the ragged white surf breaking on nearby rocks, and a huddling of pirates barnacled on those spray-lashed rocks.

"Look!" cried Ish Ulpin.

And everyone looked, and saw Whale Mike sitting where yard-arm joined mast, with Drake Douay on his lap.

"Hey, Mike!" yelled Bucks Cat from the rocks. "How's your baby?"

"He all right!" yelled Whale Mike. "We sing happy song!"

Drake had never felt so humiliated in his life.

He tried to untie the ropes which still secured his feet. But all he managed to do was break two fingernails. He began to cry with fatigue and frustration. His tears ran hot down his cheeks.

"You want free from rope?" said Mike. "That no problem. I just leave rope in case wave take you in dark. Rope for safety. I cut."

And he pulled out his sheath knife—which was almost the size of a sword—and liberated Drake's feet.

"What now?" said Drake.

"This!" said Whale Mike.

And threw Drake into the water.

"Hey!" shouted Drake, floundering in the slathering sea.

Mike laughed.

"Swim!" he said, waving in the direction of the nearby reef. "Swim!"

Drake, having no option, swam toward the reef, where barking surf chased yelping waves and devoured them in crevices and rock-traps. Then Mike dived, and swam after him. When Drake gained the rocks, he jammed himself between two of the largest and coldest and hung on tight against the threat of the surf.

"Bring your slut-hole here, darling," said Andranovory.

But, to Drake's surprise, the order was not followed up by a prompt attack. Even Andranovory was too far gone to be lusting in more than thought.

Whale Mike wallowed through the seas like something out of a bad dream. He gained the rocks.

"You all right?" called Mike to Drake.

"Fine," said Drake.

"You want cuddle?" said Mike.

"I've cuddled enough, thanks," said Drake.

"Never enough cuddle," said Mike.

And, shortly, Whale Mike, Slagger Mulps, Ish Ulpin and Bucks Cat were cuddling together in a big body heap. Drake saw most of the other pirates had also huddled into body-warmth teams. He realized it would be smart to join them, for it was cold; wind and spray were sweeping the exposed rocks. But he was too scared.

He humbled down as best he could, trying to make himself invisible. A gull winged low above the slipshod surf. How long would it be before he was too weak to save his eyes from the seabirds? The slubbering sea throttled amongst the rocks, hungering for his hot blood and his long white bones; if the storm got up again, the sea would surely claim him before the birds did.

Finding thought so unproductive of pleasure, Drake stopped the practice, and shortly fell into a fitful half-sleep punctuated by dreams and the voice of hallucination.

Meanwhile, Slagger Mulps, luxuriating in the warmth of Whale Mike's armpit, stared out to sea. Shadows smudged the far-distant horizon; he knew those shadows to be the Greater Teeth. They were shipwrecked, without a doubt, on the Gaunt Reefs; there was at least an even chance that they would be rescued before too long by a raiding ship or a fishing boat.

And almost an even chance that they would not.

"We sing!" shouted Whale Mike, with invincible cheerfulness. "Everyone sing!"

This command woke everyone who had managed to drift away into the land of dreams—including Drake. He listened with astonishment as Whale Mike started a song.

All the pirates knew it, and joined in, but Drake could not follow the lyrics, for they were so full of sea-talk, arcane slang, and dialect words native to the Greater Teeth. But the chorus was easy enough to understand: everyone howled like a dog, crowed like a cock, screamed like a cat then barked like a seal. Then clapped hands against thighs.

Drake suddenly wanted to be part of it: part of the singing, the slapping, the body-huddles, the community. It all seemed, for a moment, positively jolly. But did not dare join in. His recent experiences had left him feeling as wrecked as the *Walrus*. He closed his eyes, and, eventually, slept.

Toward noon, Drake woke from muttering nightmares to hear excited talk amongst the pirates. They had sighted a ship. As it came closer, they saw it had green sails. Closer still, and they saw its dragon figurehead.

Mulps spat, and swore.

"It's the *Warwolf*," said Mulps.

The masts and rigging of the *Walrus* advertised their presence, and it was soon clear to everyone except Drake that the *Warwolf* had sighted them. However, by the time the ship was bulking near the reefs, even he knew that rescue was at hand—not that the pirates seemed glad of it.

Keeping a prudent distance from the rocks, the *Warwolf* lowered three boats to investigate. Soon the castaways were sharing their reef with newcomers, a party of grim men tricked out with weapons and looking more than ready to use them. One was, to judge from his bearing, their leader.

He carried himself like a king.

He was tall, lean, as black as Bucks Cat and as bald as a hazel nut. He was dressed in brown leather, and wore round his hips a great big leather belt from which hung a waterproof sea-pouch and assorted ironmongery. He looked dangerous. But he had come, nevertheless, to rescue them—so, at the sight of him, Drake perked up.

"Who's the bald old coot?" said Drake to anyone who might answer.

Nobody condescended to reply, but the bald old coot

was in fact Jon Arabin, the Warwolf himself, an ascetic man with a taste for experiment and challenge. Arabin came onto the rocks like a conqueror. His eyes were a pale, sunwashed blue. Drake was startled to see such blue amidst such black. Steady eyes, yes, and a steady voice, which said:

"There's space afloat for any who'll swear loyal to me and mine. Even the Walrus. How about it, Mulps, me pretty fopling?"

Mulps spat in reply.

"I'll take no murder on my ship," continued Arabin, unperturbed. "So you must swear loyal. Mulps, play the man: free the crew from their word."

"Done," said Mulps, nodding a little. "Any rat in search of a sewer can run."

Nobody moved.

"Loyal is one thing," said Arabin. "Stupid is another."

Drake got to his feet. He felt thin, transparent, almost weightless.

"I'll swear loyal," he said.

"That's rape-meat from the last boarding!" said Andranovory. "Take a swearing from him? He can't stand a deck, far less set sail."

Arabin turned his stern gaze on Drake, who felt, for a moment, like dust being weighed against iron.

"What can you do, boy?"

"I know iron," said Drake promptly, "and I know steel. Yes, and rope. Climbing, splicing and knots. It's my father who learnt me ropes."

"Aye, boy, and buggery perhaps," said Arabin. "But can you cut?"

"Cut?"

"Aye. Cut, gut, gralloch and gash. Go nose to nose with a cutlass and swim through smirking. How about it, boy? Come here!"

Drake reluctantly ventured down to the foam-smothered patch of rock where Jon Arabin stood, careless of the sea lathering his boots. As surf sucked back, Arabin tossed a dirk so it fell between them. Drake stared at the bald man's hard bones, the rough-torn boots, the ugly chunks of callus on the knuckles, the pale blue eyes as cold as the sea and as ruthless.

"I can cut," he said, and stooped, and grabbed, and jerked the dirk to the challenge.

Jon Arabin kicked him in the stomach, and he went down hard. Heart scrambling, Drake scuffled to his feet. Sick nausea staggered him, and he knew he was dead meat: but he squared back, panting, knife held tight, and stood ready.

Arabin gave a little nod.

"Aye," he said. "You've got the makings. Get in the boat."

7

Name: Orfus pirates.

Description: league of sea-robbers based on islands of the Greater Teeth.

Language: a dialect of Galish.

Political organization: oligarchical rule through a limited franchise democracy.

History: dates back several centuries to the Summer of Three Comets, when the delinquent Harla clan of Galish traders set up as pirates on the island of Drum, a base later abandoned after a severe dispute with the local sea dragons.

Once back aboard the *Warwolf*, Jon Arabin ordered a raft to be cut loose and thrown overboard. He was obeyed.

"That's their chance," said Jon Arabin, as the bamboo raft splashed into the sea. "They can swim for it, if they wish."

"Why give them a chance?" said one of his men. "Are you in love with friend Walrus of sudden?"

"Nay, man," said Arabin. "But Whale Mike's on that reef. He gave me a chance once, aye, when the Walrus was set to drown me. I owe him the same in return."

"What's with the boy?" said a man.

"New meat," said Jon Arabin. "Get him some soup. Then to bed."

"We've no bunk spare."

"Then he can sleep on the floor. He's tired enough—aren't you boy? Aye. You'll nod away to never in an instant."

Drake was in no state to argue otherwise. Jon Arabin knew what he was talking about.

The *Warwolf* stood off from the Greater Teeth that night, and put in to Gufling the next day. A slow and weary business it was, with much sounding, towing and warping before they eased the ship in to a seacleft which fitted them as tightly as a virgin. Gufling, Drake learned, was the smallest Tooth where a ship could berth; Jon Arabin had been exiled here by debt.

From the deck, Drake looked around with eyes which had widened to accommodate the gloom. Overhanging cliffs tossed around the echoes of boots on stone, harsh laughter and shipwork hammering. The place stank of sewage, smoke and fish heads. Dogs were barking, babies bawling, and fat women yelling in a Galish patois at times scarcely comprehensible.

"Come along, boy," said Jon Arabin, striding down the gang-plank. "What are you waiting for? A whore-money proposition?"

Dumbly, Drake followed his new master—wishing, for a moment, that he was a fish, free to take the sea-path back to Stokos. They fumbled their way down cockroach-haunted tunnels to Arabin's living quarters, where a confusion of women and children filled the air with tears and laughter.

Drake was shown a place where he could sleep, a side-kennel in Jon Arabin's cave complex. It was a warehouse of sorts, holding baulks of spare timber, buckets of tar, lobster pots, fishing floats, harpoons, chunks of cork and hundreds of odds and ends of rope.

"You say you know rope, boy," said Arabin. "Well, have we got work for you! Look on it as a challenge. Do you accept?"

"Plen pro!" said Drake in his native Ligin, meaning *"avec plaisir."*

And he sat down on the spot and began rummaging through the ropes. Jon Arabin laughed.

"Lunch first!" said he.

Lunch was three different kinds of seaweed, assorted seaslugs, lobster, whore's-eggs, raw fish and roast seal, all obtained locally. Drake was glad he had learnt that raw fish was safe to eat—otherwise he might have disgraced himself by accusing Jon Arabin of trying to poison him.

"Good fish," he said.

"You'll find, boy," said Arabin, "that the Teeth must feed themselves, more or less. You'll be busy enough when the *Warwolf*'s home. Aye. Working sealing boats and fishing."

"Do I start that after lunch?" said Drake.

"Nay," said Arabin, with another laugh. "After lunch, it's ropes. Rope is your future, boy, till I say otherwise."

Drake was glad he had not been bluffing about rope. He knew knots and splices, and used them well, fashioning serviceable rope from the wreckage he was given to work with. At first he worked without ceasing, thinking himself a slave. But Jon Arabin paid little attention to his rope production, so Drake soon eased up.

And, before very long, he discovered that they practiced religion here, too, albeit in a fairly disorganized fashion.

Jon Arabin gave Drake some beer money. Once he had mastered this strange coinage—a mixture of brass triangles, bronze hexagons and copper squares, all written over with alien hieroglyphics—he multiplied it through cards. No pirate played without cheating, but, as the saying goes on Stokos, "The Demon takes care of his own," Drake reaped the rewards of the truly devout.

After scarcely five days on Gufling, he had made himself so unpopular by his large-scale winnings that nobody on the island would play with him.

"Never mind," said Arabin, when he heard of Drake's plight. "After our next trip, we'll buy back into Knock. There's ten times the people there."

Knock, Drake learned, was the largest of the Teeth.

"And when is the next trip?" he asked.

"We leave tomorrow," said Arabin.

That night, Drake indulged himself with wild imaginings in which rape, slaughter and pillage took pride of place. However, the next day, as they labored at the tedious business of putting the *Warwolf* to sea—more warping, towing and sounding—he learned, to his disappointment, that on this trip they were to be engaged in strictly legitimate trade.

To be precise, they were going to make the pearl run down to Ling, about a thousand leagues away, in the Drangsturm Gulf. Few would dare the pearl-run risks, not even pirates. But Jon Arabin, who had chanced it first a decade ago, risked it every second year.

After much labor, they cleared Gufling and set a course for the south. As pirates nimbled through the rigging, Drake wondered when he'd be taken in hand and shown how it was done. He was sure he'd manage splendidly. He was still wondering when a filthy mumbling old man confronted him. The ancient looked Drake up and down with rheuming eyes that were three parts blind, bared his lips to show toothless gums, and said:

"You Drake?"

"I do have the honor of being Dreldragon Drakedon Douay, a pirate of the Greater Teeth and a henchman of the honorable Jon Arabin, whom I hope to serve well," said Drake, with all the dignity he could muster.

"Aye," said the old man, with a cackle. "You'll serve him well enough. Come with me!"

Drake, not knowing what to expect, followed warily, a hand on the hilt of the dirk Jon Arabin had let him keep after their brusque introduction on the Gaunt Reefs. The old man mumbled to himself as they ventured into the fumbling gloom below decks. Drake caught snatches of his monologue:

". . . yes . . . valley . . . she and her twat . . . good gold and biting . . . oh you were pretty . . . hot bread for forking . . . dragons may say . . . what's with the warthog . . ."

And more of the same, punctuated with cackles of laughter and the odd bit of shadow-boxing.

Down and down they went, until they came to the deepest, darkest, dirtiest bit of the ship, where a guttering seal-oil lamp fouled the air with smoke, where rats sat on their hind legs screaming defiance, where the scuttling cockroaches were a handful apiece, where the air stank of stale cheese, grease, old fish, dead cat, offal, soft carrots and rotten potatoes. Four charcoal stoves were burning, so it was hot—as hot as sharing a bed with five fat whores and fifty pairs of woollen socks.

"Where are we?" asked Drake with something very much like dread, fearing that he knew the answer already.

"We're in the klandlay, boy."

"The kitchen?"

"Aye, that's a name for it."

"And what—well, what am I meant to do here?"

"Why so many questions when you already know the answers?" said the ancient.

He plunged his hands into a bucket of white fluid—milk?—and retrieved half a dozen eggs. What happened next would not bear description—but the crew ate the results at meal time.

So Drake abandoned dreams of larking in the rigging, of swashing onto merchant ships with cutlass in hand, of blooding virgins and breaking into treasure chests. He settled, instead, to life as the cook's boy, helping prepare and dish up meals of salt pork, seal meat, sea biscuit, salted cod, stockfish, bacon, gray peas, and rye-flour cakes fried in whale oil and served with a dole of vinegar.

As the ship ploughed south, Drake adapted to life in the fo'c'sle, a crowded bunkroom continually damp

LORDS OF THE SWORD 101

with sea-gear and loud with coughing, snoring, sneezing, scratching, farting, gossip and argument. He found it hard to make friends as the crew blamed him (not, it must be admitted, entirely without justification) for some of the more appalling culinary disasters they endured.

In the fo'c'sle there were, amongst others, a huge foul-mouthed muscle man called Quin Baltu; Jon Disaster, who liked to be thought of as hard and dangerous; Raggage Pouch, who stole anything and everything that was not nailed down; Harly Burpskin, who had more money than sense, but was evening up the balance by playing cards with Drake.

There was also Ika Thole, a red-skinned red-haired harpoon man from the Ebrell Islands. Naturally, he reminded Drake of the high-breasted Zanya Kliedervaust, whom he had last seen at Cam's leper colony. Drake, homesick, love-sick, was eager to learn all he could of Zanya's homeland. He asked Thole to speak of the Ebrells—but Thole slapped him down, called him "you greasy little quat," called him worse, and refused to have anything to do with him.

Even Burpskin, though he was prepared to challenge Drake at cards, could scarcely be counted as a friend. Drake sensed that there were strong bonds of trust and friendship between the crewmen, however much they quarrelled and fought. Working the canvas, riding out whatever weather the Central Ocean assailed them with, they relied on each other for their very lives. Drake, working as he did in the galley, was excluded from this great partnership. He was a lower order of life entirely.

He started to lust for the day when he too would be a sailor, hauling on ropes, running out along the yard-arm, standing watches at night, spitting on his fellows from the crow's-nest . . .

But when he asked Jon Arabin for permission to get started on real sailor work, his captain just laughed, patted him on the head and said:

"Wait till you grow to man-height."

Which, naturally, infuriated Drake almost beyond

measure. He would have consoled himself by getting drunk. However, with the exception of gambling, the consolations of religion were unobtainable on this dry ship. Consequently, their voyage seemed to last forever. But they were scarcely twenty days from the Teeth when, by night, they sighted a glow on the eastern horizon.

Drake saw it when he went to relieve himself at the ship's head, a perilous place built out above the water. He met Ika Thole, there for the same purpose.

"That's Drangsturm, boy," said Thole, feeling congenial because he had just come off watch.

"The flame trench," said Drake, to show that he knew what it was all about. While he resented being addressed as "boy," he was glad Thole had condescended to speak to him at all.

"Aye," said Thole.

And they said no more about it, but stood for some time watching those barbecue skies. The ever-burning fires of Drangsturm ran from west to east across the narrow isthmus which separated the Drangsturm Gulf from the Inner Waters. In strongholds such as the Castle of Controlling Power, members of the Confederation of Wizards stood guard, ready to repel any monsters of the Swarms which managed to get beyond Drangsturm.

Both Thole and Drake knew the easy motion of the ship was taking them steadily toward the horrors of the terrorlands beyond the protection of the flame trench. Shortly, the ship changed course. Near Drangsturm, the coast made an elbow and ran west. Ling lay some seventy-five leagues (as bird-flight measures distance) along that coast. So west ran the Warwolf.

That night, in his dreams, Drake did battle with the monsters of the Swarms, which he knew well enough from songs and legends common on Stokos. He dreamed that the awesome might of the flame trench failed; that the fantastic wizard-castles fell to ruin in war; that the Swarms came north; that the ancient enemy marched on Narba, on Veda, even on the towers of Selzirk the fair.

Drake woke when Shewel Lokenshield thumped him in the face with a dead fish.

"Grumph!" snorted Drake, waking in a great hurry.

"Keep the noise down," growled Lokenshield. "You were groaning like a sow in heat."

"Nightmares," said Drake, by way of explanation.

"Man," said Lokenshield, in disgust, "if you're having bad dreams already, you'll be sleeping screaming by the time we get to Ling!"

Moments later, Lokenshield was asleep again. But Drake lay sleepless, sweating in the hot, dank fug of the fo'c'sle. Worrying about Ling. Now it was so close, he was truly beginning to realize the risks they were running.

By dawn, the wind had died away to almost nothing. The *Warwolf* floated in sunlit seas with only the lightest of airs to gentle her sails. They were running— well, idling—some twenty leagues north of the coast, a featureless blue-green line on the horizon.

"The terror-lands," said Jon Disaster grandly, indicating the coast to the south. "Home of the Swarms."

"I suppose," said Drake hopefully, "that the Swarms couldn't get to us from the shore."

"Oh, the greatest of them," said Disaster, "they could fly, well, they could damn-near fly from here to Stokos."

"Oh," said Drake, feeling younger and less certain than he had for years, and hurried down below to the comparative security of the galley.

The *Warwolf* cruised along the coast to Peninsular Quanat. She rounded Cape Songala then dared the narrow strait between Quanat and Island Va. Then ran by night for Ling. Drake was up bright and early, curiosity defying fear.

"What's that island?" he said, pointing to a considerable chunk of offshore rock.

"That's Ko," said Jon Disaster. "That's where the pearls are."

"If we know where they are," said Drake, "why do we trade for them? Why don't we go get some for ourselves?"

Jon Disaster laughed, and made no answer.

Shortly, the anchor slid away to the sandy bottom of Ling Bay. Drake scanned the daunting cliffs, which were punctured with holes, caves, tunnels, shafts, windows, embrasures and vents.

"What's that which glitters?" he said, shading his eyes against the sun.

"Quartz in the rock," said Jon Disaster.

"Quartz?" said Drake, who knew nothing of any geology saving certain iron-yielding ores and the coal-strata near his parents' home.

"Quartz is cheap crystal," said Disaster. "Aye, you'll see soon enough."

Looking down into the cool, clear water, Drake saw great globular crabs picking their way across the sands like so many crawling skulls. Skylarking pirates dived to the sea, ducked each other under and wagered as to how far down the anchor cable they could swim. Drake was not tempted to join them. He was far too tense to play idle water-games.

"Shouldn't we be keeping a watch?" he said.

"A watch?" said Disaster. "Whatever for?"

"The Swarms, of course."

"Boy, like as not they'll never come. Inland, water's scarce, and little water means few of them. It's only the flying ones to fear. If those come—well, it'll be a hundred as like as one."

Drake shuddered. What on earth was he doing here? He should be back on Stokos, yes. Stokos where he would one day be king. Or would he? Would Drake's theft of a mastersword and his subsequent disappearance prejudice King Tor against him? Well, just possibly . . .

But he had a legitimate excuse! If Muck had taught him properly, he would have endured everything, anything. Surely Tor would understand that. Wouldn't he?

Drake thought; *Well, even if I don't get to marry Tor's daughter, I could always become a priest.*

Yes. That would suit him right down to the ground. If he couldn't be king, he'd be a priest instead, devoting his life entirely to religion. Yes. He'd teach his temple's women himself, personally, one by one, to ensure quality control. He was surprised he'd never thought of the idea before.

"What you thinking about?" said Disaster, seeing Drake's abstracted expression.

"Screwing," said Drake.

He stared again at the cliffs. There was still no sign of the natives of he place. Were they dead? Killed out by the Swarms, perhaps?

"Why doesn't Arabin send a longboat ashore?" said Drake.

"It's best to let the Ling take their own good time," explained Disaster. "They're not much used to strangers, for few come south by sea."

"And by land?" said Drake.

Disaster laughed.

"It's fearful rough country inland," he said. "As far as I know, even Southsearchers venture here near to never. You know Southsearchers, boy?"

"Aye," said Drake knowledgeably, though most of what he knew was vague.

At last, late in the afternoon, the Ling did venture out. They came in small outrigger canoes cobbled together from scraps of driftwood. They were a strange breed of tall, lean people with golden skins: not the glossy golden brown of an oiled suntan, but the high-pitched glittering sheen of the noble metal itself.

"Have they painted themselves?" said Drake.

"Nay," said Disaster. "That's their natural color. They're a strange folk, as I've said. Their eyes are milk-white entirely, but for the black of the pupil."

"You've seen?" said Drake.

"I've seen many things. Including the Ling stained red with blood, aye, blood from some poor fool they'd ripped asunder. They did it with fish-hooks."

Drake, fascinated, listened to the gory details of the outré tortures Disaster proceeded to describe.

The Ling hailed the Warwolf, but not in Galish. Jon

Arabin shouted back to them, and a regular palaver began in some lingo utterly alien to Drake—and, indeed, to most of the crew.

"The females would fetch a good woman-price," said Drake sagely, eyeing the distant bodies and wondering if their eyes really were all white.

"Aye, and it'd be worth our lives to take them," said Disaster.

"They don't look very dangerous to me," said Drake, with the sense of superiority which comes naturally to a big ship's sailor looking down on some little canoes.

"Oh, they're regular fierce!" exclaimed Disaster. "Haven't you been listening to what I've been saying?"

"Oh, it made a nice story," said Drake, "but no people could really be as cruel as you've said. Surely."

"Believe me!" said Disaster. "They're straight out of a nightmare, this lot. Aye, and when it comes to women, that's when they're worse. Why, if you so much as look at one of their females, they'll cut your eyes out."

"In truth?"

"Aye, I've seen it myself. Fearfully bad it was. Our last trip, our bosun raped a lass in that sea-cave there, the big one where that canoe's just coming out. Well, he thought himself safe enough once back aboard, but they took him by night, believe me. We found him come morning, floating face-down in the water just off the stern. He'd been skinned alive, to start with. His prick had been—eh, look, they're coming in."

An agreement must have been reached, for the Ling canoes were closing with the ship. Drake saw Jon Arabin striding down the deck, smiling as he came.

"Drake!" shouted Arabin. "Good news! The Ling will trade with us, taking only one hostage."

"And who's that?" called Drake.

"My own dear son," said Arabin, "the light of my life, the sun of my sky, the moon of my heavens, flesh of my flesh, blood of my blood, as sweet to me as my mother's milk."

He was very close to them now, teeth shining as he grinned.

"I didn't know you had a son," said Drake, puzzled.

"Ah," said Arabin, "but you know now."

And tousled his hair, and kissed him.

And Drake, belatedly, understood.

8

Ling: an open bay on the coast of Argan some seventy-five leagues west of Castle of Controlling Power; lies west of Peninsular Quanat and south of Island Va and Island Ko.

Ling: the inhabitants of Ling, a golden-skinned people with milk-white eyes; notable as pearl divers.

Population of Ling: 4,261 (year Khmar 17).

"You can't do this to me!" shouted Drake. He was shocked. Outraged. "I trusted you!"

"Then you can trust me still," said Jon Arabin. "This is but a little thing you're being asked to do. A few days ashore—why, that's nothing."

"Days!" said Drake.

"Oh yes. Now we've arrived, the Ling will want to make a special expedition to Ko for extra pearls. We'll wait here till they've finished."

"But this—this—the whole idea is impossible," said Drake. "To start with, I'm the wrong race."

"Don't worry," said Jon Arabin. "They're not racist. They've got no prejudice against blond-haired boys. Just keep away from their women and you'll come to no harm."

"That's not what I meant, and you know it!" said Drake angrily.

"My dear, dear son," said Jon Arabin, tousling Drake's hair again in a truly infuriating manner.

"You'll have to keep that temper under control once you're ashore. You don't want to disgrace your father, do you now?"

Drake hardened his hands to fists. But Jon Arabin just laughed. An easy, healthy laugh. Easy for him to be happy!

"Man," said Drake, "I'll never pass muster as your son. Man, you're like coal, whereas me—I'm more the color of a cockroach."

"The Ling only breed their own gold with their own gold," said Arabin. "They knew nothing of the mixing of skins."

"But they breed dogs," said Drake, desperately. "And cats, surely."

"Nay," said Jon Arabin, "for they have none such."

"Then they have mice! And rats. Don't they?"

"Man," said Jon Arabin. "Rest easy. I've told you—there's no harm here if you keep your cock in order."

"Aye," said Jon Disaster with a grin, "but if you send your cock adventuring then they'll cut you in half and tear your head off. If you're lucky! If you're not . . ."

Disaster elaborated, until Arabin, seeing Drake was getting increasingly nervous, ordered him to silence.

"Your canoe's come alongside," said Arabin. "Down you go!"

And, as the entire crew of the *Warwolf* applauded, Drake scrambled down a rope ladder to the canoe waiting to take him into captivity. The five Ling in the canoe stared up at him. Their eyes really were white. Could they then be truly human? One reached out and steadied him as he stepped from the ladder to the canoe, which wobbled alarmingly underfoot; he crouched hastily, grabbing at the sides. Men mocked him from the decks:

"Remember to smile as they skin you!"

"When they offer up bowls of sand, it's polite to eat it."

"Blow me a kiss, darling, while you've still got lips to kiss with."

Drake, ignoring them, sought arse-space on a paddle bench. It was hot. In the *Warwolf*'s shadow, small fish hung motionless, weightless, amidst masses of dark-green weed trailing away into limpid depths. Strange, to think of that garden hauling from the hull through the deep-sea waves.

"*O-lo-o-la-tra-lee-o-zo,*" said one of the five men in the canoe.

"*O-lo-see-lee-ay-lit-ay-lo,*" he was answered, by the eldest man afloat.

"*O-lo-al-o-so-lo,*" said all in unison.

Dipping their paddles in the water, they began to stroke toward the shore.

Sun and sea split from flashing paddles. Drake squinted against the glare, closing his eyes as the paddlers began an ominous high-singing chant. Hot bloodlight filtered through his eyelids. He heard distant laughter on the *Warwolf*, and wished he was back on board.

Shadows cooled out the sun. His eyes startled open. Their canoe was sliding into a deep dim sea cave. Cold blocks of white light gleamed in the rock roof. How old was this place? Who had made it? Slaves, maybe. Aye, slaves sweating under whips till they fell from exhaustion and were beaten to death by the brutal Ling.

"*O-so-lo-lee-o-lo,*" chanted the paddlers, "*O-so-say-lo, o-lo-ay-tree-o-lo.*"

The words were music. Senseless music. Perhaps the paddlers were gearing themselves up for a killing. Perhaps it was a death-chant they were singing.

Deep within the cave was a shelving beach. As the canoe scraped against sand, Drake jumped overboard and helped run it ashore, seeking—ah, desperate hope!—to win favor by showing himself work-willing. A little water leaked into his boots; he stamped his damp feet, partly from nervousness.

The much-trampled sand, grooved by canoe-keels, suggested that a dozen of the craft afloat by the *Warwolf* belonged here. Drake had a sudden, sickening

ing vision of ambush, rape and slaughter, of laughing pirates falling on the Ling to murder them for pearl-wealth.

Might that happen? Might Arabin succumb to greed, and decide to kill rather than trade? He was known to be deeply in debt, needing every scraping he could get. Was Arabin that kind of man? Need could make anyone that kind of man.

The Ling were talking amongst themselves in their fluid, fluent voices. Drake cleared his throat.

"Does anyone here speak Galish?" he said.

They fell silent.

Had his voice annoyed them? How much excuse did they need before they fell on him with flaying knives and torture hooks? He smiled nervously: then wondered if these strangers might deem even a smile a deadly insult.

"*O-o-o*" said one of the Ling, taking Drake by the hand to lead him into the secret places beyond the canoe cave.

Drake was intensely embarrassed, for on Stokos only slaves walked hand in hand. Still, he dared not protest. He sniffed the air. Imagined he smelt blood. Hot, reeking blood in great quantity.

"Grief," he muttered.

After many turnings, bends, stairs, squeeze-holes, ramps, inclines, corridors and passageways, Drake was at last shown into a large white room where great big globular crabs with claws the size of nutcrackers were crawling over the walls.

"What's with the crabs?" said Drake. "Eh?"

"*O-lip-o,*" said one of the Ling, smiling.

And gave him a little push.

Drake, fists clenched, stepped into the room.

Okay, crabs! Watch out! This is Drake Douay you've got to deal with.

Drake's guides departed. The crabs made no move against him. They looked . . . well, actually, they looked remarkably dead. Yes. On investigation, they proved to be empty shells which had been glued to the walls, doubtless by way of decoration.

Drake took stock.

He was in a square-hewn chamber dominated by a raised deck of small gray stones topped off with clean white sand. Drake entirely failed to recognize this contraption for what it was—a bed. And not just any old bed, either, but a bed for one of the High-Born. For the second degree, tradition prescribed stones minus sand. And a commoner would have slept on rocks.

Drake fingered one of the stones. It was too small to make much of a weapon. He still had his dirk, but what good was that? He should have asked to bring a sword ashore. He would have felt safer, yes. And besides—if he was playing at being Jon Arabin's son, surely he should have been kitted out with the weapons appropriate to his status. Well, too late to worry about that now . . .

Was there a toilet nearby? He needed one urgently.

The sand-topped stone-heap . . . yes, it was obviously a glorified sand-box, to be used like the one his boyhood friend, Nevil Norkin, had for his kittens. Drake promptly began to scrabble a little hole in the top of the bed. But, before he could commit a *faux pas* of enormous dimensions, a young woman entered. In her hands she carried the tail of a stingray—which, amongst the Ling, was the ultimate erotic symbol. She was naked.

"*O-ma-no-so?*" she said, a faint smile on her lips.

Drake's horror-shock immediately abolished all worries about bowels and bladder. Jon Disaster's warnings flooded back to him. Chaotic images of skinned flesh, pulled fingernails, amputated organs and gouged-out eyes tumbled in that flood.

"Go away!" he said frantically. "Go away, before someone finds us!"

"*O-lee!*" she said, in tones of protest.

Drake picked up a handful of sand and threw it at her.

"*Lee-o-me-nee!*" she said.

Drake's dread doubled as another woman entered. Also naked. The two had a rapid conference in their strange, sing-song voices, then cornered Drake and did their best to strip him naked. He only managed to preserve his honor by the most vigorous resistance.

"Jon Arabin!" said Drake. "I'll kill you when I get hold of you!"

His outburst of anger scattered the women.

"Saved," said Drake. "At least for the moment."

And he sat down in a corner, sweating, trembling, breathing heavily. This business of being a hostage was obviously going to be—to say the least—demanding.

"It's my blond good looks," said Drake. "That's what does the damage. The women get one look at me, and they just can't keep their hands off. I suppose they don't often see a fellow as handsome as me, not this far south. Well—can I help my beauty?"

Drake knew there was nothing he could do about his natural sex appeal.

"It's not my fault!" he said. "I'm innocent!"

But his innocence would do him no good if he was caught embracing a nubile young female. Oh no. Likely as not, he would be discovered by some dour, ugly representative of the older generation, who would have him killed out of sheer jealousy, if for no other reason.

"I've got to pretend I'm a professional virgin," said Drake. "Or something."

During the course of the next three days (in which he did, finally, after several blunders, manage to find the toilet), Drake was tempted by three dozen naked women. Young they were, and beautiful, faces so smooth they seemed to be wearing masks, their milk-white eyes adoring, their breasts high-sprung, their innards oiled and ready for his exertions.

Ready they were indeed, knowing their guest was Drake Arabin, oldest and much-loved son of Jon Arabin, and heir to all the Arabin dominions: the Greater Teeth, the Lesser Teeth, the larger part of three continents, and several kingdoms in the Land of the Dead besides. Yes, to Ling, Jon Arabin was a mighty king, a great warrior, a powerful wizard, a minor demigod, and the richest man in the world.

To Drake, Jon Arabin was something else altogether. He stood at a high window staring down at Ling Bay, where the distant *Warwolf* lay, and said:

"Jon, you're a sly scheming son of an octopus. And if I don't get out of here in one piece—then you're going to be in big trouble, man."

When the daughters of Ling reported the failure of their enticements, the elders consulted, then sent in their sons. By hook or by crook, they would see Drake Arabin committed in love to some flesh of their flesh before his captivity ended.

But the sons reported as little success as the daughters. The elders conferred again, then decided to bring Drake into the presence of the Great One.

When the elders came for him, Drake Douay was practising a one-man kata with a wooden sword which he had whittled out of a broken paddle.

"*O-oo-o-ooo,*" sang one of the elders, then grabbed Drake by the elbow.

"You've come to take me back to the ship?" said Drake. "Great! I thought it was just about time to be leaving."

And he threw down his waster and allowed the elders to lead him through many cool tunnels until they came to the audience chamber where sat the Great One. She was the oldest and wisest woman of Ling, a bright-eyed matriarch whose skin, in her old age, was mottled with dusky patterns which reminded Drake of the wings of a great moth.

Drake looked around the audience chamber uneasily. It was a square-cut white room with upward of fifty elders squatting on the rough brown matting which carpeted the floor. The Great One lay in state in a hammock of sharkskin. Drake, deducing her authority from her elevation, said:

"Good morning, ma'am, pleased to meet you."

"*O-layma-nooloo,*" said the Great One, making a formal response.

"Really?" said Drake. "Listen, if we're going to have a conversation, we'll need to get Jon Arabin in on this."

LORDS OF THE SWORD 115

"Jon Arabin," said the Great One.

"Aaaah!" wailed the elders. "Jon Arabin!"

And they lent forward in unison and kissed their right hand kneecaps (or, if that was forbidden by arthritis, their right hand wrists). Drake was not at all sure what to make of this. In any case, he had little time to think about it, for the Ling had begun to speak between themselves in their high-pitched sing-song voices.

"Why does he refuse the flesh of our flesh?" asked the elders.

"Because," said the Great One, "the spirit of purity burns strong within him."

"Is he then Worthy?" asked the elders.

The Great One laid her hand upon Drake's forehead. A wisp of a hand it was, too, more skin than flesh— as frail as an old leaf which has almost frayed through to its skeleton.

"Yes," said the Great One, after a lengthy pause. "He is Worthy."

Even Great Ones have their off days.

"Shall we then initiate him?" asked the elders.

"We shall. Indeed, we must. For it would be a sin to let one of the Worthy depart to the Plague Lands without initiation."

"It shall be done," said the elders.

And Drake was roughed onto a bloodstained metal rack and tied down with thongs of sharkskin. A jabber of excited faces crowded around him. Drums pulsed, nose flutes whined, witch doctors rattled bones, and an evil old gentleman made stone sizzle across steel as he honed a knife which already looked far more sharp than was necessary.

"No!" screamed Drake, writhing against his bonds. "I didn't do it! I never touched them! What have I done? Is it something I said? Is it something I didn't say? I'll do anything, anything, just let me loose! Don't hurt me! Is there anyone here who speaks Galish? Gaaa!"

"Why is he screaming?" asked the elders.

"Because the Ecstasy has possessed him," said the

Great One gravely. "it is a good sign. He shall be truly blessed."

"Here is the box," said the elders.

"Good," said the Great One.

And took the implement of initiation from the box.

Drake howled with incoherent fear as the gloating old woman held up a snake. It was small, and very much alive. It hissed, opening its jaws, showing sharp teeth. Before he had time to admire the red and orange markings twisting down its back (markings reminiscent of the forging-patterns of Gouda Muck's mastersword) it whipped free from the Great One's hands and fell to the floor.

There was an uproar as heroes competed for the precious little monster. But the man who had been sharpening the knife stayed calm. Humming gently to himself, he leaned over Drake's body and cut once, neatly, making an incision under the floating rib on Drake's right-hand side.

Drake hissed, with fear, with anger, with pain. The old woman had regained the snake. She was fondling it. Stroking it. Crooning to it. Bringing it closer. She was—no!

"No! No! No!" screamed Drake.

But she put the head of the snake to his open wound. He screamed again as it began gnawing into his vitals. It was like being stabbed repeatedly with a red-hot poker.

Then, strangely, the pain lessened. It became dull. Disappeared altogether. Yes. While teeth still tunnelled, he no longer cared. He was starting to float, hmmm, yes, drifting away on a river of deliciously warm milk.

The Great One leaned over him. He smiled up at her face, noting, for the first time, the red veins spiderwebbed in the milk white of her eyes. She kissed him, giving him her blessing for the Journey. He felt himself falling. Her face contracted to a point, then disappeared altogether. The last sounds hissed into silence.

"Who am I?" he wondered.

Idly.
Then wondered no more, for he was unconscious.

Drake did not wake to clarity, but to fever. Hot, flushed and thirsting, he endured cramps, spasms and hallucinations. He was fed strange foods and stranger fluids, which sustained life but did not cure him.

"Arabin," he said. "Get Arabin. Jon Arabin, understand?"

"*O-fo-lo-mo-lee*," said one of the young women who fed him.

And smiled, and left him.

But did not return with Jon Arabin.

Time and again Drake repeated his demand. He had to get a message through to his captain. If he stayed in this crazy place, he would die.

"I'm sick, yes," said Drake, to one of his handmaidens, "but I'll do as well on the *Warwolf* as I would here. Honest. It's the sea air, I need it to keep me alive."

The response was another smile.

Nothing more.

He could see, through his sickroom's embrasure, a slice of blue sky, occasionally decorated by patches of high cloud. Fair weather cloud, yes. In the little time he'd spent on the *Warwolf*, he'd already got into the habit of taking a right healthy interest in the weather.

"Those idle sons of sodfish will be playing around the anchor cable again, I suppose," said Drake.

Yes. Or practicing sword under the hard gaze of the ship's weapons muqaddam. Or patching sails. Or splicing ropes. Or—

But no matter. Whatever they were doing, Drake wanted to be with them. Aye. In the company of his comrades true. Quin Baltu, Shewel Lokenshield, Goth Sox, Lee Dix, Hewlet Mapleskin, aye, and Jon Disaster—he remembered them as brothers.

Finally, the day came when Drake was well enough to quit his bed and venture to the embrasure. Squinting into the brilliance of a world lit by real honest sunlight, he looked down on Ling Bay—and saw that the *Warwolf* was gone.

No! Surely not! Surely Arabin's ship of green sails lay close to the cliff, hidden by the limitations of the embrasure!

On rubbery legs, Drake staggered from the room, questing for a better view.

"Jon, Jon," he said, as he stumbled down white-lit corridors. "Jon, you can't have left me. No, say it's not true!"

How often did ships come to Ling? The *Warwolf*, or so it was alleged, visited once every two years. Apart from that—nothing.

"You'd better be there, Jon Arabin," threatened Drake. "You'd better be there, you and your ship. Or I'll damn you to fifty hells for seventy times eternity!"

Finally he found a square door cut in the side of the cliff, high above the sea. He stepped outside, into the warmth of the sun. Below lay all of Ling Bay: innocent of any ship. Clear shone the sparkling waters, as beautiful as the women of a poet's dreams. And empty.

Drake wept.

9

Saba Yavendar: one of the Nine Immortals; won poetic fame with Winesong and Warsong, written in the Stabilized Scholastic Standard (later adopted as the High Speech of wizards) of the Technic Renaissance.

Survived Genetic Mutiny and Interregnum. Joined Institute of Applied Theology (later destroyed by Founders in Wars of Suppression). After Famine Years, was adviser to Lords of the Eightfold Way (forerunner of Confederation of Wizards).

Gained great power in Empire of Wizards after Long War against Swarms, but lost all in Years of Chaos. Disappeared after offending Talaman the Torturer (aka T. the Castrator, T. the Eye Gouger and T. the Baby Strangler).

Later works (including notorious *Victory of the Prince of the Favored Blood*) popular crowd-pleasers scorned by scholarship, which must concur with Larftink that Yavendar "lived too long and wrote far, far too much." Indeed, Gatquip's long-disputed claim that the *Complete Works* can be reduced to a canon of a dozen lines demands positive reassessment.

Drake's wound healed to a crinkled red scar. His fever abated. Abandoning his bed (yes, by now he recognized a heap of stones and sand as a bed) he explored. Questing. Seeking. Searching for a way out of this warren, a way back to civilization.

He found rooms packed with dusty old bones. A

mortuary, where the unkempt dead, anointed with wild honey, lay waiting for the Funeral Winds. A strange globular room with silver walls where his weight left him, and he hung weightless in the air like a fish in water.

He took stairs which descended as well as those which went up, thinking there might be tunnels which traveled deep underground before breaking out to freedom. He found dank, gloomy, ill-lit places flooded with slimy water.

Once, he found a door which opened on a huge, utterly silent hall perhaps three leagues in length, where a dozen bulbous gray shapes, each hundreds of paces long, lay half-submerged in pitch-black water.

"Grief of suns!" said Drake. "Will I never get out of here?"

He lost his way a dozen times, and once wandered for a whole day in waterless tunnels before chancing his steps back to the inhabited areas. Nothing daunted, he set out again—but this time he carried a chunk of charcoal with which to mark his way on the walls.

At last, he squeezed out through a narrow vent to stand in harsh clifftop sunshine. He had won a view of some of the meanest terrain in creation, a desolation of stone pillars, razor-sharp shadows, thornbush, cactus, sparce acacia, gulleys, buttes, sinkholes, escarpments and ravines.

There was no sign of water.

"Desolation," muttered Drake.

He had never before seen a landscape so lonely. Utterly unmarked by human hand. He longed to be on Stokos again, ah yes, back on his home island where the terrain had been civilized by mines, quarries, slag heaps, ash pits, and other comforting signs of human activity.

I'd die of loneliness if I tried to walk across this.

He saw something glinting a few paces away. What? His hot black shadow crabbed across the rocks as he ventured to the glitter. It proved to be a chunk of sharp-cut white crystals. Very hard.

"That quartz stuff Disaster talked about," said Drake.

And wished he had Disaster with him. Or Ika Thole, yes, or even dim-witted Harly Burpskin.

"Anyone," said Drake, "as long as we've language in common."

He was talking to himself a lot, these days. Was that a sign of madness?

"I'll talk when I want!" yelled Drake, suddenly angry.

And he hurled the chunk of quartz into the wilderness. Then it occurred to him that maybe the stuff was worth having. Disaster had called it "cheap," but perhaps Drake could bluff an unwary buyer into thinking it valuable.

"Where did my quartz go?" he said.

He scrambled onto a small rock, and, from that eminence, swiftly discovered his quartz, which he duly retrieved.

"A bigger rock," said Drake. "That's the thing."

Yes. From a bigger rock he might see—well, running water, if he was lucky. Or maybe an old road which he could follow east through the wilderness, in the general direction of Drangsturm.

Drake dared a perilous scramble to the top of the nearest house-sized rock. From there, high above thorn bushes and other rubbish, he had a much better view.

No road. But . . .

Was that a building he saw? Yes. Half a league distant lay a square tower of thrice tree-height, built from massive white, blue and ochre blocks. A spike rose from each of its rooftop corners. Drake studied it doubtfully.

Could it be . . . ?

Surely not!

And yet . . . it did look remarkably like the legendary Wishing Tower known to every child of Stokos from fairy stories. And he was on Argan, was he not? Argan, the true homeland of all improbable things?

"Improbability is not impossibility," said Drake to himself, and, abandoning his chunk of quartz, he set

off for the tower with all possible speed, i.e. slowly—
the ground being regular leg-breaking territory.

At first he was all enthusiasm, dreaming of the marvelous things he would wish for. Fresh vegetables! A real live cucumber! A piece of lettuce! Then—well, the larger things. The throne of Stokos. The fair Zanya Kliedervaust, she of the red skin and the high-lofted breasts. And more height, yes, at least five extra hands of height.

"That would make me near as tall as Sully Yot," said Drake.

He remembered his last encounter with Yot, in Androlmarphos, when the crazy wart-faced fellow had tried to stab him. What on earth had made him do a weird thing like that?

"I'd never have credited him with the nerve to gut a cat," muttered Drake.

He paused, breathing heavily. This was hard work! The terrain was so rucked, hillocky and chopped about that a stone's throw of thirty paces meant a weary scramble of thrice that distance for the footsore traveler. The sun was heavy on his head. A bead of sweat rolled into his right eye. It stung, fiercely. Give up? No, never!

Drake struggled onward, shrinking as he went. Crushed by the sun.

"Man," muttered Drake, "and I was short enough to start with."

Rock caught and amplified the heat. He smelt hot, pungent herbs. Their scent made him dizzy. How immense was the world! This desolate place, far beyond all voices, was teaching him how he really measured up against the universe.

Like an ant, man. An ant trying to walk across Stokos.

A shadow flickered over the ground. Shadow of a winged creature. A monster? Alarmed, Drake glanced skywards. No, not a monster—a buzzard. It started to circle.

"Piss off, you whore-faced puttock!" said Drake.

The buzzard, a professional pessimist, continued to

circle. Drake realized its diligence might well be rewarded. If he broke an ankle out here, he was finished. Momentarily, he regretted ever leaving the safety of the tunnels of Ling. Leg-breaking apart—what would he do if he met one of the Swarms?

"I don't believe they exist," said Drake. "Who says they do? Wizards, that's all!"

Maybe Drangsturm was a great big con, yes. Maybe there was wealth beyond the flame trench, aye, gold, silver, stuff like that. Probably wizards kept people away from it by making up tales of monsters. Likely they roamed the terrorlands at will, picking up chunks of gold and similar riches.

"Swarms?" said Drake. "Bah! Humbug!"

Much, much later, grazed by rock, stung by hornet, pricked by thorn and burnt by the sun into the bargain, he gained the doorway which pierced the lower level of the ancient square-built monument, and knew at once that this was not the fairy-tale tower he had hoped for.

Unlike the Wishing Tower, this one was not inhabited by a magic dwarf, a talking rabbit, a blue-nosed leprechaun and a friendly little elf. Peering into the gloom he saw, instead, four hideous totem poles of dull metal, closely resembling the Guardian Machines described by old teachings preserved by the metalworking guilds of Stokos.

"Guardian Machines," said Drake.

He had been taught about them in his theory classes about three years previously. What had he learnt, exactly? That they were dangerous, yes. Still . . . these ones looked pretty dead.

"You awake?" yelled Drake.

The totem poles sat in sullen silence. Maybe they weren't Guardian Machines at all. Maybe they were art. Drake had heard about art—bits of odd-shaped stuff set up in special rooms for people to gawk at. It was said to be real big in Veda, the city of the sages.

Drake stepped through the doorway. Dead leaves crunched underfoot. Inside, it was cool and shady. But dry. He wished he had water.

Look around. Investigate.

Four steep stairways spiralling up into the shadows. Some barely perceptible activity going on at his feet— yes, a tribe of red ants were practicing genocide on some of their black-skinned cousins. And overhead . . . looking up, Drake saw a spider the size of a dog, which sat in a ceiling-spanning bat-catching web and glowered at him. Hastily he armed himself with a hefty stick in case the spider got any unfortunate ideas.

Then, since he had the stick in his hands, he hit himself on both shins, which hurt, but would help teach him that he was too old to believe in fairy tales.

What now?

Retreat or explore.

The view, that's the thing. From the roof, we'll see roads and stuff. Or a ruined city, maybe.

So thinking, Drake made for the nearest stairway. He was almost there when one of the metal totem poles, which was indeed a Guardian Machine, ground into life with an enormous racket of gears. Spitting blue sparks, it advanced. Drake went haring up the winding stairs—and slammed into an invisible wall, almost knocking himself out.

"Break!" screamed Drake.

He hammered the invisible barrier, butted it, stuck it with his stick, kicked it—all to no effect. Downstairs the Guardian Machine was hissing and roaring.

"Give, you ganch!" yelled Drake.

But it wouldn't. It yielded inwards slightly, but that was all. He scratched it, finding its surface cold and slippery. Beyond lay a skeleton, and the stairs leading upward.

No escape!

"*Olwek ba-velch!*" said Drake savagely, then turned to face the Guardian Machine.

Which, by the sound of it, was still at the bottom of the stairs, grinding, hissing and tearing. As he listened, the sounds lessened. Then died. Cautiously, he crept downstairs until he could see the metal monster at the foot of the stairs. Obviously, it was unable to climb. But it scarcely looked short of patience. He suspected it could happily wait until ants carried away the dust of his bones—as they would indeed unless he could escape.

There was room to squeeze past the machine.

If he was quick—

Drake dared one step downward. The machine roared and spat at him. Lightning slammed into his gut, knocking him backward. He could not breathe! Paralysed, he lay with arms outflung, mouth gaping. Then managed to gasp a thimble-sized breath of air.

As the machine roared and whined, gathering strength for another homicide attempt, Drake very slowly and very painfully rolled over and began to crawl back up the spiral staircase. The machine shot at him as soon as it could—which was just a fraction too late.

Back at the invisible wall, Drake rested, collecting his wits. There was no way out down the stairs, that was for sure.

There were no windows, but light was definitely coming down from the top of the stairs.

He studied the skeleton. Somehow, someone had got beyond the invisible wall. And had died there.

Drake reviewed the Inner Principles of the Old Science which he had learnt as part of his apprenticeship studies. He recited the Beginning:

"Cause has effect; effect has control; control requires search; search elucidates cause."

Then he recalled the first Rule of Investigation:

"Describe what you see, for perception controls process."

Drake had never put much stock in theory. In fact, he had always hated it—particularly since, being totally illiterate, he had had to memorize the whole 23,427 words of it. Being dubious about the validity of the Power Theory of Knowledge, he still resented the waste of all those bright sunny afternoons which could have been spent in healthy amusements like street-fighting, or in the practice of religion—but the Scientific Approach now seemed to be his only hope.

So he began an Investigation.

126　Hugh Cook

He described:

"Low light . . . cool . . . was warmer outside . . . stairs . . . going up . . . cracks . . . some brown stuff . . . stain? . . . bones beyond invisible . . . no, not like air . . . bit blurred . . . push . . . yields . . . slippery . . . cold . . . no shadow . . . fits to wall . . . no visible seam . . . wall same block-pattern as stairs . . . except . . . yes . . . plate of white metal set in wall . . . no rust . . . pattern of five raised circles set on metal plate . . . raised circles are . . . are moveable . . ."

As Drake fingered the raised circles set in the metal plate, something changed. What? He stood absolutely still, listening. Then realized a faint hum, which he had dismissed as a noise within his own head, had ceased to be. He could hear . . . a tiny creak from his own knees . . . the complex sounds of deglutition as he swallowed some saliva . . . and that was it.

Drake mobilized some more saliva in his mouth, then spat.

His spittle splattered against the skeleton's skull. Reaching out, he found the invisible barrier had gone. He glanced at the metal plate in the wall, and the raised circles he had fingered. Cause and effect. Yes.

"Score one for theory," muttered Drake.

With reluctance, for he hated to concede anything to Gouda Muck—or, indeed, to any other of that age group.

"But I'll give him this," muttered Drake. "Even if he was mad, the old bugger did make bloody good swords."

And he took a couple of steps forward.

Then stopped.

He could hear something. What? Yes: that hum.

"Oh no," said Drake. "Oh no, tell me it's not so."

But, on turning and trying to retreat back downstairs, he found the invisible barrier barring his way. He did another Investigation, a comprehensive one. There was no magical cause-and-effect device on this side of the barrier. Now he knew why the bones were there.

"The poor old sod starved to death," said Drake.

And, looking at the yellow bones, had a sudden intimation of his own inevitable death. Even if he got out of this alive, he would die some day. For the first time in his life, he truly understood his own mortality.

"That's the trouble with bloody-well being sober all the time," said Drake. "You get some weird old thoughts breaking loose."

Yes. The sooner he got back to civilization and got decently drunk again, the better. If he stayed here much longer, brooding about Knowledge, Theory and Mortality and such, he'd be a regular mad philosopher by the time he escaped. Stokos had had two of them, and a sorry old sight they were, too.

"Onwards!" said Drake boldly, appropriating for his own purposes the motto of the Guild of Navigators, which was not strictly his to use at all.

He swiftly found himself in a machine-cluttered room at the top of the tower. He could not tell what these amazing devices did, or where they were from, or what they were worth—but none attacked him, so he didn't rightly care.

What he wanted was a way out. Which he found, soon enough: a square hole in the ceiling. So up he went. And, after he had gazed again on the desolation of the Deep South, he started wondering just how the hell he was going to get back to ground level. If he had a rope, it would be easy.

Otherwise . . .

The walls were sheer, impossible to climb. If he jumped, the odds for breaking something were excellent. If he broke something, he was dead.

"Hoy!" shouted Drake. "Anyone here?"

He listened, but heard only a faint hissing, which could have been the sun trying to weld his shadow to the roof. Shading his eyes, he scanned the landscape. Nobody. The clifftops lay only half a league away. From this height, it scarcely looked any distance at all.

Then came the blue of the sea, and, to the north, the humped mass of the island of Ko. There was something odd about Ko. Yes: its ends were curling up in the hot sunshine, floating above the sea. Drake squinted, trying to bring them into focus. No change.

He was horror-struck. It was his fault! He must have somehow unleashed some enormously evil power which had been lurking in this tower. Perhaps that power was, right now, making all the lands and islands of the whole wide world turn up at the edges and curdle.

"Nonsense," he said to himself. "Impossible!"

Yet: some of those ancient Causes were known to have amazingly grandiose Effects.

"Well," said Drake, "we'll worry about the world when we're free in the world to worry. Right now we need a rope."

And, without waiting to worsen his sunburn, he went below decks to make another Investigation.

He found nothing remotely worth having, but for twenty-seven identical amulets. Each, together with its necklace-chain of smooth-flowing black links, had the weight of a walnut. Each amulet was a cool, glossy lozenge of jet black. On one side, a golden sun disc. On the other, raised silver decorations in the form of seven stars and a crescent moon. On Investigating the silver stars, Drake found the amulets could be made to talk.

". . . strong voice," muttered Drake. "Man's voice . . . strange . . . no language I know . . . worth a pretty, I bet . . . magic, perhaps? Spells, perhaps? . . . well . . . no harm trying . . ."

He took the amulets downstairs. Crouching by the yellowed skull of the long-dead stranger, he let the invisible barrier listen to each amulet in turn, knowing well enough that many such charms had magical powers. The barrier held firm. Drake attacked it one last time, thumping it hard with his fists.

No good.

"Still," said Drake, putting the amulets round his neck for safe keeping, "these charm-things will be worth something if I ever get out of here. Yes, wizards would pay for them, if nobody else."

He was right about that, for each amulet contained

the voice of Saba Yavendar himself. The great poet of the days of yore had once lived in this tower for half a millenium, and had whiled away some of those long years of exile by making multiple recordings of all his early works, including his *Winesong, Lovesong* and *Warsong*.

Wizards valued such things, and the High Speech of wizards was near-identical to the Stabilized Scholastic Standard which Yavendar had recorded in.

"Still no rope, though," said Drake.

But, before he slung the last amulet around his neck, he tested its strength. It was beyond his power to break it.

"With enough of these woman-fancy faggots," said Drake, "I could make a chain to get me out of here."

So he resumed his Investigations, but with no more success than before. He got angry.

"You see, Muck?" he yelled. "You see, you groggy old bugger? You can't make rope from Investigations!"

Then stopped yelling, for his throat started hurting. Thirst. Yes. That was it. He was going to thirst to death, and soon. No doubt about it. Since he was definitely doomed to die, he was all the more bitter about those afternoons wasted studying the Theory of Knowledge, the Theory of Lists, the Reductive Crisis of Categorizations and all the rest of that pretentious old rubbish which never yet helped put a sharper edge on a sword, and never would.

"Missed out on all those sacrifices, too," said Drake, gloomily.

The human sacrifices organized by the temple of Hagon had mostly been in the afternoons. Everyone agreed they were top-notch religious experience, but because of his schoolwork, he had never managed to see one.

"All those days breaking my brains," muttered Drake.

And hit a machine with his fist, hard. Then kicked it, but hurt his foot.

"Ganch," said Drake, viciously.

130   Hugh Cook

The machines were obviously built to last. Otherwise he would have relieved his feelings by smashing them to pieces. Breaking. Smashing. Yes, that rang a bell. What was it? Yes . . . the final Rule of Investigation:

"The last Test of Limits is Destruction."

At first he was chary of breaking the place up. After all, something was making Ko island curl at the edges, and the only thing he could put it down to was his own Investigations. If he started some Destruction he might end up in serious trouble.

"But there's no other way," muttered Drake, picking up the lightest available machine. "Don't take this the wrong way, little thing—it's sanctioned by the Theory of Investigations, don't you know."

And he hurled the item against the wall. It was fragile, having been designed only to store, sanitize and dispense tooth-brushes. It shattered. A toothbrush (perfectly preserved for millenia by a low-grade stasis field) fell from the wreckage.

"A little jewel-cleaner of some sort," said Drake, frowning. "What was that doing in there?"

And he Investigated, carefully, looking for jewels. There was none. But there were some thin, finely woven metal wires, sheathed in pliable jackets of different colors.

"Hmmm," said Drake. "Maybe the last rule is the best of all . . ."

And he went downstairs to retrieve the larger bones of the skeleton, thinking to use them as levers to help pry apart the larger machines.

He was still hard at it when night came. He got little sleep, for the topmost room of the tower became amazingly cold by night. By the time dawn came, his stomach was seething with acid hunger. His mouth was thick, dry, furry. He sucked on the knucklebone of a long-dead man, generating saliva to ease the dryness of his throat.

"To work," said Drake. "To work . . ."

By noon, he had smashed every device in the room,

and had woven a rope of wires which reached almost to the ground. Now he had to climb down.

"No sweat!" said Drake, using an ugly vernacular expression meaning "easy."

He was swiftly disabused of this notion, for in his weakened condition—he had lost a lot of water to the sun—he found it hard-going. By the time he reached the ground, he was in a state of wet-faced exhaustion.

He still faced the half-league walk back to the vent he had exited from. Half a league? In this spasmodic terrain, rough as a storm-chopped sea, his undulating route would stretch the journey out to nigh on three thousand paces.

Be a man.

With a third of the journey done, he slipped, fell, and ricked an ankle. Broken? Even if it was, he still had to walk on it. With his dirk, he cut himself a hefty stick to lean on. Up. On! He almost swooned from the pain—but continued.

A shadow flickered across the ground.

The buzzard?

Looking up, Drake saw something far, far above. High through the blue empyrean it flew. A great bulky body and a long, long trailing tail. It was a hundred paces long if it was a fingerlength. As Drake watched, it vanished into cloud.

What was that?

It was, he decided, a hallucination. Nothing which flew could be so big. Surely. But then, dragons—no, it had not been a dragon. A monster of the Swarms? Impossible. The Swarms were an invention of wizards, part of a bluff to keep the world from the riches of the terror-lands . . .

Again a shadow flickered over the ground.

Again Drake looked up.

It was a buzzard, that was all. Probably the same one which had been hungering after him the day before. Well, it was right out of luck, for he had no intention of dying. Not today.

"Not ever, in fact," said Drake.

As the purple shadows of evening were spreading

across the terror-lands of the Deep South, Drake gained the vent which led into the depths of Ling. He was too tired to be happy. He stumbled to his quarters, drained a bowl of water then fell onto his bed and collapsed.

"Our visitor has returned alive from the Forbidden Tower," the Watchers reported to the Great One. "How can that be?"

"Omnia puris pura," said the Great One, or words to that effect. "He found no evil there for no evil lives within him. We must increase our efforts to incorporate him."

Drake spent two days in bed, utterly exhausted. His ankle, fortunately, was only badly bruised—but, even so, he knew there was no escape for him on foot.

It was a good few marches to Drangsturm, with no wild water on the way. Even if he met no monsters, thirst would finish him for certain. He remembered the buzzard circling overhead; he shuddered. Even if he reached Drangsturm, he would be on the wrong side of that prodigious flame trench. Did it run right into the sea? If it did, how far would he have to swim to get to safety?

Forget it! He would have to steal a canoe, yes. And, while stealing a canoe, he might as well go for some pearls. What did they really look like, those 'beads without holes?'' Men deemed them fabulous wealth, but what made them so special?

Drake's desire to learn about canoes was amply satisfied in the days that followed. On showing himself interested in the sea, he found plenty of tutors eager to learn him all its aspects. (And also to seduce him—though, fearing more torture, he resisted all their blandishments.)

They taught him paddling.

They tolerated his fondness for collisions.

And then the Ling made a decision which would shortly allow Drake to satisfy his curiosity about pearls.

Drake had lately taken to pointing at Ko, and making strange noises which were clearly meant to be questions. Obviously he wanted to go to the island.

"Being pure," said the Great One, "he does not want to live as a parasite. He wishes to share our labors."

Which was how Drake got to be taken to the pearl-fishing grounds at Ko.

"It's all right," he said with relief, when they got there. "It's not melting after all. It must've been some trick of the sea making it look so. We can go back now."

But the smiling Ling still confessed to no Galish. Instead, they set a bushel of pearl-oysters in front of him, and showed him how these were opened.

Soon Drake knew why pearls were so precious: because in days of oyster-opening, in which he was sure he killed more oysters than all the world could have eaten in ninety generations, he found but one small pearl, and even that was misshapen, squashed almost flat. He had plenty of examples to compare it with, because the Ling were indulging in a positive orgy of pearling, diving from dawn to dusk.

"I'll try diving," said Drake. "It's got to be easier."

It wasn't. It was exhausting. But, as he got good at it, he relished the fierce pleasures of physical mastery. To be good at something, to be excellent—yes, that was what made life worth living.

Down in the depths of the sea he dived, swimming sinuous through translucent seas where sunlight sieved down through the blue-green fathoms, where fish flickered away into the mists of distance, or dawdled at weightless leisure between floating weed and plump red sponges.

They dived, some days, near an underwater cliff which fell away to cold, cold, black-green depths. Once, Drake swam out above that unfathomable abysm, for the sheer pleasure of terrifying himself. Once was enough.

In waters less deep, he joined the play with the big, lazy black-winged rays, ferocious in appearance but near enough to harmless unless hooked or speared. He broke open sea urchins for the pleasure of moray eels, which fed from his naked hands. When exhausted by the sea, he slept on rock ledges in the leisurely heat of the afternoon sun.

"He spends less and less time bringing up pearl-oysters," complained his comrades.

"Doubtless he has a religious connection with the sea," said the Great One. "He is engaged in her worship. Let him be."

"Oh," said the Ling.

It seemed there was much to learn about this strange, saintly son of Jon Arabin, who looked young and virile, yet refused every offer of the pleasure of the flesh.

What the Ling did not learn—for they were very innocent, and not much good at arithmetic—was that Drake was robbing them blind. He massed a hoard of twenty pearls—a fortune in other parts, if sailors' stories were anything to go by. And he dreamed sweetly about what such wealth could buy him in civilization.

Each evening, as night settled on Island Ko, he sat by a driftwood fire sucking the flesh from the claws of giant crabs, staring into the flames and imagining the soft breasts of women, the sighs of a swooning lover, the hearty laughter of a tavern, the chink of gold in a casino, the generous smiles of flattering faces admiring his silken elegance.

Finally, the pearling on Ko came to an end. The divers shifted back to Ling. And Drake was ready to escape.

He chose a canoe: one small enough to paddle himself. He scavenged a single waterskin, which he filled from the ever-replenished Inner Pool which supplied the whole community of Ling. Food was no problem: there was any amount of dried oyster flesh for the taking.

He had more than a few doubts about the voyage. It was a hell of a long way to paddle.

"But," said Drake, "I don't have much bloody option. If I can get back to Stokos, I can likely be king.

Or a priest, at least. What's the choice? To stay here and rot, that's what!"

Ling, as far as he could tell, was ignorant of both booze and gambling. And as for sex—he knew well enough that he would be tortured to death if he so much as laid hands on any of the young flesh which delighted in tantalizing him.

So early one morning, while it was still dark, Drake launched his canoe. It was, in fact, Midsummer's Day—the start of the year Khmar 18, and the first anniversary of the Martyrdom of Muck.

Drake was far out in the bay when the dawnlight, diminishing the dark, revealed a ship. A ship oncoming, a stately sight, all sail set to bear her along in the light winds of dawn. Drake stopped paddling, and sat there, hoping. The ship had green sails, yes. And—a dragon figurehead! It was the *Warwolf!* Shouting, weeping and whooping, Drake jumped up and down to such effect that he upset the canoe and precipitated himself into the water.

"I wonder," said one of the elders, observing him from the heights, "why our young guest was out on the waters so early in the morning."

"Because," replied the Great One, who was standing beside him, "he has the Power. He knew his father was returning today, so set himself forth to meet him."

"He will, then, leave us."

"Doubtless."

"What then do you see for his future?" asked the elder.

The Great One deliberated gravely, then said:

"I see him changed to a sail."

"To a sail?"

"Why not?" said the Great One. "We each of us start as a fish in the womb. Is it anymore miraculous to be changed into a sail?"

"Well . . . what else do you see?"

"Monsters . . . many of them . . . and . . . a woman. Red skin. Red breasts. Her name—no, her name eludes me."

"Is this woman then to be the mate of our noble

visitor? Or will he return here to honor us with his flesh?"

"The way is murky," said the Great One. "I see a time when he will be but a step away from a world of destinies. Much then will rely on his wisdom—and the strength of his swordarm."

Thus ran the word of wisdom in the land of Ling.

10

Name: Jon Arabin.

Alias: Warwolf.

Occupation: pirate-trader.

Status: master mariner; ship-owner; large-scale debtor; husband of Leela, Waru, Verona, Silobeth, Esylan, Tarawen, Gleneth, Parazela, Qualavinth, Janateerith, Zal, Ralathy *et al.*

Birthplace: Ashmolea.

Description: lordly lean black bald clean-shaven man with pale blue eyes, firm voice and forthright manner; wears brown leathers and big leather belt encumbered with sea-pouch and a variety of blades.

One of the first things Drake saw when he got on board the Warwolf was Ika Thole, the Ebrell-born harpoon man. Seeing Thole's red hair and red skin, Drake was instantly reminded of his true love, Zanya Kliedervaust. Zanya of the honey-colored voice! Zanya of the high-sprung breasts! Zanya the beautiful, the lush, the ultimately desirable!

How long since he had been laid?

Months!

He had an urgent desire to be back on Stokos, to be face to face with the fair Zanya, praising her with poetry, offering her flowers, stripping away her clothes.

"Zanya, no clothes can properly compliment your beauty—"

"What's that you're saying?" said Jon Arabin, coming up behind him.

Drake promptly turned and tried to punch him in the face. But Arabin caught Drake's fist, and laughed.

"Easy, boy, not so fierce."

"You toad-buggering bastard!" said Drake. "You sailed away and left me."

"Aye, boy," said Jon Arabin releasing Drake's fist and meeting his gaze without trouble. "We knew you'd be safe enough."

"Safe! Look at this!"

Drake pulled up his tattered shirt with such force that the frayed and faded fabric tore, thus exposing his scar. Arabin chuckled.

"Cut, were you? A fight over women, perhaps? Well, for the young, they're worth fighting for."

"Fight!" said Drake. "It was no such thing! They tied me down for torture! Slashed me with a knife then put a snake to the wound. A great monster, all blood and gold. It ate its way to my innards."

"Aye, boy," said Arabin, "then they cut off your head, but you grew yourself another to be looking respectable."

And he dug his fingers in deep under Drake's floating rib. Drake winced as the hard man probed and palpated.

"There's naught deep damage there," said Arabin. "Go any depth in there, and the man's dead. I'd say you got a wound, a fever with it, then some imaginings from the fever."

In fact, the snake which had eaten into Drake's flesh was still there, deeply encysted. Nourished by Drake's own blood supply, it was slowly changing. Even now, a mass of eggs was slowly ripening in its belly. Once they hatched, birthing millions of baby worms . . .

Ah, but that lay in the future, and, for the moment, what Drake didn't know about didn't hurt him.

But he was still angry.

"I hope I get a share of the profits," he said.

"Aye, boy, that you will, what's left after clearing debt. Aye, and we'll be paying to overhaul the ship as well. And does she need it!"

"Well, does she?" said Drake.

"By the oath she does," said Arabin, momentarily appalled at his ignorance. "Go see John Disaster, he's in charge of our clothing chest. Tell him I've said you're to have a new kit entire—you look rough enough to scare a scarecrow."

"Thanks for the compliment," said Drake bitterly. "It wasn't my choice to live so far from a tailor's shop."

"Once you're kitted out," continued Jon Arabin, unperturbed, "come along and watch the trading done. It's good to get to know the ropes."

"Why so?" said Drake.

"Why? Because we'll be back here two years from now."

"Hrmph!" said Drake.

He got Disaster to give him new kit—boots, linens and a set of sealskins. All the clothing was damp, and smelt rather of mold. But, thus dressed, he felt a new man.

He went to watch the trading, and saw good pearls traded for a cargo Arabin had lately loaded at Narba— canoe timber, tarpaulins, canvas sails, fresh vegetables, rice, flour, hides, furs, bone-meal, fish-hooks, harpoons, cauldrons, glass beads, casks of salt pork, siege dust, bamboo, silk, cotton, awls, needles, calamanco, mandolins and ivory.

With the trading done, a dozen girls and an equal number of satin-skinned young men lined up to kiss Drake on his lips, to force pearls upon him, to weep at his feet, to stroke his haunches and fondle his hands, while the crew of the *Warwolf* laughed, clapped, stamped and cheered.

"So much for torture chambers!" said Jon Arabin, as the last suitor quit the ship reluctantly. "It must have been the fever-dreams you were remembering."

And Drake, scratching his scar idly, was almost persuaded to agree.

Though he was glad to be back on board, he could not help noticing how cramped and dirty the ship was, and how it stank. And it was crowded, yes, after the comparative privacy he had enjoyed in the caves of the Ling.

He consoled himself with the thought that this was the last voyage of his life. Once they touched land, he would jump ship and buy a passage back to Stokos. Well—that would mean more sea, of course, but only briefly.

On reaching his homeland, he would buy himself out of his apprenticeship, pay whatever theft-fines he owed with respect to Muck's mastersword, and then buy himself a place in the priesthood of the demon Hagon. His wealth was certainly equal to his ambition.

Since it was midsummer, he was now seventeen years old plus a couple of months. In less than a year, King Tor would make a decision on his marriage prospects. Well. If he got Tor's daughter, he'd quit the temple and be prince (and, later, king). If he didn't get the daughter, he'd follow a career in the priesthood. But, either way, he'd have Zanya Kliedervaust as his pleasure-woman.

His wealth would surely make certain of that.

Drake worked on the finer details of his plans as he helped raise the anchor, laboring round in a circle, throwing his weight against one of the twelve bars of the capstan. Even with this enormous amount of leverage, all were a muck of sweat by the time the brutal weight had been broken free and hauled up high and dry.

He was summoned below decks by the cook. As Drake helped hash up some unidentifiable gunk fried in whale oil, he imagined the beautiful meals which Zanya would cook when she was his pleasure-woman. His sweet daydreams blurred unfriendly verities; even the increasingly uneasy motion of the ship failed to trouble him.

They had rough weather for the start of their trip

north. Then, when they had just cleared Cape Songala, a storm claimed them.

A ravaging wind blew from the west. After a two-day storm-fight, what little canvas they had dared carry was blown out entirely. Then the wind shifted to the north-west, threatening to drive them toward doom at Drangsturm.

Jon Arabin decided to lie-to, praying the storm would blow itself out before wrecking them. So lie-to they did: but, slowly, remorselessly, they were driven toward grief where the flame trench met the Central Ocean.

Finally, the fires of Drangsturm itself were seen glowering against the stormcloud sky. The wind's joy blew berserk. They must raise sail or die—but no canvas could stand the weather.

"Man the fore-shrouds!" roared Jon Arabin.

And so they did.

When Drake was ordered aloft with the rest, he could scarce believe his ears—but soon enough he was up there, clinging in the rigging which braced the foremast. In his darkest imaginings, he'd never dreamed himself being turned into a storm-sail, but there he was, shuddering in the screaming wind while the ship lurched and his stomach lurched with it.

Warm within his gut, unperturbed by the weather, the encysted snake fed quietly on his blood, nourished its slowly-growing eggs, and thus prepared certain profound changes for his future.

For two days more the *Warwolf* endured the storm, with her crew manning the fore-shrouds in shifts. Once she was driven within half a league of the coast, but a wind-change saved her. She sprung a leak: Arabin set men to pumping. Another started: he organized a bucket-brigade. The first mate fell down a companion-ladder and broke his neck; Arabin swore, and promoted the second.

At last the inconstant wind shifted all the way round to the south, and eased a little. The *Warwolf* ran along with bare poles. Drake, by this time, was lurching on his feet, with hardly enough sense left to understand that he was still alive.

Arabin, passing him on the deck, slapped him on the back.

"We've done it, boy!" said Arabin. "We've come through!"

And Drake, despite the intensity of his fatigue, grinned.

"Aye," he said. "We're heroes."

Both Shewel Lokenshield and Ika Thole heard him say as much, but neither of those hard men mocked him. Rather: they shared his triumph.

"How about some food for half-starved sailors?" said Ika Thole.

And Drake, understanding that the question was prompted by dire need, gladly went to the galley.

Toward noon on one rough-weather day (which day? How much storm had they endured? Blood and balls, there was no remembering) lessening winds allowed them to set a little sail. A brave sight the *Warwolf* made then, plunging through the mountainous gray seas with timbers groaning and strong men groaning in harmony.

"We'll have it sweet from here to Narba," said Jon Arabin to himself. "We're in the clear."

Many sailors' superstitions held that such talk was tempting fate. Certainly, it was over-optimistic, for that evening their troubles were multiplied by a monster.

It came flying from out of the south, laboring through the air on storm-damaged wings. Swept from the shores of Argan by the weather, too poor an aviator to fly against the wind, it had no choice but to brave on forward into the unknown. An island was what it needed, but the *Warwolf*, happening where she did, suited the brute's purposes nicely.

It came on the ship from the stern. Then flew alongside. Drake Douay saw it out of the corner of his eye.

"If that was on a chessboard," he murmured, turning and getting a good look at it, "I'd say it was a Neversh."

Since it wasn't on a chessboard, he dismissed it as

a hallucination. Harly Burpskin saw the same thing, and thought it was a demon. Raggage Pouch also saw it—and mewled with piteous fear. He knew exactly what it was. It was indeed a Neversh. And Raggage Pouch, who had once seen a Neversh kill seventy armed men on Island Burntos, feared it more than anything out of nightmare.

The Neversh flew in a great wide circle round the ship.

"Jon!" screamed Quin Baltu.

"What?" yelled Jon Arabin.

"There's a—"

The rest of Quin Baltu's words were lost in the sundering roar of a wave breaking over the ship.

"So there's a wave," muttered Jon Arabin. "So what?"

But he was worried, all the same. For, heavily laden with an enormous mass of water, the *Warwolf* seemed almost to dig into the sea. For a few moments, Jon Arabin thought she was going to sunder under there and then.

Water cascaded from the ship in torrents. Slowly, her bow began to rise.

"Jon!" screamed Quin Baltu.

"Don't worry!" yelled Jon Arabin, thinking this was no time for Quin Baltu to panic. "She's riding nicely."

"But there's a—"

There was a crash fit to rival thunder. Jon Arabin looked round wildly. Saw that the foremast was shattered, was down, broken, smashed, had fallen across the fo'c'sle, had wrecked the fo'c'sle, and was now kicking, struggling, striving, trying to resurrect itself.

Or was it?

No. On closer examination . . .

"Hell's blood and pigs' balls!" shouted Jon Arabin, in a voice that was one part fear and two parts fury. "It's a Neversh, or I'm a tadpole."

Jon Arabin could never be mistaken for a tadpole (though he had in his time been compared unfavorably with a shark, a lamprey, a vulture and a cantaloup) and there was indeed a Neversh struggling in the wreckage of rigging and canvas on the forward part of his ship.

"Jon—" shouted Quin Baltu.

"I see it!" yelled Jon Arabin. "Well, don't just stand there! Get rid of it!"

Quin Baltu started forward, obedient to Jon Arabin's command. But the next wave took him overboard.

"Merantosh!" said Jon Arabin, who was always prone to obscenity under stress. *"Na jaba na terik!"*

He looked round for Disaster, or some other man who might be fool enough to tackle the beast. None such was in sight.

"Right, then," said Arabin. "I'll handle it myself."

As these monsters go, the Neversh was fairly small. Scarcely a quarter grown, it was just fifty paces in length, from the tips of its twin feeding spikes to the end of its whiplash tail. Small, yes, yet dangerous. It thrashed strenuously, wings beating so wildly that it was impossible to count them all. Its body, rich with buoyant gas, was kicked around by the wind. Finding the mainmast with its tail, the Neversh coiled tail around mast, and hung on tightly.

"Come on, men!" roared Jon Arabin. "We're going to deal with that hell-bitch!"

Nobody paid him any attention.

The ruined foremast, which had till then been pointing forward, rolled with a crash from the wreckage of the fo'c'sle. It started dragging in the water. A snare of ropes prevented it from falling away entirely.

"Men!" roared Jon Arabin. "We act now or we lose the ship. Kill the monster! Cut away the mast! Come on! Come with me!"

But the entire crew was in panic, some men trying to launch the boats, others climbing the sheets—as if that would save them!—or taking cover below-decks.

"Grief!" said Jon Arabin.

He called up the weapons muqaddam, who had been supervising the pumping.

"Get some order in this ship," said Arabin, "even

if you have to kill someone. I'm going forward to take care of our unwelcome visitor."

The weapons muqaddam looked round, saw the nature of the unwelcome visitor, and gave a short bow.

"My lord," he said, "I will remember your heroism to your wives and children."

Then grinned, darting out of reach as Arabin swung a kick at him. They were good friends from way back.

On his way forward, Arabin came upon a party of pirates who were trying to launch a boat.

"Avast there, you landlubbers!" bellowed Arabin. "Any crow-gutted scavenger who wants to leave had better be ready to walk water!"

With a few more well-chosen words and some adroit use of his left-hand boot (always his best kicking foot, the left) he scattered the men back to their work.

Then hung on tight as a huge wave broke, sending water lathering over the ship. Amidst the lather was Quin Baltu. Jon Arabin grabbed him as he went floating past.

"You all right?" said Arabin.

Quin Baltu could only cough and gasp. He had been thrashed something terrible by the roistering ocean; he had swallowed enough salt to pickle a pig.

"Volunteers!" roared Arabin. "I need five volunteers to carry Quin Baltu to safety."

Five volunteers promptly came forward.

Drake Douay was one of them and John Arabin grabbed him.

"Friend Drake stays here," said Arabin. "It only needs four of you to carry Quin Baltu."

The lucky four hustled Quin Baltu away.

"Now you come along with me," said Arabin to Drake.

As the sea captain had caught the cook's boy in a painful wrist-lock, there was not much argument about it.

Weeping with fear and fatigue, Drake was forced along the deck toward the Neversh.

11

Neversh: flying monster with six wings; eight very short legs ending in clawed feet; massive head; thick neck; bulky bulbous body containing buoyant gas; very long whiplash tail which it often uses as a weapon; twin feeding spikes which appear to be made of solid ivory, but on Investigation prove to have a honeycomb structure; twin grapple-hooks to secure prey.

The Neversh can grow at least two hundred paces long and is alleged to be able to deflect crossbow bolts with its tail. (Nevertheless, archers have often shot down samples of this type of monster, as its gas-retaining sacs puncture easily.)

The Neversh is one of the Swarms, those colony creatures which dominate the terror-lands of the Deep South, and are only prevented from invading the north of Argan by the gulf of Drangsturm—and the wizards guarding that flame trench.

Weeping with fear and fatigue Drake was forced along the deck toward the Neversh. As Drake and Jon Arabin came level with the mainmast, Drake saw the monster had coiled its tail around the mast to stop itself getting swept away by the waves.

"We can chop the tail!" cried Drake, who wanted to go no nearer the head than he had to.

"That won't do," said Jon Arabin.

"Why not? Cut away the tail! The next wave will take it!"

"Aye! Or it might turn round to fight its way aft. Then what?"

"You tell me," said Drake.

"We lose the ship, that's what. Come on! Move yourself! No—wait!"

Jon Arabin forced Drake to the mainmast.

"We'll cut the tail?" said Drake.

"No! I've told you that! The rope—cut it loose."

Drake drew his dirk and cut loose the coil of rope which was tied (by four-dozen turns of twine) to cleats anchored to the mainmast. As the rope came free, the coils of the tail of the Neversh shifted. Drake started, fell back. Jon Arabin caught him, took the rope and slung it over his shoulder.

Then Arabin hustled Drake onwards until they were up by the monster's neck. A massive neck, thicker than a treetrunk. It seemed a dull purple color in the dark of the evening. It pulsed as the creature breathed.

"Hack it!" shouted Drake, with the savagery of fear. "Chop it and gut it!"

"Aye, boy, and have it tear the ship apart as it died. They're powerful strong, these brutes. Take half a day to die if they're cut clean in half. Help me with the rope!"

Arabin ducked under the monster's neck, mounted wreckage to gain some height, then slung the end of the rope to Drake.

"Make it fast!" said Arabin. "A loop round the monster's neck! A hangman's knot, if you know the shaping!"

"Aye!" screamed Drake, catching the rope-end.

One moment he was standing there fumbling with the rope. The next he was slammed against the monster as a wave crashed down on the ship. The burdening waters smothered him this way and that. He lost his grip on the rope, was sucked away by the wave—then held. By the Neversh.

He had been swept right up by its head. A murderous jointed claw—its nearside grapple-hook—had spiked his boot precisely where sole met upper.

"Jon!" screamed Drake.

"Hold tight, boy!" yelled Arabin. "I'm—"

Another wave drowned his words and the world. Flailing in the flurry, Drake grabbed something, a bar or pipe of sorts. The water was too heavy for thought.

Then the wave subsided, and Drake saw he was clinging to one of the monster's twin feeding spikes. Its nearside grapple-hook still held him. Its offside claw came for him. He kicked out. But it slashed into his sealskin jacket and held fast in the fabric.

Drake let go of the feeding spike. The grapple-hooks took his weight effortlessly. He dropped both hands to the offside grapple-hook. It was polished, it was cold, it was thicker than a banana. He tried to bend it or break it.

Impossible!

"O-o-o-oh!" moaned Drake.

Then the monster started straightening out both grapple-hooks, pushing him away. And Drake thought:

It doesn't want me!

Then realized the thing had no mouth. It fed with the spikes. It wanted to push him away so it could jam those spikes into his body and suck. He jerked out his dirk. He slammed the blade into one of the feeding spikes.

"Die!" he screamed.

His steel drove deep—then proved impossible to withdraw. His only weapon was useless, jammed in the feeding spike. He must cling to it: his strength against that of the grapple-hooks. He grabbed the hilt with both hands. Another wave smothered over. As foam shuddered away, Drake gasped for breath. The grapple-hooks convulsed, breaking his hold on the dirk.

"Jon!" he screamed.

In answer, Jon Arabin dropped to the deck. Too late! The grapple-hooks shoved, one last time—and Drake was rammed hard up against the wreckage of the fo'c'sle.

The Neversh lowered its head, trying to get its feeding spikes into goring position. Drake tried to push them up and away. He might as well have tried to hold up the world. The grapple-hooks pushed up and out. The Neversh was almost in a position to spike and feed.

Drake half-saw Jon Arabin draw his falchion and raise it high. The falchion, yes. A great ugly bit of metal, with the mass of it concentrated in the thickness far forward, at the optimum striking point.

Down it came, striking at the grapple-hook which had spiked Drake's jacket. The falchion descended on the grapple-hook's middle joint. It went through clean like an axe through a cucumber.

Drake was still held by his boot.

The Neversh reared up.

As the monster reared, Drake was jerked away from the wreckage. The sole of his boot tore free from the uppers. He was thrown clear. He landed on his back, hitting the deck heavily. The monster clawed for Arabin with the hook which had just lost Drake.

"Scarn!" screamed Arabin.

And chopped the hook away.

The monster swung sideways, meaning to kill Arabin with its twin feeding spikes. But those spikes slammed into sprawling wreckage, cutting the gesture short. Arabin, still in a fighting rage, hacked a great chunk out of one of them—then stopped, suddenly realizing that if he cut the spikes away, the creature would be free to pulp him with its head.

He chopped for its nearest eye instead. His falchion bounced off the armored bubble protecting that eye. Useless. Well, then—the rope!

"The rope now, boy!" shouted Arabin, wiping his falchion against his sleeve, out of habit (it usually had blood on it after combat) then sheathing it. "Don't just lie there—or we're dead! Up off your arse! Help tie this rope around!"

Drake swore, mustered himself to his feet, was almost skittled by another (small) wave, then floundered forward to help get the rope knotted round the neck of the Neversh. Soon Jon Arabin was beside him, checking the hangman's knot he had fashioned.

"Good rope, this is," muttered Arabin. Then raised

his voice against the weather and repeated himself so Drake could hear. "Valence cordage. Have you heard of it?"

"Aye," said Drake. "We use it for cliff-work on Stokos."

"Where you learnt yourself climbing."

"Aye," said Drake, a little doubtfully, though he had boasted broadly of his skills in the past, and it was too late to gainsay them now.

"Then I'll belay you, boy, and this is what you'll do . . ."

And Arabin explained.

"Mother of dogs and poxes!" exclaimed Drake, in horror.

"It's the only way, boy," said Arabin grimly.

"Do it yourself then!" said Drake.

"I would if I could, boy, but I'm no shakes at climbing. Come, let's get forward."

"I won't do it!"

"Aye, then I'll gut you here," said Arabin, and drew his falchion for further work.

"A death by steel is as good as any," said Drake, his voice sullen with fear and hate.

He was calling Arabin's bluff.

They looked each other hard in the eye. Man and boy they stood there on the heaving deck, the shadows of evening darkening all around them.

"You're dead meat," said Arabin, with death in his voice.

"Aye, and so are we all in the end," said Drake, more confident than ever that he would not be forced forward, and that Arabin would find another way to deal with the monster.

At that moment, the thing's tiny little disorganized brain finally cottoned onto the fact that it could get a clean run at its antagonists by backing off toward the stern, pulling its feeding spikes clear of the wreckage which kept its head from striking at will.

Its eight crocodile-sprawling feet scrabbled splinters from the deck as it went into reverse, dragging the Valence cordage with it. Arabin, who had the coil slung over his shoulders, had no chance to pay out any slack. Dragged off his feet, he hit the deck heavily.

The Neversh lowered its feeding spikes and charged like a bull. Arabin lay helpless. Drake ripped off his sealskin jacket and flung it to the wind. The Neversh saw something flying in the air, reared up as if to spike it—then crashed back to the deck.

Drake helped Arabin scramble to his feet. Retreating together, they paid out plenty of slack. By the time the Neversh had stopped puzzling over the flying jacket, the two humans had gained the fo'c'sle wreckage.

"Well done," said Arabin.

But Drake took no joy in the compliment. His legs gave way. He clutched the strongest bit of timber he could find, and wept. He was too tired, too cold, too dizzy. He was finished.

Arabin drew his falchion, as if to renew his threat—then a wave burst over them, knocking away the falchion and smothering them under a mountain of water. Drake, snatched from his timber, grabbed at guess—and hooked an arm round Arabin's neck. Arabin clung to the rope, the far end of which was knotted round the neck of the Neversh.

The wave eased away at last to nothing, leaving the two of them sodden, dripping, shuddering. Arabin gripped Drake by the arm. Hard. His fingers dug deep into Drake's biceps.

"It's my plan or nothing, now," said the Warwolf, his voice urgent.

Drake, released, collapsed to the deck. Helpless as a jellyfish. Arabin grabbed him by the scruff of the neck, hauled him to his feet, then laid a firm hand on his shoulder.

"Courage, boy!" said Arabin. "Courage!"

Drake stared at his captain. The sky of the man's eyes was entirely lost in the gloom. Drops of sea-spray clung to his bald head, which looked, in the gathering night, like an egg going black with rot. Beyond was the monster, wings still whirring, feet scraping and clawing as it made ineffectual stabs at the fo'c'sle wreckage. Beyond that, the rest of the ship. He half-heard the weapons muqaddam shouting orders.

All about was the wilderness of the sea, an upthrash of confused gray, smeared cloud and horizon-menacing gloom. If they were to act, it would have to be now, for soon the night would make it impossible.

"Show me the place," said Drake.

"This way, then," said Arabin.

They went further forward, paying out more rope as they went, then the Warwolf took his footing in the wreckage of the fo'c'sle and made ready to belay.

"I've lost my knife," said Drake, thinking he might need one.

"Then take this," said Arabin, drawing a fresh blade from the massive leather belt which sustained his falchion's sheath, his waterproof sea-pouch, a luckstone, and a couple of dirks like the one he offered Drake. "And keep it well, until the day you leave it in the heart of the Walrus."

And Drake, sensing this was a project dear to Jon Arabin's heart, mustered a grin and cried:

"I live for that day!"

"Aye!" shouted Arabin, with a sudden onset of something like joy, his heart made glad to see Drake showing spirit. "So do we all!"

Then Drake braced himself on the edge of the ship, tested the rope, and made ready to do on the heaving hull what he had done often enough before on his father's coal cliffs.

Over the side he went, rappelling down, warding himself off from the hull with his feet, fearing at any moment to be dashed against that wooden cliff and shattered entirely.

A big sea came shuthering up around him. Lost in the wave-sway, he clung to the rope as best he could. And broke free of the waters. Gasped for air. And was gasping still as a greater sea-thrash smashed him loose from the rope.

In the sea's despairs he tumbled. Then something brutal crunched him. He grabbed it. And, as the waters lumbered away, found himself clinging to the shank of the anchor. He swung his legs over its arms, and, as the seas roistered around him, clung to the ugly mass of barnacle-crusted iron.

Something like a snake whipped round his neck as he clung amidst cataracts. As the waters baffled away, he fought with the strangling thing.

"Demon's grief!" he said, getting it free at last.

And found what he held was no snake but the end of the rope. Swiftly, he hauled in as much slack as he could, and took a couple of turns around the anchor before the next sea. Then, between one assault of the sea and the next, he knotted the Valence cordage as best he could, hoping the rope lived up to its reputation. His hands ran dark with his blood, for he was gashing himself on barnacles in his haste.

"Done!" said Drake.

And a sea came up and almost did for him.

As the waters dipped away, he risked the hard part— and started to climb the rope. It had just a little slack in it. But, as he climbed, the Neversh on the deck above jerked its head, pulling the rope taut. Drake was almost tossed off. But he was strong, yes, and desperate, and clung on with a grimness death itself would have envied.

He gained a little more height, then felt a strong hand grab him. It was Jon Arabin, who hauled him up to the deck. Drake fell into his master's arms, and was held in the refuge until his shuddering eased.

"Now, boy," said Arabin. "Do you know how to release the anchor?"

"No," said Drake, honestly.

"Then I'll manage that myself," said Arabin. "Stay here."

Then Arabin sought out the trapdoor he knew to be in amongst the wreckage of the fo'c'sle, and crawled down through that narrow way into the utter dark below, where the hugeness of the anchor cable coiled in the rat-haunted gloom. He found the safety chain, unwound it from the grab cleats, jerked it clear—and heard the rope begin to whip away as the anchor fell sheer to the seas of night.

The anchor hit the sea, dragging the Valence cordage down with it. The cord tightened round the neck of the Neversh, jerking the monster sideways. Screaming, it fought against the weight. For a few moments it held its ground. But the pain was intolerable. At last, it let go of the mainmast with its whiplash tail, and, wings beating, clawed feet skidding across the deck, was dragged to the side and pulled over.

The Neversh smashed into the water and disappeared from sight.

"Drake!" yelled Arabin.

But the word was savaged by surf and by water-slop, tangled by ropes and baffled by echoes. What Drake heard was only an incomprehensible cry of human anguish. He was sure something terrible was happening to Arabin below decks. For more than a moment, he was tempted to ignore the cry. Then it was repeated.

"Courage, man," said Drake to Drake.

And crept through the dark wet scrabble-wood wreckage of the fo'c'sle, until he heard Arabin call out yet again—and recognized the shout as his own name.

"What is it?" yelled Drake. "Rats?"

"Rats?" roared Arabin. "What are you blathering about? Is the monster over?"

"Aye," said Drake. "Over, and sunk from sight!"

"Good, then," said Arabin.

And grabbed in the dark for the anchor axe which was always kept handy in case the ship had to quit a mooring in a hurry, cut away its restraining cords with one of his dirks, then hacked and chopped until he had cut clean through the cable, setting the anchor free to fall away to the cold dark hell of the seabed, dragging the Neversh with it.

Shortly, Arabin was on deck again, with Drake. As they picked their way back to their comrades, he said to Drake, as quietly as the weather would permit:

"Few enough have seen that and lived. Fewer still have helped tackle it. You did well."

And that accolade, Drake knew, was to be valued more than the honors of many a kingdom.

"Now get yourself down to the kitchen, boy," said

Arabin. "We've a hard night coming on, and the men will be wanting their soup."

And Drake went, thinking his captain a hard man.

"Where have you been?" demanded the cook, when he got below.

"Helping Jon Arabin."

"With what?"

"Oh," said Drake. "With—"

Then paused, finding he had no wish to avaunt about his feat. For he had faced the worst kind of arse-opening terror, and to tell the tale would be to relive it, at least in part.

"With ropes and cordage and stuff," he said, by way of explanation.

And then pitched into the work the cook gave him, and was soon too busy to think. And, while he did not appreciate the wisdom of the captain who kept him so busy, he got the benefit of it regardless.

And through all these alarums, the snake in Drake's belly slept soundly, planning its changes for his future.

12

Drangsturm Gulf: a U-shaped indentation—roughly a hundred leagues wide and two hundred deep—in the coast of Argan.

North, the Gulf opens to the Central Ocean.

East is Narba, Provincial Endergeneer, the settled lands of the Far South, the Castle of Controlling Power and Drangsturm.

South is a desolate terror-coast on which lies Ling Bay.

West is unknown territory which legend holds to be haunted with monsters of the Swarms, and—in addition—trolls, basilisks, gryphons, dragons, crocodiles and two-headed giants.

Need it be said?
Drake's resolution not to boast about his part in killing the Neversh held good for precisely two days. After that, he was hot for fame, glory and recognition. But nobody paid him much attention, with the exception of Harly Burpskin.

"It's a nice story," said Burpskin, having heard Drake's tale, "but a mite improbable, to say the least."

"Man, the Neversh was there," said Drake. "You saw it yourself."

"Aye, and waves washing over the deck. Likely the brute was carried off by such."

"Wait till we come to harbor," said Drake. "Then you'll see my story proved. For you'll find the anchor's missing."

"What signifies a missing anchor?" said Burpskin. "Expense, that's all. It's no new thing to lose an anchor. Aye, and a replacement will have to come from the voyage profits, before we get our share."

So much for fame and glory!

Since even Burpskin refused to believe him, Drake abandoned efforts to persuade anyone else. At least for the moment. His just recognition could wait till they reached land.

If they ever reached land.

The *Warwolf* was leaking badly, shipping water almost faster than it could be pumped out. The wind, which had shifted to the east, was still almost storm-force. Under a sky of dark and ragged fractonimbus, the *Warwolf* toiled through the buffeting waters. The rolling seas crashed into surf, strewing foam across the ocean.

Jon Arabin, eyes red-rimmed, searched the blurred horizons for sight of land. His ears ached from the constant wind and cold—a cold he'd never known before in these waters. His right hip was aching, as it always did when he was cold and tired.

Worse, he was lost.

He judged they were still in the Drangsturm Gulf—but where? As his ship groaned and shuddered, struck by another smash-fist sea-shock, he winced, as if it was his own body which was being pounded. Blood of a shark! What had he done to deserve such weather?

He reviewed his options. He could put out sea-anchors and do his best to go nowhere. In that case, the *Warwolf* would sink. He could try the long, laborious business of tacking against the easterly wind, trying to make for Narba. If he did that, his ship would sink all the quicker.

Alternatively, he could let the wind drive them to the western side of the Gulf of Drangsturm. During his many voyages in these waters—aagh, and how he longed for the fair weather of those long-ago cruises!—he had seen its mountains often enough on the far horizon. He had never been there. He had heard tales, of course . . .

But what choice did he have?

"The ship must live," said Arabin.

And, reluctantly, ordered the *Warwolf* to run for the west. Night came. By morning, the wind had eased to scarcely more than a moderate gale; foam from breaking waves was still lathered across the sea by the wind, but it was possible to talk without shouting. The very sounds of the ship were easier; her timbers were hurting still, but were no longer in agony.

"Good," said Arabin.

And ordered the lookouts to keep a sharp watch for land. Though, to be honest, he still had no idea how far they were from shore.

Shortly after he had instructed the lookouts, he was met by a delegation led by Quin Baltu. With Baltu were Jez Glane, Salaman Meerkat and Peg Suzilman. Arabin saw at a glance they were tired, angry, hostile, determined. All were armed.

"Morning, boys," said Arabin.

"Aye," said Baltu, sourly. "Perhaps the last morning some of us will see. Unless we turn, man, and run east."

"Why should we do that?"

"Because," said Baltu, "that's what the boys want."

"What's this?" said Jon Arabin. "Mutiny?"

He spoke as if in jest—but he was worried.

"Not mutiny," said Baltu, bracing himself against the ship's swagger. "We want to fix things right with a friendly talk."

"Aye," said Glane. "Friendly talk, that's the thing."

Arabin looked around for some staunch, honest men he could call on for help if it came to a fight. But nothing was in sight but Drake Douay, who was keeping as close as possible to his captain, hoping to win promotion from cook's boy to sailor.

"Drake," said Arabin, in a lazy voice. "Get to the kitchen for some soup. I've six great rats and a blue-eyed raccoon in me belly, all clamoring sore with hunger."

"What kind of soup do you want?" said Drake, casting an eye over the opposition.

Jez Glane was old and useless. Suzilman was also old—but wiry. Meerkat, slim, quiet and dark, was an unknown quantity. But Baltu—well, the big bloke could smash just about any man aboard.

"What kind of soup?" said Arabin. "What is there?"

"Oh, dragon soup, shark soup, mushroom soup or carrot soup."

"Nay, man," said Arabin. "They all sound too fancy for me. I'll have what you usually serve up— that boiled dishwater with bits of dead men's bones afloat in it."

"Man, we're right out of that stuff," said Drake, "since we're so far from ditches and graveyards. I tell you what, I'll get you a bowl of the cook's sawdust soup. That should suit!"

And Drake set off at an easy pace, meaning to summon not soup but reinforcements. But Peg Suzilman and Salaman Meerkat drew blades against him. Drake stopped where he was. Despite the death-cold wind, he was suddenly hot—hot and sweating.

"What's this?" said Drake. "You've a lust for fresh meat, have you? Man, I'd make a stringy dinner, I'll tell you that for nothing. All grit and gristle. Ease up with the steel till we get to the west. There'll be good hunting ashore, I'll bet."

"Aye," said Jez Glane, in a voice which quavered a bit. "Things hunting us, I'll warrant. Huge things with teeth, aye, claws, like scythes, feet like hammers."

"What nonsense is this?" said Jon Arabin.

"No nonsense, friend Warwolf," said Quin Baltu. "We've all heard the horrors of the shore you're making for."

A wave-burst scattered cold, cold sprays across the deck. Drake waited for Arabin to speak—but Arabin said nothing. He was trying to stare down Quin Baltu. A fruitless exercise. Drake was edgy.

Come on, Jon. Do something!

160 Hugh Cook

But Jon Arabin had no miracles proof against mutiny. He knew these men well: they had been with him for years. They would never turn against him without the best of reasons: a marrow-gutting fear which overwhelmed all loyalties and every hope.

"You hear us, Jon?" said Jez Glane, in something of a whine. "It's that we don't want to die, aye, that's why we're here."

"I run to the west for life, not for death," said Jon Arabin.

"You can't fool us," said Quin Baltu. "It's a gamble you're taking, risking our lives for unknown gains in the face of horrors we've all heard spoken of."

"Much is spoken but little is truthed," said Drake, eyeing the blades which still confronted him, and wondering if he dare risk a dash for safety.

"Man," said Baltu to Arabin, entirely ignoring Drake. "We can't run west. There's fearful danger there."

Death, danger, fear. That was what they spoke of. But most of the damage was being done by cold, hunger, fatigue. A day of calm, a good sleep, a couple of hot meals, and they'd be new men. But—Arabin glanced at the wild horizons, and knew hope of such was not to be rewarded.

"Mayhap we run to danger," said he. "But choice is not in my gift. We find safety to west—or we sink and drown."

"There's worse deaths than drowning," said Baltu darkly.

"Aye," said Meerkat. "To be breathed on by a basilisk, that's one. That's murder. Why, the very look of its eyes will kill."

"And there's crocodiles!" said Jez Glane. "Logs which turn of sudden to dragons without wings! They eat you, man, gnaw your kneecaps then chew off your prick."

"Is that so?" said Jon Arabin. "Then you've got nothing to fear!"

This raised no laugh. Well, it had been worth a try.

"Boys," said Jon Arabin, "I'll level with you. We

run with the weather for the west—or we sink. If the ship goes down, we have to take to the boats. And how would you like that? A small boat, no shelter, no land for a horizon or more."

"We'd live," said Quin Baltu, staunchly. "Danger known is better than unknown. Turn east, man! If the ship sinks, the boats will still get us to Narba. I love small boats. I could sail in such from here to the Teeth if I had to."

"Man," said Drake, grabbing a stay as the ship lurched in a truly horrible fashion, "what's this nonsense about the unknown west? Man, there's been cruises there in plenty, and will be hence."

"Aye," said Jon Arabin, taking Drake's hint. "Boys, my great-grandfather sailed these waters for year on year. Aye, and buried treasure on some westward island. That's family tradition."

Hope, yes. That was what these men needed. Hope of an island, a landfall, a safe shore. Wasn't that the ultimate function of leadership? To give hope.

"You talk of an island," said Baltu. "But words are one thing, land's another. Will you swear your island?"

"Our island waits to west," said Arabin. "I swear it on my mother's honor."

He apologized, secretly, to his mother's shade. Well, that wasn't the first of his misdeeds she'd had to put up with—and it probably wouldn't be the last.

"He swears!" said Jez Glane.

Eager to believe it might be true. For Glane, unlike Baltu, was not fond of small boats.

"He swears, yes," said Quin Baltu. "So his great-grandad sailed these waters . . . but we can't trust such stories, generations old."

"Then trust to fresher news," said Drake.

"What do you know about it?" said Meerkat, whose sword was still ready to slice at a moment's notice.

"Lots!" said Drake.

Verily, he knew the last thing he wanted was to be adrift in a cockleshell craft which might overturn and leave him floundering in the sea more than a horizon from shore. Been there, done that! All very well for Quin Baltu to talk with love and longing about adventures in small boats on the storm-tossed waves—but Drake would rather risk monsters.

"You claim, perhaps, to have been west yourself?" said Peg Suzilman.

"Nay, man," said Drake. "But my king has. King Tor, aye. A huge ogre, as wide as tall. Sits on an iron throne, eats frogs, drinks blood, gives out justice. He went there right enough, yes, but five years ago, chasing a vision of gold and diamonds. He found none such, but came home safe with news of goodly islands. Aye. Sweet water and fields of lilies."

"How do you know of this?" said Peg Suzilman.

"My father sailed with the king," said Drake. "Aye, and on the shore he found a tower. Tall it was, with Guardian Machines within, great brutes of clattering metal which spat death and chased him up some stairs. There he was trapped by an invisible wall and—"

Drake proceeded to tell the story of the find of the magic amulets, the destruction of the machines at the top of the tower, and his father's escape on a rope woven from wires of weird manufacture.

He saw Glane, Suzilman and Meerkat were close to believing him. But Quin Baltu was not.

"Man," sneered Quin Baltu, "that's a right daft story. Little lockets which talk! You expect me to believe a nonsense like that?"

In answer, Drake hauled out one of the lockets in question. He had been wearing it next to his skin, for luck.

"Man," said Drake, dangling the glossy black lozenge in front of Baltu, "this is one of those lockets my father found. He gave it to me for luck."

"I see a pretty trinket," said Baltu. "I hear no voice."

"Then watch," said Drake.

And he manipulated the seven silver stars built into one side of the amulet, and set the thing talking.

The voice of the poet Saba Yavendar contended

against that of the wind. While he spoke in the High Speech, which none on the *Warwolf* could understand, Quin Baltu listened long and hard. Then looked Jon Arabin in the eyes.

"Jon," said Quin Baltu. "We've been a long way together."

"Aye," said the Warwolf.

"Jon, I trust you."

"I trust you too," said Jon Arabin. "And I love you as a brother. Despite these moments. Go below, boys, and get yourself some soup."

So the mutineers departed. And Arabin standing easy on the rolling deck, let his arms hang slack by his side, then made every muscle in his body shudder and shake in the exercise known as Five Horses Dancing. Then he did the Three Breaths and a single Focus, and felt stronger. He looked at Drake, who was tucking away his curious amulet. Right: teaching first. Then settle curiosity.

"What brought those men to the edge of mutiny?" said Arabin. "Did they hate me? Or what?"

"Nay," said Drake. "It was despair "It was despair which took us so close to death. Despair—that's the great sin, man. That makes all the others possible. But you—you gave them confidence. That's what makes you leader."

"You think well," said Arabin, surprised.

At Drake's age, Arabin (dreaming of future glory while he endured the infinite boredom of schooling) had thought of leadership in terms of machismo. One man—the ultimate killer—to brute it over lesser mortals by death-skills alone.

"We're taught to think on Stokos," said Drake. "Not that I can always see the use of it, since there's not much money in thinking. As to leadership—why, my uncle, Oleg Douay, he spoke of it often. For he was mixed up in wars and such in his youth."

"Well," said Jon Arabin, teaching done and curiosity still to be satisfied, "tell me now, friend Drake. Whence came that trinket? From the west?"

"Nay, man," said Drake. "From the moon. My

father flew there when he were but a boy, riding on the back of a great gray goose."

"I see," said Jon Arabin. "Then how about you flying below to get me some soup?"

"Dragon soup or sawdust?"

"I'll take the seal soup," said Arabin. "It seems the least likely to kill."

It was a long, uneasy day. Arabin worried incessantly. What if reefs and rocks infested these uncharted waters? What if he failed to find safe harbor to the west? An island, yes, that was what he needed. Not anything fancy. Any chunk of rock would do, so long as his ship could shelter in its lee.

Leadership is the science of hope. Yes. But if he found no landfall to the west, what good was hope?

By the time night came, heavy rain was falling. A solid, sullen downpour. Rain! In the Drangsturm Gulf, at the height of summer! Craziness . . .

What should he do? Heave to? Or strive blindly through the night? There were so many unknowns: the weather, the distance to shore, what depth of water they could count on. How much longer could the ship stand staunch against the seas before ripping in half?

Jon Arabin made a round of his ship, and decided he knew one thing for certain: his crew could take very little more of this.

"We run for the west tonight," said Jon Arabin, with every appearance of confidence. "I know just where we are, aye, from the taste of the spray. Come morning, we'll see land—I guarantee it."

Faint hearts were heartened by this bluff, and through the night the *Warwolf* ran. Jon Arabin slept little, yet thrice dreamed his ship wrecked.

The weather eased further overnight. Come morning, they were cruising in a moderate breeze amidst herds of brisk white horses that were champing across the seas toward the western coast of the Gulf of Drangsturm, which lay in plain view maybe twenty leagues away.

About three leagues south was a considerable mass

of land which might have been either a peninsular or an island. It terminated in a rugged cape.

"Is that an island?" asked Drake Douay, pointing south.

"It surely is," said Arabin, hoping he was right.

"What's it called?"

"It has no name as yet."

"Then I name it Island Tor," said Drake. "Yes. Tor, in honor of the king of Stokos. How about those mountains on the western shore? Do they have a name?"

"Not as yet," said Jon Arabin, amused.

"Then . . ."

Drake thought about naming them the Zanya Kliedervaust Ranges. But that sounded clumsy. He cast around for a better name, and soon had one: the Dreldragon Teeth. Perfect!

Sight of land put new life into the crew. They worked with a will, and, shortly, the *Warwolf* rounded the cape Jon Arabin had seen to the south.

An ironbound coast slanted away to the south-west for about a dozen leagues, terminating in a second cape, which they rounded at mid-morning. From here, the eastern coast of Tor slanted away to the south-east.

Was Tor an island or a peninsular? The difference was vital. If a peninsular, then it adjoined the terrorlands of the Swarms, and was probably infested with monsters. If an island, it might be safe. Providing the legends of giants, basilisks and such weren't true . . .

The sun broke through the clouds. The wind dropped. They cruised in the lee of the putative island through a blue-green sea of idle wavelets. It grew hot. The damp decks steamed. Men stripped to the waist, soaking up the sunlight. This was more like it! This was how the Gulf was supposed to be in summer!

A league along the coast, they came upon a bay of beauty. Sailing close inshore so Jon Arabin could check it out, the *Warwolf* lost the last of the wind. She floated in a delicious calm. The crew crowded the larboard railing, staring at paradise. A lean white beach of crisp clean sand. Behind the beach, rough grasses of a brilliant green. Inland from that, deep cool forest of a darker green. Jon Arabin gazed long on that forest. The wood itself was wealth.

He heard the rattle-cackle of staccato bird-talk coming clear across the water. A flight of parrots burst to the sky, hustling across the heavens like splashes of animated rainbow. There was a disconcerting arthritic crackling in the background. What? He'd heard it before, hadn't he? Yes, years ago, in Quilth. Cicadas, that was all. Millions of them. They'd do no harm . . .

At the southern end of the beach, a stream ran swift and bright. Good water! The rocks of the southern headland were of limestone. There would be caves in such rock. Arabin felt a pang of heartbreaking nostalgia and homesickness, for limestone was the ruling rock of Ashmolea; he had loved its landscapes dearly in his youth. How many years since he last saw Ashmolea? Many!

"This looks great!" said Drake, admiring the pale sands, the grass, the forest. Dry land! Dry land! A bare rock covered with seagull dung would have looked sweet to him at that moment.

"Aye," said Arabin. "It's a good place. What do you want to call it?"

"Zanya Bay," said Drake promptly, for he owed his true love that much.

"Jon!" cried Baltu. "Is this the island you promised us?"

"It surely is," called Arabin.

"Then tell us about it!" yelled one of the men.

Other voices took up the cry. They wanted to know where they were, how long they'd be here, when they'd see the fleshpots of Narba. Jon Arabin gestured for silence.

"Men!" said Arabin. "This is island Tor. It's named for the king of Stokos, a fearless ogre who explored these lands in his youth. The father of young Drake Douay voyaged here with the king, and brought Drake proof of the truth of his story.

"This place of beauty here is Zanya Bay, where the

king careened his ship. A good careenage it is, too, as you can tell at a glance."

"Good, sure," cried a pessimist. "But for the Swarms!"

"This is an island," insisted Arabin. "No monsters tread these forests. And look west! You see the west of the Drangsturm Gulf, some twenty or thirty leagues away. See those mountains? Those are the Dreldragon Teeth, famous in the legends of Stokos. Such heights are far too bitter-cold for the Swarms. We're safe! So now, boys—to work!"

"Aagh, you can slag work up your poke-hole!" shouted a dissident, anonymous in the crowd.

And others shouted similar.

Exhausted by weather, labor, nightmare, fear, short rations, seasickness and wakeful nights, they had no taste for work. The very last thing they wanted was to careen the ship. If the shore had been grim, barren, bitter and stony, Jon Arabin might have won their co-operation—but, as it was, paradise beckoned. Arabin found himself facing a seething, shouting mob. His crew was on the edge of mutiny.

"Men!" shouted Arabin. "Let's talk money! Let's talk wealth! There's treasure on this island!"

"What treasure?" yelled Raggage Pouch. "I see nothing but trees!"

"Man!" shouted Jon Arabin. "And how much is lumber worth in Narba? Eh?"

And he began to talk money. When he had finished, Quin Baltu backed him up:

"It's true what Jon says. Timber's a good price in Narba. If we patch the ship proper, we can leave with riches."

But the men still refused to careen the ship.

So they struck a bargain. The ship would stay afloat. Divers would make emergency repairs to the leaking hull from the outside; other men would work from the inside. Meantime, the rest of the crew would work the forest for a cargo of timber to enrich this voyage. In return for Arabin's concessions, the crew swore to overhaul the *Warwolf* properly once back at the Greaters.

An anchor was fashioned from a net filled with ballast blocks. Divers were nominated and repair parties chosen. Hunters were put ashore to kill fresh meat—even parrots would be welcome. A boat went for fresh water, so the *Warwolf* would have ample supplies of such if she had to leave without warning. Suzilman volunteered himself as an expert on timber, and was given charge of forestry operations.

By noon, everyone was working at their tasks with confidence.

But Jon Arabin was desperately anxious. What was this place? An island or a peninsular? He had to know! He called together his three most expendable men: Harly Burpskin, Raggage Pouch and Drake Douay.

"Boys," said Jon Arabin, "I've got you together quiet-like so we can talk in confidence. When my great-grandfather sailed these waters, he was a fearsome pirate. Aye. And he buried great treasure on an island in these waters. Mayhap it was this one . . ."

And Arabin described the treasure-burial place. It was in a cave set in a headland on one side of a sandy bay. A cave lined with emeralds.

"The treasure sits in an iron box which is enchanted," said Arabin. "It cannot be moved unless you say the magic word: Ponk!"

"Ponk," said Drake, savouring the word. Then: "Is there another magic word needed to open the treasure chest?"

"There is," said Arabin. "But only I know that word. But . . . if you find the treasure, we'll split it. Equal shares."

"What about the emeralds?" demanded Raggage Pouch.

"Ah, those," said Arabin. "Well . . . what you can hack out of the walls of the cave is yours to keep."

"Why are we so privileged?" said Drake.

"Because the rest of my crew deserves no share of treasure," said Arabin, "for they have come far too close to mutiny. Aye. Whereas I never saw any of you in that mutinous mob."

All three, in fact, had shouted against the hard labor of careening: but none of them confessed as much to Jon Arabin. Instead, they congratulated themselves on his trust, and began dreaming of how they would spend their share of the treasure.

Thus it was that Drake Douay, Raggage Pouch and Harly Burpskin provisioned one of the *Warwolf*'s boats and then, by oar and by sail, began to circumnavigate Island Tor.

Drake was intensely proud to have been chosen for this expedition. The honor confirmed his own high opinion of himself. All eagerness and expectation, he stared at the lush green shore, on the lookout for headlands and caves.

A few leagues south-east of Zanya Bay, the explorers came upon a U-shaped harbor perhaps two leagues wide and two deep. Drake saw at a glance that, compared with Zanya Bay, it offered infinitely better protection from hostile winds.

"Jon Arabin should know about this place," said he. "Let's turn back to tell him."

"What fool's talk is this?" said Burpskin. "Do you want to get rich, or what?"

"I want," said Drake, "to have a ship to go home in. This place would see the *Warwolf* safer than where she lies now."

"Aagh," sneered Raggage Pouch, and hawked, and spat. "Talking like a ten-year salt-sea sailor, aren't we now? You're young, you're a landlubber, you know nothing of it."

"I say let's look after us," said Burpskin. "That's the important thing. Who knows? The treasure could be hidden in this very harbor."

"You're crazy," said Drake, infuriated by such short-sighted selfishness. "The ship's our survival. The ship comes first, aye, before wealth, food, sleep or leisure."

"That's captain's talk," said Pouch, with contempt. "We've seen you sniffing round Jon Arabin, haven't we just? You're thinking you want a career of command, perhaps? Well—why should we risk our fortune to get you launched on such?"

"I'm thinking I want to stay alive," said Drake, starting to get angry.

Thus began an argument which took so long that it was night before they finally beached their boat. They continued the argument round the campfire. It was not exactly an auspicious start to their journey.

And things got worse rather than better.

They found bays, headlands and caves, but never the cave they were looking for. They argued further, of course; they forgot precisely what Jon Arabin had told them, and proceeded to invent the details.

Drake learned a considerable amount about getting along with disagreeable companions. He also learned the hard way—about winds, tides, and small boat management. And where to camp and where not to camp.

And he suffered.

He was bitten by mosquitoes, stung by a scorpion, spiked by thorns and agonized by poison ivy. Food ran out. The three survived on seaweed, whore's eggs and rock-oysters. Then, when they thought they had almost circumnavigated the island, they wrecked their boat on its most northerly cape.

Jon Arabin had given Drake up for dead when the lad came staggering out of the forest one evening, thin, tired, ragged and footsore.

"Where have you been?" said Arabin.

"Chasing a treasure that never was," said Drake, in something like fury. "Your great-grandfather never sailed these waters! Or if he did, he never left treasure here."

"Yes," said Arabin. "But you should have known that much to start with."

And Drake realized this was true. He had let greed overbalance judgment.

"So why did you send me round the island?" said Drake.

"To see what you're made of," said Arabin.

"Does this mean I get to be a sailor?"

"No, for you've obviously lost me a boat. And what have you done with Burpskin and Pouch? Have you eaten them?"

"Came close to it," said Drake. "They gave up. They're two days north—two days as the survivor stumbles."

"Inland?" said Arabin.

"No. Shorebound, on a beach at the foot of the cliffs of a cape to the north of here. There was a way up the cliff, aye, easy climbing, but they were both too gutless to try it."

"Then I'll send a boat," said Arabin.

And did.

Then settled down to interrogate Drake, for he wanted to learn as much as he possibly could about Island Tor. Who knows? He might someday be forced back here again.

As Drake ate parrot-meat and ironbread, and answered Arabin's questions, he became quite proud of his achievement. Yes. Despite all difficulty, he'd managed. He'd not like to do it again, but . . . it was worth doing once.

Jon Arabin tested me. Aye. Well, I hope he's happy. For I am.

Seventeen days after she had arrived at Zanya Bay, the *Warwolf* put to sea again. She had a new foremast made of roble cut from the forests of Tor. The worst of her leaks had been repaired. She had a cargo of summerpine, cedar and bamboo, also cut out of the hinterland. That should fetch a good price in Narba—and should help pay for the permanent repairs which were still needed to make the *Warwolf* truly seaworthy.

They sailed north, rounding the island's northernmost cape. Then the wind got up and attacked them. A howling wind from the east. Despite Arabin's best efforts, they were forced westward, coming closer and closer to the mountain heights dominating the mainland.

Rumor held that the white enamel of those fangs was water curdled by cold. The Galish termed such stuff "muff." Jon Arabin, who was much-traveled, knew it well: Drake, on the other hand, reserved judgment, withholding belief until the day he could walk on it.

If the wind kept up, that day might be soon.

Finally, when they were almost on the rocks, the wind died. Jez Glane claimed it was prayers to his god which had stopped it: and he converted three people to the worship of that god (the great white star-dragon Bel).

Drake was not interested in Glane's god.

He was, though, intensely interested in what he could see on the shore.

"Look!" he cried. "Something moving!"

There were many things moving on the narrow coastal plain between the waters of the Drangsturm Gulf and the heights of the Dreldragon Teeth. It was too far to make out details, but clearly they were bigger than buffalo. Some were as big as cottages.

The entire western coast of the Drangsturm Gulf was, for as far as they could see, swarming with monsters of the Swarms.

Jon Arabin vowed that he would never come this way again. Not unless his life depended on it. His dreams of making a fortune from the timbers of Tor faded to nothing on the spot. Forget it! This place was far too dangerous!

Jon Arabin paced up and down the deck, waiting for the wind to get up again. But the ship floated in a deathly calm.

"Right!" said Arabin. "We'll drop anchor!"

The net filled with ballast blocks which served them as an anchor slid away into the sea. And, on hitting the bottom, tore apart.

"Anch ench unch!" said Jon Arabin.

Then apologized to his mother's shade, for he had once promised her he would never again use such obscenities.

A shadow flickered over the deck of the *Warwolf*.

He looked up. Only a buzzard. But it could just as easily have been a Neversh.

"Lower the boats, boys!" roared Jon Arabin. "We're going to sweat the ship out of here."

Arabin gave Drake command on one of the smaller boats, to see how he would do.

"The ship's survival is our survival," said Drake, to his boat's crew. "So pull, boys, pull!"

And, on this occasion, nobody disputed his judgment.

Fingerlength by fingerlength, the *Warwolf* was hauled away from the shore. Hands blistered. Eyes burnt with sweat. Men cursed, strained and swore. But they put distance between them and the monsters.

Then, finally, the wind got up. From which direction? From the west!

"A miracle!" said Jez Glane. "All power to the great god Bel!"

Jon Arabin, who had his own gods to worry about, paid no attention to Glane.

"Let's hope we're favored fair to Narba," said Arabin grimly, knowing—everyone aboard had reason to know by now—that the winds of this strange season were powerful weird and treacherous.

Fortunately, Arabin's wish was granted, and, four days later, a bullock team was hauling the *Warwolf* up the ship canal to the Inner Dock of Narba.

13

Place: Narba, a low-lying city connected to the Central Ocean by four leagues of ship canals.

Population: either 98,476 or 117,290, depending on which census one believes.

Rule: by elected City Fathers working within the General Terms of Alliance of the Consortium of Provincial Endergeneer.

Religion: Revised Atiniunism, Elchwade Transubstantiation and the Reformed Rites of Devotional Quelochianism.

Location: on the Salt Road on western coast of Argan, north of Drangsturm and south of Stokos.

Drake leaned on the ship's siderail, watching the bullock teams at work. It was intensely pleasant to watch work being done, yet to know that one's labors were at an end.

"Tonight," he said, dreamily, "I'm going to have a hot meal, a woman with smooth thighs, and twenty-five beers. Not necessarily in that order."

"Doubt it," said Ika Thole, who was standing to his left.

"I can afford it," said Drake.

"That's not the point," said Jon Disaster, who was standing to Drake's right. "Jon Arabin won't let us off the ship till all the work's done to his satisfaction."

Drake remembered the near-mutiny at Zanya Bay. Arabin's authority had proved slim enough then. How could a single ship's captain hold back a crewload of pirates who were hot for boozing and whoring?

"I don't think," said Drake, "that Arabin will get one whit of work out of us till we've had our fill of pleasure."

Thole and Disaster simply laughed.

When the *Warwolf* reached the Inner Dock, she was immediately boarded by fifty grim men in mail, armed with swords and halberds.

"What's this?" said Drake, wide-eyed. "Murder?"

"Nay, man," said Jon Disaster, lazily. "This is but the harbor guard, come to help our captain keep his authority."

While most ports would have lynched them on arrival, Narba welcomed them. The Orfus pirates mostly preyed on ships sailing out of Runcorn, Cam and Androlmarphos. Narba merchants never invested in that north-trade, but financed, instead, ventures half a thousand leagues south-west to the Scattered Islands.

Narba profited from the Orfus connection, buying north-trade plunder, and selling everything from siege dust to lime for wormbags hung from each ship's bow to discourage ship-worms. But the good people of Narba had learnt long ago that no pirate captain could keep a lusty crew from temptation without ample armed assistance.

Drake, who had not worshipped the Demon for what seemed an age, was eager for religion. But shore leave was refused for twenty days—the time needed to finish repairs to the *Warwolf*. The harbor guard maintained a watch by day and night, preventing a single pirate from stepping ashore till all the work was done.

Drake bitterly resented this labor, for he would never benefit from work on the *Warwolf*. He was quite determined that he would never sail another league on the ship. At least now they were in port they had fresh food. Hot meat dripping with red blood. Crisp crunching fresh vegetables. Fresh fruit. The dense red meat of plums, the quivering aroma of peaches . . .

Then at last the work was done. Arabin told the harbor guard he no longer needed their help. He set the crew at liberty for the day. And Drake was, for the moment, free.

Fully intending that moment to last a lifetime, he packed his treasure: pearls, magic amulets and gambling profits. All pearls but three went into his boots; the three shared pocket-space with coinage and magic amulets. For luck—he might need it in this foreign city—he still kept one amulet slung round his neck so that it lay next to his skin, close to his heart.

Turning his back on the *Warwolf*, Drake had no second thoughts whatsoever. He had stomached as much whale-oil cookery as he could bear. He was sick of damp gear, canting decks, sea-boils, bully-boy crewmen, wet ropes, wind, rain, sunburn, and all the other inconveniences of life at sea.

For a man with no prospects, piracy no doubt had its attractions. But Drake would likely enough find himself heir to the throne of Stokos, if he played his cards right. Aye. And owner of the high-breasted Zanya Kliedervaust. At the very least, he would be a priest of the temple of Hagon—which was in itself a very fine thing to be.

After his long captivity in Ling and his subsequent privations at sea, Drake found Narba to be an amazement of colors, smells, bustle and voices. And temptations.

First off, he bought himself a whore. Was he then unfaithful to his true love? No, for it was Zanya Kliedervaust he conjured into his mind to intensify his lust as he rode his woman.

"That was nice," said Drake, exiting from the knocking shop. "What next?"

Since he was young, and over-excited by growth hormones, what came next was another whore. Then, driven more by ego than desire, he bought himself a third. But his flesh failed him.

"Never mind," she said. "It happens to every man sooner or later."

"Then what do I get for my money?" demanded Drake.

"Something nice," she said.

And gave him a rub-down, squeezed his blackheads and washed his hair, all the while talking about how strong and handsome he was. All of which combined to restore his flesh for a third endeavor.

After that, Drake, who was still as devout as when he had left Stokos, went looking for a bar so he could complete his worship of the Demon. He soon found a pleasant enough place, with sawdust on the floor, men sitting at rough-wood tables eating oysters, and a stack of ragged claws in the free lunch bowl. However, Drake thought the publican regarded him strangely when he walked in, so he said to the man:

"I'm a pirate off the *Warwolf*. Any objection?"

"None," said his host.

But peered again at a sketch kept hidden behind the bar, glanced back at Drake, and, after pulling a couple of mugs ("Set them up in twins, I don't want to be wasting my time"), sent a runner to an inn lying handy to most of the dockside bars.

Drake had only just started his fourth mug when into the bar, as if by coincidence, came Sudder Vemlouf, whom Drake knew from old times back on Stokos.

"Sudder, me old mate," said Drake jovially. "What are you doing here? Sit down, man, and have a mug. Bar! A couple of ales and a dash of cold potato."

He was feeling generous, in part because the beers had warmed him nicely, yes, slurring the sharpness of the harder edges of the world.

"I was never any friend of yours," said Sudder Vemlouf, as the drinks were served.

"Sure no, you were neighbor to old man Muck. And how is the scratchy old bastard, anyway?"

"The Blessed One is in good health," said Vemlouf formally. "And he is far from happy with you."

"What? Upset about the mastersword, is he? Oh, I admit everything. Don't worry. When I'm home, I'll rich him up till his eyes pop. I've got the money now."

"You have no need to travel home," said Vemlouf, "for justice has found you here."

And, so saying, Vemlouf suddenly drew a knife.

A professional killer would have gutted in quick and low, and would have been halfway to the door before anyone realized a man was dead. But Vemlouf raised his knife on high like a ham actor in a melodrama.

"Die!" he screamed.

And, both hands clasping the hilt, he brought the blade down.

There was a certain ritual quality to the way he struck. He was slow, yes—but the beers had done their damage. Drake flung up a warding arm—too late! The steel bit through his sealskins, slammed into his chest—and skidded off the amulet.

"Get away with you!" said Drake, giving Vemlouf a shove which sent him staggering backward.

Vemlouf glanced at his unblooded blade, and then, with horror, at Drake.

"You—you live?"

"Bloody oath I live! Now get out of here, before I kick your ring through your breakfast!"

"Demon-son!" hissed Vemlouf, tightening his hold on the knife.

"Oh, jalk off!" said Drake, as Vemlouf stalked toward him.

Then, seeing the man seriously intended to kill him, Drake picked up a bar stool and defended himself. But Vemlouf managed to give him a nasty scratch on the back of his hand. Drake, rather put out by that, broke his arm, knocked him unconscious, then threw him to the floor and jumped on him.

"Damned if I like your choice in customers," he said to the barman, and left to find a quieter bar where he could practice religion in peace.

The next barman he encountered also had a hidden sketch, and also sent a messenger to a certain inn—only this time, of course, there was nobody to respond to the news.

"Who's drinking?" asked Drake of all and sundry, as a young man with sudden money necessarily must.

It turned out that everyone was. And, while demolishing a pearl's worth of ale, they were happy enough to listen to Drake hold forth on his recent adventures. Only one sceptic was unkind enough to dispute his tall tales about Ling.

"Where did all that fresh water come from?" asked he. "And how did those cold cold lights keep burning?"

"By magic," said Drake solemnly.

And would have come no closer to the truth even if he had managed to break into the armored vaults holding the automated desalination plant, the Ground Effect generator, the Control, the Planet Link, and the other sophisticated machinery installed when the Plague Sanctuary was first established at Ling, many thousands of years before, in the nightmare years known as the Days of Wrath, which were now almost less than a memory.

"Magic?" said the sceptic. "It was a place of wizards, then? Or was it?"

Wiser heads suppressed him before Drake could be bothered to find an answer, and the flow of ale continued unabated.

With so many eager co-religionists to help him worship, Drake was fairly deep in the clutches of faith by the time the bar was enlivened by the arrival of Jon Disaster, Goth Sox, Hewlet Mapleskin, Lee Dix, Shewel Lokenshield and others.

"Good to see you boys," slurred Drake. "Have a beer—I'm buying!"

Well, one thing led to another, till finally—and not for the first time—Drake's religious fervor got the better of him. He woke up the next day with a large-sized gap in his memory, and found himself at sea again. He had no money, no pearls, and no magic amulets—but for the one worn secretly against his skin for luck. He had also lost his boots.

What was worse, his penis hurt so badly he feared he had picked up a heavy dose of clap. But, on inspection, he found he had been tattoed with a snake design while stone cold unconscious.

"All right," he demanded, "which of you jerk-offs did that?"

"Who are you calling a jerk-off?" rumbled Shewel Lokenshield.

"Not you, you prickless wonder," said Drake promptly, thus precipitating a fo'c'sle fight, which he lost.

The next day, his vital organ began to swell with blood poisoning. Consequently, he was a little down in the mouth. The other pirates, though, were in high spirits, for they were returning home wealthy. Jon Arabin organized deckside games of knuckleskull, First Off and Quivliv Quoo, which Drake, sore and sulking, watched from the sidelines.

However, by the time they raised the Greater Teeth his condition was improving, and he no longer lived in fear of imminent amputation. All he had to worry about was surviving until he could make a break for freedom.

But would he ever get another chance? He had blown his best opportunity, back at Narba. And even if he struggled back to Stokos, how would he cope with Gouda Muck? The old man must be lunatic to be sending armed assassins to revenge the theft of the mastersword with murder.

"The bugger's insane," said Drake to Drake. "But old, yes. Can't last much longer. Ten years, at most. Yes—that'll finish him."

It was easy to say, but—ten years! That was more than half Drake's lifetime.

"I can't possibly wait that long," said Drake. "Anyway, attack's the best defense. Aye, that's for certain. First chance I get, I'll be back to Stokos to kill off old man Muck. King Tor won't hold that against me, I'm sure. In fact, once he understands what's going on, he'll probably help me. Aye. Likely pay good gold to see Muck wasted."

Or so Drake hoped.

The *Warwolf*, returning rich, avoided Gufling, and made instead for Knock. It was at that time early autumn. The year Khmar 18 was still young, and Drake was only 17 years old. (Though, if challenged, he would have claimed to have been 18, on the grounds that a couple of months would take him through to age 17½, and the missing half-year was not worth worrying about.)

It was a while since Jon Arabin had dared the approaches to Knock, and he disgraced himself by getting the *Warwolf* stuck as they were approaching the Skerry Passage at low tide. His own men thought it was hilarious. So did the crew of a sealing boat which slipped past a little later, returning from a hunting expedition laden with bloody booty.

"The Walrus will laugh himself sick to hear of this!" cried one of the sealers, from the deck.

"He lives, then?" called Arabin.

"Aye! Lives, farts, shits, shags—and swears you left him on the Gaunt Reefs to drown."

"That's a lie!" shouted Arabin. "He had his choices!"

"That's as may be—but all his crew swears with him. They say the only thing you took from the rocks was a sweet-faced playtime boy."

This news did not improve Jon Arabin's temper. Nor Drake's.

"Does Andranovory live?" he yelled.

"Who?" shouted one of the sealers.

"Atsimo Andranovory. A great big dirty brute with a great big beard which stinks like a bilge broom. A black beard, with black hair to go with it. Aye, and a great big chest."

"For sure he lives," called one of the sealers. "Why? Are you lovesick for him?"

"Aagh, jalk up, you ganch," yelled Drake.

Thus starting an exchange of obscene insults which continued—pirates could sometimes show remarkable stamina—until the sealing boat was out of earshot.

Thinking of Atsimo Andranovory, Drake experienced a little frisson of something which was most certainly not pleasure. He remembered that ugly inviting him to suck, then stringing him up on refusal. He remembered . . . swinging from a rope, yes, tied to a spar by his ankles . . . an agony which seemed to go on forever . . . Whale Mike singing a lullaby . . . the cold on the rocks . . .

He would never forget. Although even now the details were hazy. So much had happened since!

"What's your interest in Andranovory?" asked Jon Disaster, as they waited for the incoming tide to float the *Warwolf* off the rocks she had grounded on.

"I told him the truth about his ugliness," said Drake. "Tell me—what's between our captain and this Walrus?"

"Man," said Disaster, "That Walrus isn't properly human. Slagger Mulps, they call him—that's his proper name. He's weird, like. Thin as an eel, with gangling arms with two thumbs on each hand. Green hair, green—"

"I know all that," said Drake, impatiently. "I've been up against him before. But what's his quarrel with Jon Arabin?"

"Why, man, friend Walrus has been the Warwolf's favorite enemy, ever since the day he seduced one of Arabin's wives. Aye. Got over-excited. Bit off her left-hand nipple. From whence Arabin loathes him."

"Are we at war then?" said Drake.

"There's no war between pirates, lad. Not on the Greater Teeth. Not in theory, anyway."

"Why call me lad?" said Drake, feeling he deserved better than that (and feeling, too, that there might be war on the *Warwolf* in a moment, unless he got an apology).

Jon Disaster laughed.

"Man, you want to be more than a lad? Then use your time well. Here at the Teeth, you can learn boats proper. Take every chance to go boat for the fish and the seals."

"I've no need of more boat learning," said Drake. "Why, I sailed round Island Tor entire!"

Jon Disaster had the gall to chuckle.

"Not quite," said he. "The judgment of sailing is

whether you finish with the same boat you start with. And there, I think, you can hardly claim success."

The rising tide took them clear of the rocks with no damage worth speaking of, and, later in the day, they docked in the Inner Sleeve, a rock-locked harbor on Knock.

Drake, remembering the narrow slot they had squeezed into at Gufling, expected another equally claustrophobic prison-hole. But the Inner Sleeve proved to be a regular little harbor. Admittedly, it was sunless-gloomy, sunk between ramparts of rock. Nevertheless, with care and effort a dozen ships could have berthed there, and in fact nine were in port when the *Warwolf* tied up.

One of the nine was the *Walrus*.

This had not always been a pirate ship. Indeed, some months earlier it had been an honest slaver, and, bearing the name *Gol-sa-danjerk*, had sailed from Androlmarphos with a cargo of felons—one of whom had been Drake Douay.

The green-bearded Slagger Mulps had captured the *Gol-sa-danjerk*, and had put a prize crew on board. Thus, after he had been rescued from the Gaunt Reefs, he had still had a ship to his name. And there, on the deck of it, he stood, arms folded.

Also on deck was Atsimo Andranovory in all his glory—grinning as he recognized Drake. He had a good head for faces.

"Hello darling!" he called. "Like to give me a suck?"

"I'll see you suck on this first!" shouted Drake, drawing his dirk.

"Once you've taken it up the arse I'll love to," retorted Andranovory.

And of course their dialogue did not end there, for, being who they were and where they were, they vented their spleen with all the eloquence available to them, which was considerable in both cases. And the crews of both ships jeered or cheered each sally, depending on their allegiance.

And while this was going on, a couple of workaholics who had no appreciation of theater were busy tying up the *Warwolf* and lowering the gangplank.

And then the men of the *Warwolf* came swaggering off the ship like the heroes they were. For had they not faced storms, aye, and hurricanes, and tornadoes too? And had they not fought monsters, yes, doing battle with half a dozen Neversh for the possession of their ship? And had they not drunk five pubs in Narba stone-bone dry, a feat which fifty eminent philosophers and a panel of high-class theologians and overpaid jurists had declared to be nine-tenths impossible? And had they not been to Ling, and deflowered five thousand of the virgins of the place, yes, and pleasured the mothers of those girls as well?

But the heroes of the *Warwolf* failed to meet with the universal applause they deserved, for the crew of the *Walrus* (idle slobs, scabs and fish-fornicators that they were) jeered at them because they had been engaging in honest trade, of all things, which was surely anathema, even if it was for pearls, aye, and dangerous, and highly profitable into the bargain.

"What's lower than a merchant-trader?" cried a crewman from the *Walrus*.

"A coward!" came the reply.

And the fight was on.

In the fracas, Drake went chest to chest with Bucks Cat and sustained three broken ribs, a mild concussion, a black eye and a seven-stitch gash to his left forearm. But he thought it worth it, for he was now well and truly one of the crew.

And, indeed, Drake got a crewman's share of the voyage profits, which Arabin had withheld till then so his men would not booze away the money in Narba. By now, Drake knew that the strange coinage of the Greater Teeth was actually the common currency of Narba, the only port which would trade with them. He also learned that the more sober-minded pirates banked there, and the lucky few who survived to the age of arthritis retired there to drink away their dotage in comparative comfort.

The *Warwolf* would not put to sea again for some time, not least because Jon Arabin would be busy with his harem, which he was having shipped from Gufling. Jon Arabin was ascetic yet devout, and his own religion—the Creed of Anthus—enjoined each man "to plant a tree for each you cut down, and father a man for each you kill."

Jon Arabin, having done a lot of killing in his time, was always kept busy when he was at home. Unfortunately, his frantic exertions tended to lower his sperm count below the level at which impregnation was likely. Fortunately for the ease of his conscience, other men helped him out behind his back, and he was now three killings in credit.

Just because they were not at sea did not mean there was no work to do. Jon Arabin was true to his vow to have the *Warwolf* overhauled. So there was sanding, sawing, hammering and whitewashing, and there was a drydock to be pumped out, and then there was singeing and scraping to clean the hull. The garden of weed Drake had first noticed at Ling was torn from the hull in wet reeking clumps, or burnt off along with goose neck barnacles and other rubbish.

And then, since Jon Arabin had decided to experiment with mailletage (that is, covering the timber with nails) there was a blistering amount of hammering to be done.

Crewmen from the *Walrus* dropped by on a regular basis to jeer at the sailors doing this slave work. Jon Arabin had gone into debt after he lost his ship on the shores of Lorp, and was taken prisoner by the most vicious people to be found in all of Argan. He had spent three miserable seasons eating sheep's guts and pigs' eyes before the laborious efforts of some trusted retainers had delivered his ransom. He was now finally out of hock, but still could not afford to buy new ship-working slaves.

Finally, after a crewman from the *Walrus* was found floating face-down in the Inner Sleeve with fifty-seven nails hammered into his head, the teasing stopped.

While all this work was going on, the encysted snake

buried deep within Drake's gut quietly allowed its flesh to dissolve. A mob of eggs hatched in the wreckage of its body, and myriad worms began to infiltrate Drake's bloodstream. They embedded themselves in the walls of his duodenum, set up residence in the portal vein, squatted in his liver and crept up to his brain; they housed themselves in his stomach; they invaded his lymphatic system and burrowed into his bones. And multiplied.

Drake became feverish.

For five days he endured high temperatures, rigors and blistering thirst. Arabin's own women took care of him. They soothed him, sang to him, sponged his forehead and fed him crab soup, fish roe, sea slugs, pulped sea anemones and other invalid food.

And then the fever broke.

And Drake felt fine.

He felt better than he had ever felt before in his life—and this was scarcely surprising. For the snake which had eaten its way into his flesh in Ling dated its ancestry back through the millenia to a tailored organism especially designed to complement the other defenses of the Plague Sanctuary. The worms which had metastasized throughout his body were fulfilling the designs of an ancient science, normalizing his body functions, enhancing the action of his immune system, detoxifying poisons and killing off disease organisms.

The worms were rapidly finishing off an obscure low-grade viral infection distantly related to glandular fever, the start of a tubercular infection, two exotic venereal diseases which had not yet had time to debilitate their victim, a troublesome amoeba which had recently begun to cause him some intermittent diarrhoea, and a couple of wild and wonderful infections (native to the Greater Teeth) unknown to any standard classification.

So, while Drake had always been comparatively healthy, he now felt really good. So good, in fact, that he had to celebrate his recovery with a drink or three.

He did so—but even after his fifth mug, he felt scarcely more than a tingle.

"What're you selling me?" he demanded. "Water?"

"You young pups," said his barman, shaking his head. "You don't know your limits. But I'll help you find yours."

And he mixed Drake a Skull Splitter, a popular cocktail consisting of equal measures of vinegar, methylated spirit, absinthe, vodka and apricot wine.

"Drink this!" said the barman.

"Ah!" said Drake, as the poison went burning down his throat. "That tastes better."

A warm glow filled his stomach. He waited for a sense of langorous well-being to cozy his soul, for the harsh outlines of the world to soften and the burden of gravity to be at least partially nullified. But nothing so pleasant happened.

Instead, after a few moments, the warm glow was gone, and he was back where he started.

"Look, man," said Drake, "I don't know what fancy kind of colored water that was, but I'm buggered if I'm paying for it."

"It's strong enough for most folks," said the barman, aggrieved. "Why, three of those and Slagger Mulps was legless."

"Sure, but I'm not a wimp like the Walrus. I'm a drinking man, the real article. So pour me something stronger. If you know how!"

"Aye," said the barman, sensing a challenge here to his professional reputation. "I can pour stronger, if that's what you want. But I won't be responsible for the consequences, mind."

"I'm ready," said Drake, fiercely. "Hold back on nothing!"

Upon which the barman opened his bottom locker and pulled out strange vials, tubes, tubs, boxes, casks, jars and bottles, and mixed the most brain-blowing cocktail imaginable. Hemlock went into it, and paint, and tar, lamp-black, weedkiller and plutonium, the ink of a cuttlefish and the gall of a basilisk, a smidgin of belladonna and the blood of a (reputed) virgin, some powdered cannabis leaf and half a gram of heroin, some white of egg and some fermented fish, ground glass, tobacco ash, chopped-up leopard's whiskers, fine-ground horn of unicorn and two tomatoes, some mandrake, ginseng, tannin and quinine, chopped shark's liver seven days old, some high-grade lacquer and sulphuric acid, with lashings of honey to make the whole brew palatable.

In honor of the occasion, the barman unearthed a very old and ancient tankard made of glass—the only one of its kind on all the Greater Teeth. He poured the cocktail into it, slowly. The thick black liquid sat there, bubbling softly. The barman sprinkled some cinnamon on top and ceremoniously set the offering down in front of Drake.

"Get this dog-defecating fornicator inside you," said the barman, with unwonted enthusiasm. "That'll put hairs on your chest!"

Drake picked up the tankard with both hands, looked at it steadily, then sipped it with unaccustomed caution. Then:

"What the hell," he said.

And drank the rest down as a thirsty man would drink weak ale.

The barman watched expectantly, waiting for him to drop dead, or melt, or explode. Instead, Drake swayed a little. All color left his face. He coughed once or twice, rather harshly, then spat out a little blood. Then, fairly rapidly, the color returned to his face, his stance steadied, and he wiped his mouth and said regretfully:

"Well, it's a good drop, to be sure. Almost as good as a blow on the head. But the effect wears off powerful fast. Make me another one."

But the barman shook his head.

"Boy," he said, "if that won't kill you, nothing will. One shot of that, and you should stay drunk till your grandchildren celebrate seventy. It ain't natural to drink that down and still stay speaking, far less standing. Boy, take it from me, and I'm an expert. Someone's worked the Black Arts on you, young man. They've taken away the gift of liquor—and all of liquor's friends."

This was the opinion of a true professional, a specialist in chemical debauchery. As the words sank in, Drake shuddered. Someone had cursed him! Someone had doomed him to a life of perpetual sobriety!

He found it hard to think of a worse fate, but, after some reflection, imagined one—and hurried off to find a pirate whore to make sure it wasn't so.

14

Name: Sully Datelier Yot.

Birthplace: Stokos.

Occupation: disciple of Gouda Muck, worshipper of the Flame, apostle of Goudanism.

Status: once Muck's apprentice, but now an Instrument for the Practice of the Revealed Disciplines of the Flame.

Description: lank pale stripling barnacled with warts.

Present location: the slave holes of Knock.

It was standard pirate practice to feed competitors drinks while gambling. Drake, doomed to be sober, kept his suffering as secret as he could, and enriched himself.

Choosing games like backgammon and dice chess, where there is a strong element of skill, Drake would gamble, drink, play drunk, raise the stakes, make a drunk's blunders, raise the stakes again—then use a sober man's wit, as if by accident, to find the tactics to sweep the table.

And the things he won! Pearls, diamonds, snuff, gold, jade, silver, a wad of cocoa leaf, and one-night stands with the wives of twenty different men.

Yet profit is not all, and scarcely compensated Drake for lost pleasures. For now, when raucous drunkards sang and shouted, it was no longer the warm hubbub of friendship which he heard, but the braying stupidity of morons and madmen. Sober, he no longer laughed to see a helpless dipsomaniac resorting to tortured spastic contortions to get a mug to his lips. He no longer fell about with rejoicing laughter when one man vomited over another: instead he was bored. And remote. And cold.

He found himself living his life as though he had just come back from a funeral.

He saw now that the cozy togetherness of drinking sessions was an illusion created by the alcohol. Each drinker was in fact drowning in a separate pool of booze. But Drake, who could no longer drown himself, envied them.

When he was not gambling, Drake would usually quaff an ale or two in company to quench his thirst, then have half a dozen or more out of sheer good manners, plus a couple on top of that just to keep up his reputation. The beer made him piss more frequently, and that was it.

Soon, most pirates began to latch on to the fact that young Drake had a harder head than he pretended. But they did not stop gambling with him. No: ego compelled them to sit at table with him, downing the drinks and raising the stakes, to see who would slide under the table first. Drake once or twice consented to lose, and disappear beneath the table.

"See?" said the pirates, each to each. "He's got his limits just like any other."

And returned, in force, to test him again the next day.

On occasion, evil men spiked Drake's drinks with drugs and poisons. Sometimes he felt slightly dizzy, and once, having swallowed enough cyanide to kill a horse, he became positively breathless for thrice three dozen heartbeats. But always the worms within his body brought their complicated chemistry into play, and the ancient genius of the genetic engineering of a lost and forgotten civilization preserved his flesh from yet another toxic onslaught.

Drake could no longer fuddle his wits with alcohol, or die from poison, or vanish into the world of drug-dream hallucinations. And the disease which could kill him had yet to be built. Sex still had its consolations, but these, of course, were momentary. The beauty of drunkenness is that it can last a lifetime—which, in the case of the Orfus' pirates, it often did.

Drake won much money but few friends. Lonely, he bought companionship in the form of a dog, which he named King Tor.

The dog is the favorite beast of the Demon, being undiscriminating in its appetites, and dirty, and loud, and ugly, and the habitat of vermin, and not very bright. Drake loved dogs. He bought King Tor a spiked collar, sharpening the spikes until they glittered. He decided to train this new companion to kill rats and fight alongside him when the Warwolf's heroes rumbled with the men of the *Walrus*.

As a sober man gambling with drunks, Drake was now so prosperous he was getting into money-lending and agiotage. Stokos was, without doubt, the best place in the world to live—but the Teeth were the place to get rich.

Drake began nurturing dreams of enhancing his earnings by setting up his own branch of the temple of Hagon. Surely worship of the bloodlord Hagon was precisely the right religion for the Greater Teeth. Yes, and he should practice being a priest right here and now, since he fully intended to buy into the priesthood on his return to Stokos. That was only natural, seeing as how he was so devout.

With establishing a templed in mind, Drake attended the Slaving Day Sales in the middle of winter, intending to buy the first of his women. But there was nothing worth having, if one did not like fat—and Drake didn't. What he did find was a familiar face, Sully Datelier Yot, in chains.

"Why Sully Yot!" said Drake cheerfully. "What brings you to the fair islands Teeth Major? A little far from the forge, aren't you?"

Yot made no reply, but sat there snivelling. Something—fear, perhaps, or maybe a virus, or possibly just the cold of the midwinter island air—had set his nose to running.

"Why so quiet?" asked Drake. "Cat got your tongue? If not, I've got a dog that's eager to have it."

And Drake stroked Yot's cheek softly. Yot pulled away. But he didn't go far, since he was roped to a floor-shackle.

"Darling!" said Drake. "Why so cold? When we last met at 'Marphos, you were so eager to embrace me. Yes. You had a knife in your hand at the time, unless I misremember."

He remembered perfectly. When he had fled from Stokos, Yot had pursued him to Androlmarphos, and had made a determined effort to kill him.

"Do you want to buy him?" asked a voice.

Drake turned. His interlocutor proved to be Simp Fiche, one of the crewmen from the *Walrus*.

"Are you selling this . . . this thing?" asked Drake idly, not really caring too much one way or the other.

"I bought it myself just today," said Fiche.

"What for?" asked Drake. "It's not good for much."

"I bought it to torture to death," said Simp Fiche, giving an honest answer; he was bored, and needed some cheap and harmless occupation to while away the rest of the day.

"Why, that shows good judgment," said Drake genially. "I'd like to torture him myself. Would you sell me a piece of the action?"

"No," said Fiche, who was an inveterate gambler. "But I'll wager with him if you like. Dice-chess, the best of three games. My meat against . . . shall we say a pearl or three?"

"Bloody oath no!" said Drake. "I don't risk jewels to buy scum. Your meat versus my left boot—which I'll fill with liquor if you win."

"How about meat versus dog?" said Fiche, who had seen King Tor and liked the look of him.

"No!" said Drake sharply. "My final offer—I'll

wager with both boots, the left full of ale, the right full of mead."

"Done," said Simp Fiche, seeing these were the best odds he was going to get offered.

And they sat down to gamble.

Now the game of chess is, of course, very old and very solemn, its intricacies sufficient to tax the highest of intellects. But when the dice get rolling, freeing each player to make (sometimes) as many as a dozen moves at once, then most of its niceties vanish. The stately clash of armies degenerates into something more like a free-for-all brawl, a gutter fight with flails, whips and hatchets.

Drake and Simp Fiche played ferociously. They rolled the dice and scrambled their pieces over the board, whooped with delight or cried out with anguish, punched themselves in the head as punishment for gross stupidity, jabbed gloating fingers at each other's misfortune, and overall comported themselves more like cheap drunks in a casino than solemn chess players.

Men gathered to watch as the titans did battle. Their warriors hacked and slaughtered. Their Neversh clashed in the skies, bringing death and disaster. Battering rams converged to crumble castles. Wizards raged, and, raging, fell. In less time than it takes ordinary chess players to make their first three moves, these dice-chess players had swept nearly everything from the board but the hellbanes—which are, as every player knows, beyond capture.

And Simp Fiche had won the first game.

Drake drew the second but won the third—so the best of three left them even.

"Flip a coin, then," said Simp Fiche, who was all played out and a little bit weary.

"Fine," said Drake.

And took from his pocket one of the coins he had gained through agiotage: a bronze bisque from the Rice Empire, with the disc of the sun gracing its face and the crescent of the moon riding its reverse.

"Sun or moon?" asked Drake.

"Moon," said Simp Fiche, who had a touch of vampire in his ancestry, and had never liked the sun.

Drake tossed the coin to Yot.

"Flip it for us, boy," said Drake. Then, as Yot sat limp and sniveling: "Flip it! Or we'll gouge your eyes out here and now!"

With the greatest reluctance, Yot's fingers crabbed their way to the coin. He took it into his shivering hand and gave it a little flip. It fell with the sun uppermost.

"Fair enough," said Simp Fiche gravely, and got to his feet and wandered off as the spectators began to disperse.

Fiche had already decided that any stray cat he could catch would probably give him as much sport as Yot would have done.

"Let's go home, darling," said Drake.

And releasing Yot from the floor shackle, led him away by the rope round his neck. A few pirates made jokes about mutilations. A strong smell of dung began to permeate the air; the pirates laughed outrageously.

Shortly, Drake showed Yot into his cave.

"Sit down there," said Drake, "while I sharpen some torturing knives."

Yot sat meekly, without attempting to jump him. Drake was disappointed. He wanted a desperate fight, yes, and the pleasure of wrecking Yot in combat before killing him. But Yot had no more spirit than a dead fish.

Whistling tunelessly, Drake began to sharpen his favorite knives.

"Drake," said Yot, in a pale voice, "I can . . . I can be of use to you."

"Can you now?" said Drake. "I don't really think so. I've got more taste than to want to bugger you. And I'd never let you suck anything you might just possibly bite off, But I can use you for fish bait—if the fish aren't too fussy tomorrow. And that's about all that you're good for."

"Drake, I can—I can tell you things."

"Tell me things? Like what? Like the precise and exact taste of Gouda Muck's asshole?"

"Drake . . . things about home. You know. Cam. Your uncle. Your parents. Drake, your brother Heth."

"Yes, and how hot the sun was, and how cold the rain," said Drake, pretending news of Heth meant nothing to him.

But Yot knew better.

"Drake, I saw Heth just before I left Stokos last, and that was recent. He was come to Cam to marry."

Drake gave no verbal acknowledgment of interest, but the intensity went out of his knife-sharpening. Stokos! Cam! His uncle! His parents! Heth!

"Your uncle paid for the marriage. Yes, that's why it was in Cam."

Drake pretended not to hear, but his sharpening strokes got slower and slower, and little tears pricked his eyes. It had been so long since he saw the Home Island last, so long since he wandered its streets of forge-hammering and coal dust.

"Tell me then," said Drake at last, emotion beginning to choke his voice. "Tell me about all of it."

So Yot began to talk, and fear gave him eloquence. The words poured out of him, and what he didn't know he invented.

Before he had gone too far, Drake was offering him some ale to moisten his throat. Then, after a few tales more, he insisted that Yot must eat, yes, and change into fresh sealskins which Drake would lend him. And when at last Yot had talked himself out, Drake sat rocking on his heels for a while, stroking King Tor with an absentminded hand and brooding.

"Well now," said Drake, "that was worth hearing and all. Come—there's a banquet tonight to mark the end of Slaving Day. It's a good do, or so I've heard. Will you come with me? We'll get some real food and good drink with it, then talk some more."

"If you don't mind," said Yot, still in that same pale voice, "I'd rather rest a bit if I may."

"For sure," said Drake, content, and glutted with nostalgia. "You can do what you want. We'll be together plenty in the future, as we make you into a pirate."

"I'm not sure I've really got what it takes to be a pirate," said Yot.

"Don't run yourself down," said Drake. "Be brave! Be strong! Be confident! Come now—rest, and we'll talk again tomorrow."

So Drake took himself off to the banquet, alone, and a great treat it was. Musicians from the kingdom of Sung played for them, so they ate to the accompaniment of the skirl of the skavamareen, and the uproar of krymbol and kloo. Naked bodies danced for their delight, and performed charades of love by flaring torchlight. There was food by the table-load, with plenty of lobster, crab, gaplax and crayfish. It was a well-organized affair, with an unending supply of good drink, and plenty of buckets to vomit into.

Drake indulged himself, drinking cold rice wine and warm brown beer. It bolstered his ego to know the others were admiring him as he quaffed down quantities of alcohol which would have killed an ordinary man, and, what's more, would have embalmed the corpse into the bargain.

The banquet finally reached the rowdy stage, with knife-throwing and wrist-wrestling, a brawl, and some extra-special entertainment laid on by Jon Arabin, who whipped one of his wives raw in public, having caught her out in adultery.

Drake left shortly afterwards, staggering markedly as he quit the banquet, so his future gambling partners would register the fact that he could indeed get drunk like other mortals. Actually, he was not even slightly tipsy—but, by the time he reached his home cave, he was staggering a little for real, out of sheer fatigue.

A low-burning whale oil lamp showed Drake that Yot was curled up in a corner. A number of things in the cave had been shifted—his bean bag, rocking chair, laundry basket, sea-chest, water cask, oil barrel, fishing tackle, harpoon rack and wardrobe. Had Yot been searching the cave? Or had some villain taken advantage of the banquet, and of Yot's deep sleep (or complaisant terror) to rummage the cave in search of Drake's fabled gambling treasure?

Drake was too tired to care either way. He knew Yot was no danger to him, for Drake was now the nearest thing to a friend that Yot had in all the Greater Teeth. And as for the gambling treasure—why, that was safely hidden in five separate places, and even at low tide the shallowest of those places demanded a three-fathom dive.

"We'll have to teach you to be a guard dog as well," said Drake to King Tor, scratching that dignitary behind the ears. "Or maybe I should start keeping geese."

And, with that, he laid himself down on his pallet and pulled the blankets over himself, without bothering to undress or take off his boots. King Tor nosed his way under the blankets. Drake took the dog into his arms, and they cuddled together in an indiscriminate heap, sharing each other's fleas.

Very late at night, as Drake and dog lay snoring, Sully Datelier Yot roused his flesh to wakefulness and got to his feet. He extracted a shark-killing knife from the tangle of Drake's fishing tackle, raised the blade to his lips and kissed it. Then, shaking with fear but unshakable in his resolve, he bent over his sleeping enemy and struck with all his force.

The knife went home.

"Die, Demon-spawn!" screamed Yot.

And struck again, even as Drake heaved up from the bed. Drake rolled away, pulling a blanket with him. He swore viciously and whipped the blanket at Yot's knifehand. As wool entangled steel, Drake closed the distance.

They grappled, all knees, elbows and panting bones. Drake got a stranglehold. With hands that were wet with blood, he choked his enemy, squeezing his fingers deep and hard to the windpipe.

Once sure that Yot was dead, Drake threw the body outside, and hurled the bloody dog-corpse after it.

"Sleep with the man you murdered!" shouted Drake

at the corpse. "It's your one chance to sleep with your betters!"

Then stalked around his cave, kicking things until he had exhausted his anger. Then started to shake, as the shock of his brush with death set in. Then began to cry, first for poor King Tor, and then for his own exiled condition, and then simply because he was overtired and heavily stressed.

Then he did the sensible thing, which his mother would have recommended had she been there, and went back to sleep for the rest of the night. Only his mother would have insisted that he take his boots off first.

When morning came, Drake was disgusted to find that Yot was still alive. He had thick black bruises on his throat, true, but could still walk and talk and breathe, eat and drink—he was, in short, a living demonstration of the difficulties attendant on killing a properly constructed human being.

Abject in fear, Yot knelt at Drake's feet, snivelling once more.

"Give me one good reason why I shouldn't kill you," roared Drake. "Just one!"

"I had to kill you," sobbed Yot. "I had to. I didn't want to, but it was my duty. I like you, Drake, honestly, but you're—you're a son of the Demon."

"By the oath I am!" said Drake. "And proud of it! That's the way my father raised me, and that's how he'd have me be!"

"No, not that kind of son. A true son. Flesh of the Demon's flesh. Spawn of his spawn. He came from the halls of hell to take your mother by night."

Drake considered this intriguing notion for a few moments.

"I've never heard such nonsense in all my life," said Drake. "But supposing it was true, I'd take it as a compliment. To me, for my parentage. To my mother, for attracting such high-born attention. And to my childhood's father, for winning a woman the Demon himself would want."

"But it means you're evil, don't you see? The Demon's

the enemy of the Flame. That's why Gouda Muck sent us."

"Sent you?"

"Yes. Fifty of us. All over the world. Looking for you. To—to—well . . ."

"To kill me?" asked Drake.

"Well, yes."

At first Drake was incredulous. Then he remembered his last visit to Narba. Then an old face from Stokos, a past neighbor of Gouda Muck, had made a diligent attempt to knife Drake properly.

"Fifty looking for me!" said Drake. "How many worshippers has the Flame claimed, then?"

"Well, half of Stokos, by now," said Yot. "The king himself has converted. There's talk of outlawing the temple."

Drake felt as though he had been punched in the stomach. All the wind was quite taken out of him. But once he had got over the shock he started to get angry.

"Now look here," said Drake. "This nonsense has to end, and here, and now. Recant! Renounce the Flame. Look, there's fire—the oil-lamp's wick. Piss on it, Yot, piss on it now, or I'll kill you!"

But Yot would not. He wept with fear, he begged, he pleaded, but even in the face of death he would not defile the Flame.

"And you still think you have to kill me?" said Drake.

"I must! I must!" wept Yot.

Drake, seething with anger, roped Yot properly and put him on the market. Yot so disgusted him that Drake didn't want to be associated any further—not even for the time it would take to torture his captive to death.

"Ready meat waiting!" shouted Drake. "Best stuff for fish bait, torture, raping!"

But interest was slack. Slaving Day had glutted most people's tastes, and the Bacchanal of the banquet had left just about the entire pirate population of Knock with a hangover.

Drake grew hoarse with shouting. He cooled his throat with an ale, then thought to ask:

"You say King Tor has converted to—to—"

"To the Faith," said Yot. "To Goudanism."

"Then does Tor believe that I'm—"

"Tor is a true believer!" said Yot. His voice was shrill with fear and hate. "He knows you're the son of the Demon. He's ordered that you be handed over to Gouda Muck if you ever set foot on Stokos."

"Then what?"

"Then our all-sacred Muck will have you skinned alive. That's just to start with! Oh, you'll wish you were dead! You'll scream for the privilege of dying! But Muck won't let you go that easily. He'll make you suffer."

Drake felt all broken-up inside. This was really the end! He could never go home. Goodbye to his dreams of a place in the priesthood! Goodbye to his hopes for marriage to Tor's daughter and a claim to the throne of Stokos! Good-bye—ay yes, farewell forever!—to the high-breasted Zanya Kliedervaust.

"This is bad news, truly," said Drake, "I . . . I thought to go back to Stokos someday. Not least to see my lady."

"And who's that?" said Yot.

"You wouldn't know her," said Drake. "She was red of skin and red of hair. She was aged about twenty or so. Tall, yes, mayhap a head higher than me. Breasts beautiful, high-riding like buoyant boats."

"Are you talking about Zanya?" said Yot. "Zanya Kliedervaust?"

"You know her!"

"Why, of course," said Yot. "She's one of Muck's favorite disciples."

"Then she's—she's with Muck?"

"No," said Yot. "She's left Stokos entirely. Gone to do missionary work. To convert the world to Goudanism!"

"Where has she gone?" said Drake.

"Why should I tell you?" said Yot. "You're the Demon-son! And a nasty stunted ugly runt!"

And Yot spat in Drake's face.

Whereupon Drake grabbed him, intending to cut his throat on the spot.

"What's this?" said a jovial voice. "Business or pleasure?"

Drake relaxed his grip on Yot. He looked around and saw that a rough-smelling pirate had happened along, an evil brute with a most unlovely bearded face, with pouches under bloodshot eyes, with lice scattered like dandruff through greasy locks, and with splashes of black blood from his most recent murder still splattered across his clothes.

It was, of course, Andranovory.

"I came here intending to sell this—this thing," said Drake. "But it seems nobody wants to buy such rubbish. So I've decided to cut its throat to get rid of it. Would you hold it still? It's wriggling. Aye! And trying to bite!"

"Hold still!" barked Andranovory.

And Yot ceased his struggles immediately.

"Why, An'vory, man," said Drake, in reluctant admiration, "You've sure got a way with your voice."

Atsimo Andranovory made no immediate reply, but studied Yot carefully.

"You meant to sell this?" he said, after a pause, idling a finger across Yot's neck while the apostle of the Flame cringed and whimpered. "For how much?"

"To you, he's free," said Drake, who could think of no worse fate for Yot than sale to Andranovory.

Andranovory laughed.

"Done," said Andranovory, and cut Yot's bonds.

Then tossed the boy a knife.

Startled, Yot caught it by the hilt, and stood there looking most uncertain.

"You're my shipmate now," said Andranovory. "My bloodbrother true. My enemy's enemy is good enough for me. Come, man—I'll take you to meet our captain. Aye. The Walrus—Slagger Mulps himself. He'll be heartened by the sight of a fine young fellow like you."

"How about a drink first?" said Yot, feeling he needed something to steady his nerves.

"Why, sure—that's an excellent idea," said Andranovory.

Then Andranovory laughed again at the outrage on Drake's face, and went swaggering off to the nearest beer stand to celebrate his victory.

15

Name: Menator.

Birthplace: by the side of the Salt Road some seven leagues north of the Castle of Controlling Power.

Occupation: adventurer (and, previously, Galish merchant, horse thief, outlaw, and joint ruler of the kingdom of Talajar).

Status: warlord.

Description: a man as bald as Jon Arabin, nose broken, blue rose tattooed on left cheek.

Drake was sue Slagger Mulps would be too smart to want anything to do with a useless piece of wart-faced filth like Sully Yot. But, to Drake's disgust, Yot was aboard the *Walrus* when it set off on a raiding expedition the very next day.

He won't last, though. No. The first time he has to fight it out for real, blade against blade, he'll run screaming. Aye. This first voyage should finish him for piracy.

However, three days later the *Walrus* returned after a bloodless victory. Off the coast of Chorst, Slagger Mulps and his men had caught a trading ship. Rather then stand and fight, the crew of their quarry had set fire to their vessel and had then abandoned ship, making for the nearby shore.

Every man from the *Walrus* swore they had rescued

treasure from the burning ship. As they did no extra boozing, gambling or whoring, Drake guessed they were bluffing—but he had no way to prove it.

After a two-day rest, the *Walrus* set sail again.

One more chance for Yot to get himself killed, then.

But Drake could not help envying Yot. He was sick and tired of the Teeth, bored with fishing, sealing, and the routines of gambling. He found himself longing to be at sea again. Which was perverse, surely, for the sea was big and wet, cold and unfriendly, daunting and merciless.

But there's companionship there. Aye. The ship's life's one life shared. Yes.

How long would it be before Jon Arabin took them to sea again?

Ten days after midwinter's day in Khmar 18—that is, soon after Drake learnt of his place in the demonology of Goudanism—Jon Arabin called a crew-conference.

A number of Arabin's wives were pregnant, so he could face the prospect of more murder with equanimity. With the *Warwolf* properly overhauled, he was ready to try an audacious plan formulated during his long and bitter captivity in Lorp: to raid Cam, in Stokos, and sack the Orsay Bank.

"It's far," complained the faint-hearted. "And it's winter."

"For sure it's far," said Arabin. "But Narba is further, let alone Ling. You've all at least been to Narba. As to the season, why, winter means they won't be expecting us. Anyway, it'll be warm enough down in Stokos."

Drake was enlisted to draw maps of Cam, and help model the harbor for the inspection of Arabin's officers.

"We'll come as a merchant ship," said Arabin. "We'll fly the flag of Chi'ash-lan. We'll have silk on our backs, sheep on the deck, and a bare-breasted woman as figurehead. By night we'll raid the bank. Quick, aye, in and out. Meanwhile, our fire parties set flames amidst the city. Thus chaos while we retreat."

206   Hugh Cook

It was a cunning plan, yet simple. And extremely dangerous—which was part of the reason why Drake had mixed feelings about the operation.

Previously, a voyage to Cam would have meant an ideal opportunity to escape. But flight to Stokos was now the last thing on his mind. Gouda Muck would have him skinned alive then burnt at the stake—or worse.

He would love to see Stokos again, if only for a day. But should he raid his own people? Even if madness had made them flame worshippers, they were still the true blood of Stokos, the meanest wight amongst them worth more than any ten uitlanders.

"Troubled?" said Arabin, sensing his confusion. "Worries about killing your own, is it? Well, I'll give you a choice on this venture. Will you come, or not?"

"I'll think about it," said Drake.

And think he did.

The *Walrus* returned to Knock after a successful raid on the docks of Runcorn. This time, Slagger Mulps and his men proved their success by spending gold like water. Sully Yot made a special point of flaunting his wealth in Drake's presence, while boasting of his daring. Drake, violently jealous, thought Arabin's plan might be worth pursuing if only to win triumph equal to Yot's.

But, while Drake was still weighing the pros and cons, all plans for the raid were interrupted by the unheralded arrival of a foreign adventurer. Menator, he was called: and he came to the Teeth with five ships, three hundred men, and half his own weight in gold.

Almost immediately, he gained a reputation for ambition. Then came public proposals so brash and rash they made Arabin's outrageous plans seem the ultimate in conservative caution. Word went out to all the islands of the Greaters, and the pirates began to gather in to Knock.

The pirates met in general assembly to pass judgment on Menator. Crowding a huge cavern lit by light filtering down twenty air shafts, and by half a hundred smoking torches, they gave off a communal stench which could have seriously competed with a legion of dead seals or any army of dung-soaked dogs.

Drake, in the middle of this mob, was surprised at what a crowd they made.

Menator spoke eloquently in the Galish Trading Tongue. He was, after all, the only person present who had Galish as his native tongue, for all that it was their lingua franca.

He wished to unite them for war and for conquest. To bring Stokos under their yoke. To seize the Lesser Teeth. To build an army. And then to start empire-building in earnest.

Some men jeered, and Drake was one of them. Menator became angry.

"The Greater Teeth could control all the west of Argan," said Menator. "If only you could see it. But no. Here you sit, on your walrus-infested rocks—"

This provoked mirth in certain quarters, scowls in others. Menator, puzzled by this reaction, looked around carefully then continued:

"You sit on your rocks, fighting for fish with sharks and skua gulls, when you could rule in palaces of silk and gold, with hot wet women tight between your legs. All it takes is will. An alliance of will. Believe me."

Promises of paradise will always find buyers, and Menator's speech met with an enthusiastic reception.

"So," said Menator, thinking this was all going very nicely, "is it agreed?"

"Hang about!" shouted several voices. "We haven't heard the other side, yet."

The pirates wanted a proper debate. They believed strongly in democracy: meaning, among other things, a full and frank discussion of issues of public importance. Menator, who had never before encountered such plebian lower-class attitudes (he came from the better class of Galish merchant, and had mixed with the right kind of people for most of his life) was shocked.

Still, there was nothing he could do about it.

First speaker for the negative was Slagger Mulps, who provoked applause just by rising to his feet. Since he was so very tall, he could be seen by almost everyone. And his shock of green hair identified him even in that poor light. His supporters started to chant in unison:

"Walrus! Walrus! Walrus!"

Raising one of his double-thumbed fists on high to acknowledge this applause, Slagger Mulps swaggered to the podium (a heap of ale casks stood on their ends) and Menator was forced to yield it to him. The din slowly died down.

Drake, who had brought along some dead fish, threw one. But missed Slagger Mulps—and hit Menator slap-bang in the face. There was a roar of applause. Some of Menator's men drew weapons—but their leader brought them to order with a few curt words.

"Boys," said Slagger Mulps, with a grin. "At least you can say this for the Teeth—we've got plenty of fish to spare."

(General applause. From Menator, a scowl.)

"And," continued Slagger Mulps, "if the Teeth are infested with Walrus, what's wrong with that?"

(Mixed laughter, cheers, boos. Several dead fish were thrown, but missed.)

"These rocks have got a lot going for them," said Mulps. "For a start, they're ours. Nobody else wants them. But once we go seeking hegemony over foreign lands, well, then we're into some really heavy competition."

(More noise from the audience. A loud-voiced obscene joke about "herd riding," which was the literal translation of the Galish Mulps had used to say "hegemony.")

"Of course," said Mulps, "we could do it if we really wanted to. World conquest would be easy compared to sharing these islands with the Warwolf."

(Uproar. A walrus head was suddenly raised on a battlespear in the middle of the crowd. Scuffles broke out, continuing until the head had been hauled down and kicked to pieces, thus ceasing to become an object of contention. Slagger Mulps, unperturbed, continued.)

"But, boys, why try enslave the world? We all know how useless slaves are. Won't work unless kicked, and then so tough in the arse you'll as like break your toes as bruise them. Free men work best, boys, as do they now—loading the finest silks and the silkiest women on ships which by the morrow, mark my words, will be idling straight toward our jaws.

"Boys, let's think real. A conquered city sounds sweet, but like as not we'd burn it down the first time we set out to party. Here's a cheer for the Teeth! The walls are solid. They don't rot, they don't burn, or crack if you smash a skull against them. Why, on rock like this, you could even break up the pig bones which skull-plate the Warwolf!"

(Renewed uproar, continuing until the Walrus, satisfied with his eloquence, bowed gracefully and yielded the podium to the next speaker.)

The next speaker was Atsimo Andranovory. The great big barrel-chested black-bearded brute confronted the audience in silence, swaying slightly. Drake, gazing on him with hatred, bitterly regretted the fact that he had no more fish left to throw. Suddenly, Andranovory gave a prodigious belch. Someone clapped. Someone cheered. Then Andranovory vomited—then collapsed. The whole gathering applauded this performance.

As the drunken sot was carried away, Jon Arabin took the stage.

"Ladies and gentlemen," said Arabin, looking around. "I mean, of course, the gentlemen of the *Warwolf* and the ladies of the *Walrus,* and—"

(Furious shouting. Raucous cheers. Prolonged fish-throwing, most of it, again, inaccurate.)

"Ladies and gentlemen—may I speak?—thank you!—much as it grieves me to agree with Slagger Mulps, he's given us a lot of common sense. He got it from the fish guts his mother weaned him on. And, in any case, as the saying goes, even a blind walrus knows a dog from a virgin's gracehole."

(Pandemonium. An outbreak of predictable behavior. Consequences of such behavior, some of them blood-stained. Peace restored, mainly through use of cudgels.)

"Strange it is for Warwolf to sing in harmony with Walrus," said Arabin. "But on this occasion, I can do nothing else. We've heard easy talk of conquest. Aye. Conquest of Stokos. But who here knows the place as more than a name? I tell you this—I do. For one of my crewmen is Drake Douay, a native of the place. A strong fellow, not lightly scared."

Hearing such praise, Drake was filled with a glow of pride. Ah, Jon Arabin! He knew quality when he saw it!

"With Drake Douay," said Jon Arabin, "I've lately been planning a raid on Stokos, so I know the strengths of the place well. They've people by the tens of thousands. They make weapons for the world, so they won't be short of steel if it comes to a fight. Worse, they've a breed of ogres on that island.

"Twice the height of men they stand—aye, as tall as Whale Mike. Where are you, Mike? Ah, there he is—over there, in the corner. But Mike, he's slim compared to these ogres, for they're built near as wide as they stand tall. How can humans fight against such?

"If you ask me, this man Menator's got no true plans for conquest. Instead, he hopes to wish us away to Stokos, so we all get killed in senseless battles. Then he can rule the Teeth, while we rot in hell, getting laughed at by our ancestors. But even if we did win Stokos, what good would that do us? Not much, say I."

Then Arabin outlined the case against empire, speaking fluently, cogently, and with much gutter-wit (compared to which, what had gone before was mild).

Arabin truly doubted that Stokos could be conquered by the Teeth. He also knew that any quest for empire would involve an enormous amount of killing. He would have to breed furiously to pay off his death-debt. Meaning more expense, and more squalling daughters cluttering his caves (why no sons?). And—he was starting to feel his age, perhaps—he just did not think he could stand it.

After Arabin, many minor luminaries spoke (including Bluewater Draven, captain of the good ship Tusk). Some were for, but most were against. The pirates of the Teeth were, for the most part, too idle, lazy, cowardly, shiftless and gutless to make good imperialists.

Finally, after some discussion—which left seven pirates dead—the proposal for empire was lost.

Menator, finding the pirates would not support his drive for empire, announced that he would satisfy his ambitions without pirate help. He planned to begin by conquering the Lessers.

However, since it was winter, and the weather was bad, it was scarcely the time to hazard the dangerous waters of the Lessers. Menator therefore exercised his men by raiding the coasts of Dybra and Chorst, carrying off skinny sheep and half-starved goats.

Meanwhile, Jon Arabin resumed planning for a raid on Stokos.

In some ways, Drake regretted the fact that Menator had failed to win pirate support for his dreams of conquest. Their chances of success were small, but . . . what was the alternative?

The alternative was a lifetime of episodic raiding, long interludes of monotony, the shiftless company of drunken cronies, the repetitive comedy of the gambling tables . . .

Which was not enough.

For Drake wanted to make something of himself.

All through the years of his early youth he had imagined himself becoming, eventually, a swordsmith—a respected master craftsman whom the best men on Stokos would admire. When Muck's madness had ruined that dream, he had cherished ambitions of marrying into the royal family, or becoming a priest of the temple of Hagon. Now . . .

Now he was tempted to put his sword at Menator's service. Their chances were slim, yet . . .

We have but one life. If we don't get what we want

from it, then what's the point of having it? Better slim odds for success than certain odds for defeat.

To stay a pirate was to be defeated. There was no job on the Teeth. No pride. No trust. Yet . . .

I'm scared, and that's the truth. This Menator's at least half mad. And . . . to leave Jon Arabin . . . why, that'd be a wrench, for sure . . .

Drake brooded about it while the winter rains and the winter seas launched onslaught after onslaught on the beleaguered desolation of the Teeth.

Thirty days after midwinter, Drake was practising a one-man kata in the privacy of his home cave when he was interrupted by Harly Burpskin.

"What is it?" said Drake. "Does Arabin wish to see me?"

"Nay, man," said Burpskin. "It's strangers."

"Strangers?"

"They're sitting in the Inner Sleeve."

"Pray, how sit they there when the water's a full three fathoms deep?"

"They're not swimming, man," said Burpskin. "They're on a ship."

"What ship?" said Drake.

"The *Tarik.*"

"I know it not," said Drake. "Where has it come from?"

"From Stokos."

"Stokos!"

"Aye. With some mighty strange people aboard. Stranger still, when I mentioned we owned a Stokos boy, they proved to know you."

Drake needed to hear no more, but hastened to the Inner Sleeve. Once he left the protection of the tunnel system, he found the day cold, moist and gray. Rain was falling from a coal-scuttle sky, dimpling the waters of the Inner Sleeve where floated helpless turds, drowned kittens, the corpse of a rat and several ships. One of the ships was a dingy thing painted in colors of earth and clay. A tarpaulin was stretched above her open hold.

"That's the *Tarik*," said Burpskin. "Go to the hold, man. You'll find a friend there."

"A friend?"

"Aye," said Burpskin, stepping back into the shelter of a tunnel.

"Aren't you coming?" said Drake.

"I've seen your friend once. That's enough for me."

Drake looked dubiously at the Tarik. Was this a trap? Only one way to find out . . .

He walked through the rain, stepped onto the greasy gangplank, skidded, and almost fell. As he gained the deck, his heart was scrambling; he was panting with excitement. He strode toward the open hold.

Stout green bamboos held up a ragged brown tarpaulin in which an enormous weight of rainwater had pooled; the bamboos were bending beneath the load. Cautiously, quiet as a cockroach gliding through shadows under the threat of a hunting hammer, Drake eased himself in under the shelter of the tarpaulin and peered into the hold.

There in shivering gloom a great, sad creature sat on a pile of moldy sacking. The creature was almost as wide as it was tall. Its shaggy black hair trailed down around the huge flaps of its ears. Its blue eyes, set amidst gray skin, looked tired and defeated. Light gleamed faintly on its downward-jutting tusks. It was King Tor.

Yes, Tor—who, by Sully Yot's account, had converted to this weird religion founded by Gouda Muck. Adherents of that faith believed Drake Douay to be the son of Hagon, the incarnation of absolute evil. So prudence dictated a retreat.

Yet Muck's but a mouth talking. And haven't I got a mouth myself? Aye. I'll argue it out with the king. I'll talk him sweet to sense—or die trying.

"My lord . . ."

Tor looked up. He saw Drake. His nostrils flared. He came to his feet with a roar. As his head hit the tarpaulin, he thrust up with his arms. The water pooled in the tarpaulin was flung skywards. As it cascaded onto the deck, Tor roared, then shouted:

"Dreldragon! It's Dreldragon! Dreldragon Drakedon Douay!"

At his shout, men came bursting out of the cabins in the poop of the ship, and came racing down the wet, greasy deck, skidding and sliding as they came.

Drake fled.

He sprinted over the water-wet deck, slipped, fell, bruised his shin, gained his feet—and ran straight into the arms of a tall broad-chested man.

Drake struggled. He tried to kick, claw, scratch, bite, butt, spit, punch and swear. But even swearing was nigh impossible with his enemy holding him so tight.

"Ease up, man," said his captor, with something of a laugh. "It's me."

Me? By the voice, "me" was Heth.

Drake eased up, and looked at the face of the tall, well-built man (his hair as blond as Drake's) who was holding him now like a lover. It was indeed his brother Heth.

"Heth," said Drake. "Oh, Heth . . ."

And began to weep with relief.

As the two brothers embraced, the rest of Tor's men gathered round. Amongst them was Levil Norkin, Drake's boyhood friend. And Oleg Douay, his uncle—the finest swordsmith on Stokos.

"Hey!" yelled King Tor, peering out of the hold. "Come in out of the rain. Come down here—I don't want my finest fighting men dying of pernicious anaemia."

On Stokos, it was a firmly-held belief that prolonged exposure to cold rain caused anaemia. Drake had endured so much bad weather on his adventures that he doubted it could be as destructive as Stokos thought—yet he willingly got himself out of the rain.

In long conversations with Heth, Tor and others, Drake learned of the disaster which had befallen Stokos.

After Tor had converted to Goudanism, the temple of Hagon had been destroyed. Goudanism had been made compulsory.

"It had its advantages," said Tor. "With the temple destroyed, the people spent little on whores and gambling. That made it much easier to collect taxes."

"Aagh," said Drake, and spat. "Taxes!"

"Government costs money," said Tor, "and there's no way around it. Why, building roads alone—that's a heavy job for taxes."

"Roads!" said Drake, with contempt, thinking he'd find much better ways to spend money if he were king.

"Roads," said Tor, "are necessary, look at it how you will. And they don't build themselves. Anyway—quite apart from the matter of money, the priests of Hagon had been taking more and more power for themselves. So I was glad to see them broken."

"And then?" said Drake.

Then Gouda Muck spoke madness. He said that only those born pure in flesh had rights to life. He set down codes for eyes, teeth, limbs, hands, hair and height. He declared all those not matched to his codes were evil."

"And," said Drake, "you . . . ?"

"I was too tall to start with," said Tor. "His codes were built for humans. But I'm an ogre, and proud of it. What's wrong with being an ogre, I ask you?"

"Why, nothing," said Drake. "I honor ogres so greatly that I once asked to marry into your family. I'm still good to the offer, man. Where stands your daughter now?"

"My beautiful Hilda," said Tor, "is held prisoner on Stokos with her mother."

And he began to weep. There are few things more lugubrious than an ogre in the depths of despair.

"Never mind," said Drake. "We'll rescue her. Aye. A war for Stokos! We'll win. Then chop up Gouda Muck, aye, cut him into seven thousand pieces."

"With the help of the sea gods," said Oleg Douay, cheerfully, "we may well manage to do just that."

"How stand things on Stokos now?" said Drake.

"After Muck made his codes," said Heth, slowly, "some tried to kill Tor. Others fought beside him. We lost."

"Lost badly?" said Drake.

"Badly enough," said Heth.

"Who rules then, on Stokos? Does Muck rule?"

"No," said Heth. "He's set up Sudder Vemlouf as ruler. Perhaps you've heard of him."

"Aye, that I have," said Drake. "He was Muck's neighbor for year on year. I met him last in Narba, where he tried to kill me. He thinks me the son of Hagon."

"If you are the son of the Demon," said King Tor, through tears, "then I'm with you all the way. Muck talks purity, but what that means is death, murder, blood, killing, the overthrow of rightful rule, the end of law, mad torture, fear, suspicion, and worse."

"If we struck at Stokos with force," said Drake, "how many living there would help us?"

"Many," said Heth. "For many favor Muck only since they thought he'd win. If once they thought he'd lose, they'd sing different, that's for certain."

"But before we can talk of striking," said Oleg Douay, "we must have strength to strike with. The gods help those who help themselves, you know."

"You must," said Drake, "meet a man called Menator."

"Who's he?" said Tor.

"He was once king in a place called Talajar, which is in the Ravlish Lands," said Drake. "When he lost his kingdom in war, he fled. He came to the Greaters with five ships, three hundred men and half his own weight in gold. Since then, he's been trying to persuade us pirates to a war of empire."

"Why talk of yourself as a pirate?" said Tor.

"Why, man, for sake of honesty," said Drake. "For that's what I be, right now."

"No," said Tor, laying one of his immense hands on Drake's shoulder. "You are a warlord in the armies of Stokos. You are the betrothed of my daughter, with all that that implies. I name you Lord Dreldragon; I name you heir to the kingdom of Stokos."

Drake saw Heth grinning at him. Olegy Douay was smiling, obviously pleased. Levil Norkin gave him a

clenched-fist salute. Drake felt giddy. Then, unable to help himself, he shouted his triumph to the world, with all the strength and eloquence at his command:
"Wow!"

Menator swiftly came to agreement with King Tor. If Menator supported Tor in the conquest of Stokos, then Tor would give men, gold, weapons and ships to help Menator win an empire. His position bolstered by this agreement, Menator once more sought to win agreement from the pirates.

Drake was now wildly enthusiastic at the prospect of an invasion of Stokos. They would win. He would marry Hilda. And then he would find someone who knew where Zanya Kliedervaust had gone to, and he would send agents forth into the world to hunt her down then drag her back to Stokos to be his pleasure woman.

He was upset to find that, when he lobbied for King Tor, others failed to share his enthusiasm. Jon Arabin was still dead against a war of empire. Drake, who had no inkling of Arabin's religious objections to such a war, said:

"Jon, you must support King Tor!"

"Who are you to tell me what I must and must not do?" said Jon Arabin.

"Jon, it's for your own benefit I'm saying this. Here's a great chance, man! Wealth, fame, power! When I'm king on Stokos, you can be lord of all my seapower."

"And what makes you think," said Arabin, "that I should rejoice at the prospect of serving under a greasy under-sized mannikin who's been for so long my cook's boy?"

Without waiting for a reply to that question, Arabin turned his back on Drake and strode away—leaving Drake feeling cut to the quick.

As the pirates once more gathered in from the islands for a general assembly on Knock, Drake made further attempts to recruit Arabin to Tor's cause—but was again rebuffed. He saw his chances of power and kingdom slipping away from him. In desperation, he ventured to the cave where Slagger Mulps lived, determined to lobby the Walrus.

"The situation," explained Drake, "has changed. It's no longer a few wild pirates seeking invasion of Stokos. No—it's civil war we're planning. Once Tor steps ashore at Cam, half the city will rise to his support. We've no longer ogres to fight against—the ogres are on our side."

The green-haired pirate chief was suspicious.

"What's in it for me?" said Mulps.

"Survival," said Drake. "Muck has strange ideas. If he gets to rule the world, you die."

"How so?" said Slagger Mulps.

Drake explained Gouda Muck's ideas about what flesh should live and what flesh should die.

"I've got no prejudice myself," said Drake. "Why, man, I seek to marry an ogre—and they're as weird as ever was, or ever could be. So it matters not to me that your hair is green, aye, and your eyes as well. But Gouda Muck would have you killed for such."

Drake by now knew that Slagger Mulps was intensely sensitive about his odd appearance. So he played on that as best he could—but, when the day of the meeting came, Drake was still unsure which way the Walrus would speak and vote.

Once more the pirates crowded into their huge meeting cavern. This time, Drake did not come equipped with dead fish, but with a speech carefully worked up with help from both his brother Heth and his uncle Oleg Douay.

Drake was the first speaker.

He climbed onto the podium and faced the mob of pirates. He breathed their stench, and breathed, too, the fumes of half a thousand pipes—a ship laden with tobacco had recently been captured by the Teeth, and many of the pirates were doing their best to dispose of its cargo.

In that cave, dimly lit by air shafts and torches, Drake recognized scarcely a single face. He was speaking to strangers who, if displeased, might throw things—or tear him apart in the mindless rage which could so easily overthrow the sanity of a crowd.

Drake felt unsteady on his feet. There was a strange taste at the back of his throat—a taste like metal. His mouth was dry. He cleared his throat, then hawked, and spat.

"Aagh," said Drake.

"Stand up!" yelled a wit.

"Man," said Drake, "if the good King Tor was here, I'd stand on his shoulders. Then you'd see me right enough. But Tor can't be here today. Not today. Not any day. And why? Because he's too great-girthed to dare our tunnels. You've seen him, aye. Surely. That's a monster true. Our monster, if we turn our will to Stokos."

That opening was impromptu. But, while it had not been planned, it had come out smoothly enough. Now for the prepared speech. Drake looked out over the heads of his auditors. His first move was designed to slit Jon Arabin's sails right down the middle. Very well then.

"Boys, some of you know me, some know me not. I'm Drake Douay. Born on Stokos, aye, and there on Stokos raised. When last we met together, boys, all crowded here as close as buggery, you heard the good Jon Arabin speak well of me.

"Friend Arabin, my captain true, he named me as the one man who knows of Stokos as more than a name. I told Arabin well enough of Stokos, aye, and of the ogres. Hence Arabin spoke against a war on Stokos. And rightly so—for who here could chest it out with an ogre?

"But times change. Now the greatest ogre is ours. King Tor, that's him. He'll not fight against us. No. He's ours. He's with us. And so is every other ogre born on Stokos. For Stokos has fallen to the madness of an old man called Gouda Muck, who hates all ogres and has sworn to kill them out."

"With reason, perhaps," yelled an anonymous heckler.

"This Gouda Muck has got no reason," said Drake,

"for he speaks against copulation, aye, against men with women, against men with men, against cats with dogs for all I know. He stands against drinking, too. And rules out gambling. He worships what he calls purity, by which he means the end of joy, starvation of the flesh and all."

Then Drake proceeded to paint a picture for the pirates. They would land on the coast of Stokos. They would rally the countryside. They would march on Cam. The people would rise against Gouda Muck. Tor would be victorious.

"Then," said Drake, "we can break apart the Orsay Bank. That's fabulous wealthy—and Tor, he loves it not. Yes. King Tor has sworn that our reward will be every treasure looted from the bank. That's wealth for all. Wealth almost beyond imagining."

Drake spoke the truth. Tor had no love for the Orsay Bank, and was ready to sacrifice it to the pirates.

Drake, having said his piece, sat down. Pirates whistled, stamped, shouted, clapped and threw things. A mixed response, in other words.

What now? Will Arabin speak?

Drake knew Arabin would find it difficult to win much credibility if he chose to speak as an expert on Stokos. Drake had indeed slit Arabin's sails—and he knew Arabin would be furious. Someone was coming to the podium. Who? Why—

Grief of death! It's Sully Yot!

Up on the podium climbed Sully Yot. The lanky wart-faced youth looked flushed, manic, wild-eyed, half-crazed. He screamed at his audience:

"Evil! Evil! Evil! Tor is evil! Gouda Muck has spoken! Praise to Muck! He learns us truth! Some flesh is pure, but other flesh is born to evil. Tor is a monster. Monsters are not human. Tor has teeth which are wrong, limbs which are wrong, hands which are wrong. Only those with a fist of five digits are human. Tor has six fingers."

"Hey!" yelled the Walrus. "What's this nonsense about the fist deciding the man?"

"It's not nonsense," shouted Yot. "It's truth!

LORDS OF THE SWORD 221

Muck's truth! I've heard the news from Stokos! Muck has spoken, Muck has revealed. Muck is the High God of All Gods. And you—you've two fists on each hand. You're a monster too. You don't deserve to live. You—"

Sully Yot was hauled off the podium and pulled into the crowd. For a moment he vanished. He resurfaced briefly, then disappeared again. People were fighting, some obviously trying to kill Yot, others to protect him. Finally, Yot was hauled to safety.

By Quin Baltu, Ika Thole, Shewel Lokenshield, Peg Suzilman, Jon Disaster and Jon Arabin. By Harly Burpskin, Raggage Pouch, querulous old Jez Glane and slim dark Salaman Meerkat. By Lee Dix, Goth Sox, Hewlet Mapleskin and others—the entire crew, it seemed, of the good ship *Warwolf*.

Drake groaned.

"What is it?" said his brother Heth, who was standing next to him in the crowd.

But Drake had no chance to answer, for uproar broke out as a very angry Walrus gained the podium. Slagger Mulps displayed his two-thumbed fists to the crowd then made them into fists.

"These hands," shouted Slagger Mulps, "these hands are ready for war."

He wrenched down his trousers and showed off his male pride.

"And this—this, boys, this is ready for war as well. I'm built for action, that's the truth."

He pulled up his trousers.

"Arabin," said Mulps. "Arabin so old that every bit of hair has fallen from his head, he can stay behind on the Teeth. Aye. Mount sentry over rat, mouse and cockroach. But I'm for war, boys. War. Conquest. Gold.

"Last time I spoke, I spoke against empire. But times—well, as Drake Douay says, times change. We've got a king on our side. An ogre on our side. All the ogres on our side. Half of Stokos on our side. That alters odds. I'm in for gold, conquest, wealth, women. Who's with me?"

A roar of approval showed that most of the pirates

were. Drake knew that many other people would speak before a final decision was reached. But he was already sure of what would happen: the pirates would vote for empire.

After much heated discussion—in which another half a dozen pirates died—the reavers of the Greater Teeth did indeed vote for a war for empire. And Jon Arabin sent Harly Burpskin to tell Drake Douay that his days with the *Warwolf* were finished.

Drake had expected as much.

He did not rightly understand why Arabin was still against empire, but knew his public opposition to Arabin must end their friendship. But to be an outcast still hurt. He had admired Jon Arabin, had rejoiced in Arabin's approval, had struggled hard to win promotion from ship's boy to crewman—

And now it was all over.

Still, he was in amongst friends. His brother. His uncle. His king. And others from Stokos. And they had their own ship, the *Tarik*, to make ready for a preliminary probing raid on Cam.

The probing raid was a disappointing, almost fruitless affair. The *Tarik*, with Drake aboard, sailed the six hundred leagues or so to Cam. As they dared the approaches to the harbor, three ships came out to meet them. Those ships chased the *Tarik* right round the shores of Stokos. Finally, in bad weather, the *Tarik* shook off the pursuers, and headed north.

They had learnt that Sudder Vemlouf, ruler of Stokos, had a navy of at least three ships.

"What we should do," said Drake, "is go in force. Aye. Half a dozen ships. Or send in spies. Perhaps we should ask Sully Yot to spy for us—he's got Muck's trust."

"That's an excellent idea," said King Tor.

So Drake arrived back at Knock with his hopes high. Sully Yot would be asked to spy for them; Yot would refuse; Yot would be thrown to the sharks or tortured to death, which would be a just and proper punishment for killing Drake's much-loved dog. (And, of course, for attempted murder of Drake Douay.)

When Drake landed on Knock, he was disgusted to find that Sully Yot had sailed with the *Warwolf*, bound on a raiding expedition to the Ravlish Lands.

"What else is new?" said Drake.

The latest excitement proved to be the challenge which Lord Menator had sent Slagger Mulps. It seemed the Walrus was demanding to be Grand Admiral of the Fleet of Imperial Conquest. Menator had doubts about his worthiness, but had given the man a chance to prove himself.

If Slagger Mulps could sail to the terror-lands beyond the protection of Drangsturm, capture one of the monsters of the Swarms and bring it back to the Greaters as proof of his prowess, then he would be "seriously considered" for the position of Grand Admiral.

"It sounds to me," said Drake, sagely, "that Menator thinks Mulps is too big with ambition. So Menator wants to kill off Mulps. But he doesn't want the blood to show too clearly on his own hands."

Drake's analysis was correct. Menator wanted to appoint only his own men to positions of power. Menator knew such a policy would not win approval from the pirates—so he had chosen to try to kill off Slagger Mulps subtly, by tempting him into accepting a suicidal dare.

To Drake's surprise—and to the surprise of others—Slagger Mulps took up the dare, and began to ready his ship for a voyage south.

"The man's mad," said Drake to Drake. "And I'm glad I've no part in that madness."

Slagger Mulps was due to sail on the first day of spring. The day before the *Walrus* set sail, Drake was called to a conference with King Tor and Lord Menator. It was Menator who did the talking.

"We've thought long and hard about this challenge we've set for Slagger Mulps," said Menator. "We can't think of any way for him to cheat—but he's a pirate, so there's no telling what devious tricks he'll turn to. Thus we want someone aboard his ship to be our eyes and ears. To report true as to where he goes and what he does."

"Man," said Drake, "then don't look at me. I crewed with Jon Arabin, sworn enemy of Slagger Mulps. If I were to go aboard his ship, his crew would kill me. Why, my own worst enemy sails with the *Walrus*. That's Atsimo Andranovory, a man made for murder. So I'll stay with King Tor, thank you very much."

"You'll do no such thing," rumbled Tor. "You'll sail for the south with Slagger Mulps. Not least because I need to test you. You've been chosen to marry my daughter. You've been chosen to inherit my throne. I need proof I've made the right choice."

"Why," said Drake, "surely you can trust your own judgment."

"In my youth," said Tor, "I studied the Inner Principles of the Old Science, just as you did. From that, I learned that judgment is best supported by experiment."

"I see," said Drake. "Perhaps . . . perhaps a test to destruction."

"That depends on what you're made of," said Tor.

"The *Walrus* sails tomorrow," said Drake. "Have you jacked this up with Slagger Mulps? Is he happy to have me on board? Have you got a promise of safe conduct out of him?"

"We've not spoken to Slagger Mulps," said Menator.

"Nor will we," said Tor.

"Then how," said Drake, in something close to despair, "how do I get on his ship? And if I do—how do I survive?"

"That," said Tor, "is your first test."

16

Name: Slagger Mulps.

Alias: the Walrus.

Birthplace: Chenameg.

Description: very tall; very thin; long sharp nose; green hair; green beard; green eyes; long arms and double-thumb fists.

Career: started life as a gardener's boy, then had to depart hastily from Chenameg. Lived as a limmer in Jone (in Selzirk) until sentenced to life as a galley slave after being caught raping a pig in a public toilet hard up by Ol Ilkeen. Liberated after five years when Abousir Belench, an Orfus pirate, dared a dawn raid on Lake Ouija. Thereafter prospered as a blade of the free marauders.

Status: Orfus pirate; cave owner and slave owner on Knock (largest of the Greater Teeth); ship's captain.

Ship: the eponymous *Walrus*.

"This good place," said Whale Mike.

He held aloft his lantern. By its yellow light Drake saw three stoves, heaped sacks of charcoal, a huge hammock in which a horse could have slept in comfort, casks which presumably held ale or stuff yet stronger, hams hanging from hooks, strings of onions, boxes, crates, ropes, a heap of timber and a rack of tools.

"This place is huge," said Drake.

"Well, I not small," said Whale Mike. "This ship, she was *Gol-sa-danjerk*. That her name. Now she *Walrus*. This was hold, but I make changes."

"Have you always been ship's cook?" said Drake.

"Oh, I many things. But I good cook. I do that long time. Cook always eat well—that not so?"

And Whale Mike laughed.

Drake looked at the array of tools—hammers, mallets, chisels, awls, a variety of saws and other implements.

"Who owns these tools?" he said.

"Oh, they mine," said Whale Mike. "I carpenter. I do many jobs. We not got big crew. Some of these jokers, they not so smart. They not understand carpentry stuff. But that no problem for me. I smart joker."

Drake thought Whale Mike's estimate of his own intelligence was, to say the least, optimistic. But he did not say so. Instead, he said:

"Thanks for bringing me aboard."

"That okay. You my friend. That not so?"

"Definitely so," said Drake.

"You sleep," said Whale Mike. "You get rest, talk good tomorrow. You have to talk fast, that not so?"

"Very much so," said Drake.

Wondering how he would fare on the morrow when he had to face the Walrus.

"Under there," said Mike, pointing to the shadows beneath a rack of hams. "There sacks. That comfortable, that not so?"

"Surely so," said Drake.

And crawled in under the hams, and laid himself down on the sacks. It was comfortable enough. He stared up at the bulky shadows of the hams. How well were they secured? It would only need one to fall . . .

Whale Mike began to hum a happy song. What was he doing? He was sitting on a coil of rope, working on something. What? Ah . . . the tooth of a whale.

The lamplight gleamed on Whale Mike's sallow, swollen face. No ears. Was it cold, having no ears? What was it like to be stupid?

A shadow jumped onto Mike's shoulder. A ghost? A demon? No—a cat. Slowly, Mike turned his head until he was staring the cat in the face. Was he going to bite it? Eat it? Tear it apart and gullet it raw?

As Drake watched, Whale Mike kissed the cat. That settled it! The man had to be soft in the head!

Footsteps thumped over the deck above. A voice called down the companion-way which led down into Mike's all-purpose cabin.

"Mike?"

"Yo!" said Whale Mike.

"We're bringing the water aboard. Can you give us a hand?"

"No problem," said Mike.

The cat jumped from Mike's shoulder as he stood up. Though he was more than twice Drake's height, his head did not quite touch the ceiling. He must be very important to rate so much space. But of course—when there was a battle to fight, or an anchor to pull up, or a monster to kill, Mike must be the ideal person for the job.

When Mike left, Drake began to explore. The cat—perhaps it was psychic—immediately hid.

"Puss puss puss," said Drake, trying to tempt the cat into kicking range.

The cat prudently stayed hidden.

Drake examined Whale Mike's scrimshaw. The whale's tooth was being worked into a representation of the writhing bodies of a dozen naked men and women. It was obscene. Fascinating. And very delicate. Done with great skill.

"He must've stolen it off someone," muttered Drake. "I hope he doesn't wreck it trying to finish it."

He heard heavy feet and profound thumps up above as barrels of water were brought on board the *Walrus*.

"I must be crazy," said Drake.

Stowing away on the *Walrus* at risk to his life—yes,

maybe he was a bit crazy. How would he explain himself to Slagger Mulps on the morrow? Perhaps he could ask Whale Mike to hide him here for the entire voyage. No. That was too dangerous. Mike might get sick. Or die. Or fall overboard. Or the ship might flood. Or sink. There were a thousand ways in which he might be discovered.

He would have to win over Slagger Mulps. Get protection from Mulps. But . . . what if Mulps once again handed him over to Atsimo Andranovory? Drake remembered Andranovory demanding a suck. Having him hauled into the sky on a rope. Remembered his long agony as he swung from the end of the rope . . .

Drake poked amongst the casks and cases, looking for something to eat. The air was heavy with the smells of onions, smoked seal, hams, dried fish, herbs and spices. He cut himself a bit of ham. Chewed it slowly.

Perhaps Tor means to get me killed.

King Tor was strange. Sometimes he seemed to have perfect confidence in Drake. Other times, doubt ruled his mind, demanding that he set Drake tests.

Maybe he's one of these people who's not sure of his own mind. Maybe. He's not much of a leader, perhaps.

Jon Arabin never changed his mind like that. Yet, even so, circumstances had brought about a change in Drake's relationship to Arabin. There was every chance he might end up as an enemy.

And Slagger Mulps . . . man, I've got to make friends with him. Now that's crazy. Wild.

Yet not impossible.

The lamp flickered, and went out. Drake stood in the darkness, trying to orientate himself. Where was his bed of sacks? With hands extended like the feelers of an insect, he began to explore the night. Barked his shin against a crate, and hissed. Something hissed back at him. What?! Oh—only the cat, of course . . .

Drake found the mess of sacking where he was to sleep, and settled himself down. Brooding on his future. To become a friend of the Walrus? An enemy of the Warwolf? It was all too possible.

He lamented the instability of human relationships. Life would be so much easier—and so much safer!—if one kept the same set of friends and enemies for a lifetime. At least he could be sure of Heth.

Blood, that's the stuff. Family.

He bitterly regretted being parted from Heth. He wished he was back on the good ship *Tarik*. Would he see Heth again? Why, of course he would. At journey's end . . .

Drake heard a thump of boots coming down the companionway. Suppressed laughter. Who was that? Not Whale Mike, by the sound of it. Smaller people. Two of them? Maybe three.

"Gragh!" said a gutteral voice.

Then hawked. Then spat.

"The grimby cludge keeps a lantern lit, mostly."

"Andranovory?"

"We'll manage."

A tight, confident, well-controlled voice. Clear. Sharp. Ish Ulpin? Possibly . . .

Sounds of collision.

"Mal skok!"

A chuckle.

"Oh, An'vory, man! You're so much fun when you're happy!"

That, unless Drake was very much mistaken, was Bucks Cat.

"Here's a cask," said Andranovory.

Muffled fumbling. Happy splash of liquor running into a crock? Bottle? Mug?

"A toast . . ."

A clink of mugs in the night.

"A toast to what?" said Bucks Cat.

"Victory," said Ish Ulpin. "We'll play this Menator's games for now, but when we're ready . . ."

"Throats open," said Andranovory.

"Oh man, oh yes," crooned Bucks Cat. "I'll slice the little one myself. Imagine—him as king?"

All three laughed.

Drake began to sweat. He knew exactly who those three were talking of. Just his luck! He remembered how Bucks Cat and Ish Ulpin had forced him into the sea, a horizon away from Stokos. They were true killers. They would abolish him without a moment's hesitation. If they caught him.

Someone touched Drake. On the buttock. He almost screamed. Then realized it was only the cat. The cat began to crawl onto him. Ugh! What's the difference between a cat and a rat? More fur and a thicker tail, that's all . . .

"There must be stronger stuff than this," said Andranovory.

"Sure to be," agreed Ish Ulpin. "But we'd have Ockle's luck searching by dark."

Ockle? Ockle's luck? What the hell did that mean?

"Oh man," said Bucks Cat, with a chuckle. "I thought you would've worked it out by now. The stove's still hot. One is, anyway."

Movements in the dark. What? Hiss of—pain? Anger? Someone finding a hot stove the hard way, maybe. Sound of cloth tearing. For what? To wrap around fingers for handling a hot stove, perhaps. Protest of metal. A stove door? Opening? Gleam of red coals. Flare of flame. A twist of cloth bursting into light. Flames rising to reveal—

"The lantern," said Ish Ulpin, as the twist of cloth in Andranovory's fingers burnt itself out. "I've found the lantern. Give me another light, I'll get it going."

The lantern would reveal everything.

Drake grabbed the cat—which could not have been psychic after all, or it would have understood its danger.

He flung it through the night.

A scream. A shout. A prolonged yowl. A furious seething hissing and spitting. Several obscenities.

"Hey!" said a familiar voice. "What going on down there?"

"We're just leaving," said Ish Ulpin.

"Oh, you leave all right," said Whale Mike, clambering down into his private domain. "Who this?"

"Let go of my beard!"

"Oh! An'vory! Walrus, he speak to you three times

already. You drink too much. You drinking now, that not so? You stay out of here. And what you do my cat? She not happy. I hear that."

"Your crazy cat attacked us," said Ish Ulpin.

"That not so," said Whale Mike. "That cat not stupid. You step on her, maybe. Who this?"

"This is me, Bucks Cat."

"So you've got all three names now," said Ish Ulpin. "There's nobody else down here. If you want to play the child and tell the Walrus, you know what names to give him."

"This not child stuff," said Whale Mike. "This serious. There only so much food, only so much drink. We got long way travel."

"You talk like a sheep-shagging schoolmaster," grumbled Andranovory.

"What you know about schoolmaster?" said Whale Mike. "You from Lorp. They got no school there. This serious matter."

"Okay, okay, it's serious," said Bucks Cat. "We got the message. How about letting go before you break my arm?"

Mike obliged.

Ish Ulpin, Bucks Cat and Andranovory quit the hold in a hurry. Whale Mike lit the lantern from the stove, nodded at Drake, then tempted his cat into his arms for comfort.

"What they do to my cat?" he said.

"Andranovory got hold of it," said Drake. "He was going to push it into the stove."

"Oh, that just like An'vory," said Whale Mike. "He not so good. He drink too much."

"But the cat fought back," said Drake. "Man, that's a beautiful cat you got there. I love cats."

"That good," said Whale Mike, stroking his cat and kissing it once again. "That mean you smart. All smartest people like cats. Not like dogs. That dog, that stupid animal for stupid people."

"Verily," said Drake.

And, before he slept, he helped Mike slander dogs

at length and in detail, and praise the race of cats to the very heavens.

At dawn, the *Walrus* put to sea. Toward noon, Drake stumbled onto the deck in company with Whale Mike. The Greaters were but a smudge on the far horizon. But, much closer, visible in every detail, was the unlovely Andranovory.

Who gaped at Drake.

"Hoy," said Andranovory. "That's—that's—"

"This my friend," said Whale Mike. "We go see Slagger Mulps."

"You—I—hey, boys!—there's—"

Andranovory swayed on his feet. He was drunk—hence his incoherence. There were ragged red cat-scratches on his right-hand cheek.

"Come," said Whale Mike. "This way. Come."

And Drake, very shortly, was shown into the captain's cabin, which was set in the poop of the ship.

On the *Walrus* everything was dirt, filth and disorder. Her crew was not even in the habit of coiling ropes properly. The captain's cabin made a startling contrast to this general disorder, for it was neat, whitewashed and scrupulously clean. That Drake noted at first glance.

Then noted no more, for a sickening fear seized his senses, and he thought he would faint. His heart leaped like a frog trying to jump out of a water-barrel. His mouth tasted worse than it had when he had addressed the pirate's general assembly. He felt giddy.

Slagger Mulps sat behind a desk where charts were spread out. He looked at Drake, then looked at Whale Mike.

"Leave," said Mulps.

"Okay," said Mike cheerfully.

And withdrew his head and shoulders from the cabin, closing the door after him. Mulps watched Drake, saying nothing.

"I—I suppose you want some explanation, man," said Drake. "It was Menator sent me here. Lord Menator. He dared me aboard. I think he means to kill me by this dare. I think he means to kill you, too, aye, given time. Kill both of us. That's what this voyage is for. To be the death of us."

"Why should he do that?" said Mulps.

"For empire, man," said Drake. "We're both lusting after leadership. Aye. Me to be king on Stokos. You to be admiral. That speaks ambition. Hence danger to Menator. He knows as much, so kills while the killing's easy."

"I've thought as much myself," said Slagger Mulps. "The danger is to both of us. That makes us friends—perhaps. But . . . if you will sail with us, then you must swear yourself to secrecy."

"Secrecy?" said Drake. "About what?"

"Why, about the secrets of this voyage south, of course."

Drake thought. He had little choice. But—

"I'll not swear," said Drake, "if your secret touches on the lives of King Tor or Jon Arabin."

"I thought you enemy with Arabin," said Mulps. "You spoke against his speaking at assembly. That hardly leaves you friends."

"Aye," said Drake, "but we've not yet come to blood. I want to leave some hope between us for the future."

Slagger Mulps considered this.

There was much bad blood between Walrus and Warwolf. Could he afford to have Drake Douay aboard when Drake still had residual loyalties to Jon Arabin?

"What would happen," said Slagger Mulps, "if it came to a fight between Walrus and Warwolf?"

"Man," said Drake, "that's nothing to do with the voyage here. All I ask is to share your dangers, aye. At journey's end, I'll be back with King Tor. I'll say good words for you with the king. That's worth having, isn't it?

"But I'll say this—I've got some fair thoughts left for Jon Arabin, but I've none left for one of his crew. That's Sully Yot I'm talking of, the wart-faced one. He tried to kill me—killed my dog while trying. He turned against my king. That's treason, man—to speak against the king.

"While shouting filth, he said hard words about another fellow I could mention. Not to be too subtle—yourself. Man, I know I spoke bad words in a worse temper when we first met. But since then—you know yourself I've sworn to marry Tor's daughter. I've pledged my flesh to an ogre. Whatever words I've spoken, I've no prejudice. My actions prove that.

"Man, I say this—you're as human as any other. Aye. Green hair, green eyes, the works. And I say this, too—if by one chance in a thousand million we clashed with Arabin on this voyage south, I'd fight for you and yours. At least till Sully Yot was dead at my feet."

Drake ended his speech. Stood there. Trembling. Slagger Mulps stared at him. Broken loose by the ship's motion, a slim piece of sharpened graphite slid across the charts, fell off the table and broke as it hit the whitewashed floorboards.

"You speak well," said the Walrus. "I tell you this. The secrets of this voyage touch not on the lives of Arabin or Tor. So swear to keep our secrets."

Drake consented to place his hand on a virgin's breech-cloth—an article which Slagger Mulps regarded with superstitious awe—and swear himself to secrecy.

"Now all can be revealed," said Mulps.

Drake bated his breath and waited for revelation.

"We run to Narba first," said Mulps, in a conspiratorial whisper, "there to sell a cargo of seal furs."

Drake snorted, and breathed easy.

"Is that all? Is that the ship's secret?"

"If it were known we were engaged in honest trade," said Slagger Mulps, "it would shame us for thrice five generations."

"Aagh, Jon Arabin runs for pearls, and makes no secret of it," said Drake.

"Yes—but the pearl run reeks of danger. That's different from braining baby seals and ripping their bodies naked."

There was, Drake had to admit, a difference. But he

could not help thinking the secret ridiculous. Surely there was more to know.

"What special plan have you for capturing a monster?" said Drake. "They're fearsome fierce, these monsters of the Swarms."

"Courage will serve us," said the Walrus, blandly. "We'll have men killed in the attempt, doubtless, but we'll win through in the end. You'll have your opportunity to cover yourself with glory."

Drake, at that moment, would rather have covered himself with a blanket. He had not slept very well the night before. As nervous tension ebbed away, he felt weak with fatigue. But there was one thing he needed before he could really relax: a safe-conduct pass or its equivalent.

"Man," said Drake, "as maybe you know, I've tangled with a few of your men in the past. They're more likely enemies than friends. So I'd like you to get your men to swear to my safety."

The Walrus laughed.

"I'm not your mother," he said. "You'll have to stand up for yourself. That's a test of your worth—to make peace with the crew."

"Another test!" said Drake. "These tests will be the death of me!"

"Mayhap," said Slagger Mulps. "But that's your problem, not mine. Now out—I've got to chart the details of our trip to the terror-lands, aye, the terror-lands of the Deep South."

Out on deck, Drake looked around for Whale Mike, who was nowhere in sight. In his hold, doubtless. Drake hastened there—but was intercepted by Andranovory.

"You!" said Andranovory, swaying.

"What do you want?" said Drake.

"This!" said Andranovory.

And punched Drake in the gut. Hard. Drake took the blow easily, and punched back. His fist sank into Andranovory's belly as if the man were made of marshmallow. The black-bearded brute grunted in surprise, and sat down on the deck in a hurry.

Drake was about to put in the boot when he saw he had spectators. Bucks Cat and Ish Ulpin were watching him.

"Drake!" said Ish Ulpin. "Over here!"

Reluctantly, Drake went toward Ish Ulpin. The lean, pale man looked as if he never saw the sun. Big black Bucks Cat stood beside him, grinning as merrily as the knife-scar on his throat.

"Whale Mike tells us you're sailing south with us," said Ish Ulpin.

"Aye," said Drake.

"We hear tell that the Warwolf tangled with Swarms and such on her last voyage south."

"That's true," said Drake.

"Then sit down, man. Take a seat—aye, there on the rope, that's comfortable enough. Tell us about it."

"And why would you want to hear?" said Drake.

"Why? Well, we'll be tangling with such soon enough, won't we now? It's nice to know what we're up against."

Drake realized that Ish Ulpin really did want to know. On inquiry, he found that nobody aboard had been further south than Narba. The waters of the Drangsturm Gulf were, to the crew of the *Walrus*, largely an unknown quantity. So Drake settled himself, and began to tell his tales.

Drake was a good story-teller. Under pressure—with a life to lose if he failed to interest—he became an even better story-teller. Others of the crew gathered round to listen.

One tale led to another, and thus, as the days went by and the ship cruised steadily south, Drake got to know the crew well. Bucks Cat—who proved to be boisterous, good-humored, intelligent, and perhaps the most competent sailor aboard. Ish Ulpin—who, as Drake had suspected, was a dangerous man, too careless with himself to value others.

Tiki Slooze, a feeble, querulous man who reminded Drake of Jez Glane. Rolf Thelemite, an intense character who claimed to be from the fabled islands of Rovac (claiming, too, that his blade was firelight steel from Stokos—though he never let anyone see it). Simp Fiche, whom Drake had met before—he lived for rape and torture.

And others. Ching Quail, Trudy Haze, Praul Galana, Morton Seligman, and close to three dozen more.

Drake found himself popular. Except with Andranovory. But that drunken bully was scarcely loved by the rest of the crew. Nor was he a match for Drake in a fight.

So far, so good. But what happens when we get to the terror-lands? What happens when we get to the Deep South?

Drake expected at least some men to jump ship when the *Walrus* reached Narba. But, though all the men got shore leave, none fled. All, it seemed, were ready to brave the terrors of the lands beyond Drangsturm. To do battle with the monsters of the Swarms. To dare the horrors of creatures worse than nightmare.

And Drake?

He was fearful. Yet was proud. And fiercely ambitious. He had to survive this test. To win the hand of King Tor's daughter. To win the throne of Stokos. And prove himself equal to the heroes of the *Walrus*, who faced the prospect of absolute horror with calm— almost, indeed, with indifference. Who would have thought they could be so brave?

They're brave, perhaps, because they think no Swarms exist. Aye. But they do. I've seen them, clear enough. The Neversh—chest to chest. And the other monsters, crowded on the shore.

As the *Walrus* braved south, Drake developed a nervous tic. He slept poorly—woken often by nightmares. He got acid indigestion. Under the stress of fear, he became irritable, short-tempered. Then at last, by night, he saw the flames of Drangsturm reflected from clouds on the horizon.

Come morning, the *Walrus* anchored by a small offshore island. A day's sailing—or less—would take them to the shores of terror beyond the protection of Drangsturm.

"What island be this?" said Drake, staring at massive low-slung buildings on the island.

"This is Burntos," said Bucks Cat. "Landguard troopers are garrisoned here. They hold the island against any monsters of the Swarms which fly this way."

"It's a low, barren, ugly place," said Drake. "What do we want here? We've food, water—everything but women. Have they a brothel ashore?"

"Not that I know of," said Bucks Cat. "But with luck, they've got a monster they can sell us."

"Sell us?" said Drake.

"But of course. We need a monster to show to Menator."

"But—but—but we—"

Bucks Cat slapped his thighs, and threw back his head and laughed uproariously.

"Oh man!" he said. "Are you innocent!"

"What's the joke?" called Praul Galana.

"This young hero here," said Bucks Cat, pointing at Drake, "he really thought we were going to hunt the terror-lands for a monster. Oh man! That's rich!"

Bucks Cat laughed till tears ran down his face, and others laughed with him.

"But," said Drake, starting to get angry, "the day we left Knock, I spoke with the Walrus. He told me true that we were hunting monsters. Aye. He spoke of death and glory."

"Well, man," said Bucks Cat, recovering himself a little, "he likes a joke too."

"How did he know of this Burntos place since he's never been this far south?" said Drake.

"Oh, we hear of this place in Narba," said Bucks Cat. "It's no secret."

"Well," said Drake, "if you never planned to dare the terror-lands—how come everyone was so hot to hear my stories?"

"Why, for you tell a good tale, and that's reason enough," said Bucks Cat. "Besides—we're not home dry, are we? If there's no monster for sale ashore, maybe we will have to hunt one.''

And, thought Drake, maybe, even if they secured a monster, bad weather would see the *Walrus* endure some adventures as wild as those which had befallen the *Warwolf* in the waters of the Drangsturm Gulf. Though he had to admit the weather had treated them fair enough so far—the *Walrus* had had dry skies, hot days and favorable breezes ever since leaving Narba.

Drake was on the first boat which went ashore to Burntos. The others with him were Bucks Cat, Ish Ulpin and Slagger Mulps. In honor of the occasion, the Walrus had shed his sealskins, and had dressed himself in silken robes embroidered with astrological symbols. Drake thought he looked daft—but the green-haired man was obviously very pleased with his appearance.

The boat scraped against stones.

Drake jumped into the sea, and helped haul the boat ashore. A single old man was picking his way along the shore, gathering driftwood. Otherwise, nobody was in sight.

"Hey," yelled Bucks Cat. "You got any monsters for sale?"

The old man paid them no attention.

"Maybe he speaks no Galish," said Drake.

"Maybe he's deaf," said Slagger Mulps.

"Maybe," said Ish Ulpin, "selling monsters is against his religion."

"Chel!" said Slagger Mulps, meaning "avanti!"

And led the way toward the low-slung buildings. Massive buildings. Built of huge stone. Slit windows. Strange, narrow doors.

"Drake," said Slagger Mulps, as they came on the nearest building. "Inside. Sus it out."

Drake, with some trepidation, ventured through the narrow door. He found himself in a long, cool, gloomy room. On either side were rows of pallets. On every pallet were identical stacks of folded blankets and folded clothing. At the end of every pallet was a pair of boots. A little dust danced in the shafts of sunlight come through the slit windows.

Drake went outside.

"Man," he said, "this place is for sleeping."

They explored further. Finally, surmounting a small rise, they gained a view of a huge paved square. Half a thousand men—or were they statues?—were standing there. In rows. Spears in hand. Utterly motionless.

"Here's our people," said Slagger Mulps.

"A parade," said Ish Ulpin.

And spat, in disgust.

"What are they doing?" said Drake, bewildered.

"Soldier stuff," said Bucks Cat. "This is—this is kind of holy. I've seen it in the Rice Empire. We'd better stay clear till they've finished."

Drake watched.

Nothing happened.

Were these real soldiers? Impossible! Surely they were statues.

Then—

One of the spearmen went down. Crunch. Falling flat on his face on the paving stones. He stayed down. Nobody spoke. Nobody moved. Shadows shifted slightly as the sun eased itself across the sky. A fly settled on Drake's face and began to feed. He slapped it. Then was embarrassed by the noise. But nobody looked in his direction. A tiny dust-devil whirled across the courtyard, then faded to nothing.

The soldier who had collapsed was still flat on his face.

"Craziness," muttered Drake.

And turned away from the parade. If everyone on the island was going to stand paralyzed in the sun, maybe this was a good time to go looting. He wandered off amongst the buildings, peering through the slit windows. Eventually, he came upon a kitchen. Inside were upward of a dozen women, hard at work preparing corn and potatoes for a meal.

"Flesh is hope," said Drake.

And dared himself to the door of the kitchen. Being as attractive to women as he was, with any luck he could chat up one of the ladies and get in a quick one before the soldiers finished their daft parade.

As Drake stepped into the kitchen, the women stopped their work and looked at him. A couple spoke to each other in some foreign tongue, then giggled.

"Hi, girls," said Drake.

As he spoke, a tall red-skinned woman came out of a side room, her arms white to the elbows with flour. She glanced at him indifferently. Was it . . . Zanya? Yes! It was Zanya!

"Zanya!" yelled Drake.

She looked at him again, shrugged, picked up a rolling pin and retreated into the room she had come from. Drake hastened to the door of that room. And was met by a brawny purple-skinned man who was not entirely a stranger.

"Greetings, Oronoko," said Drake.

"Fa'unu a'fukutu," said Oronoko.

And scooped up Drake, carried him to the door of the kitchen, and threw him outside in the dust.

17

Zanya Kliedervaust: priestess of the Orgy God of the Ebrell Islands; renounced her position and formally abjured alcohol, sexual intercourse, sunbathing, the eating of sweet things and all the other pleasures of the flesh after seeing her mother, father, brothers, sisters, cousins, uncles and aunts die of venereal disease, alcoholism and obesity.

Quit Ebrell and traveled west in the company of Prince Oronoko of Parengarenga, questing for purity. Arriving at Cam on the xebec which rescued Drake Douay from the Central Ocean, sought work at the leprosarium.

Was converted to the worship of the Flame by Gouda Muck; became an apostle for Goudanism and left Stokos to preach the Faith in foreign parts.

The wizard Miphon was cleaning a xyster when Drake Douay was brought into his clinic by one of the women from the kitchen. Blood was dripping through Drake's blond hair and sleeking down his weather-battered sealskins. A drop of dark red fell soundlessly to the cool gray flagstones of the floor.

"Welcome," said Miphon, speaking in the Galish Trading Tongue; and, smiling to reinforce his welcome, he laid the xyster down on a well-scrubbed table of sun-bleached driftwood.

"*Tach smin hebalar,*" said the woman from the kitchen.

Miphon, who did not speak her language, waved her out of the clinic. Choosing to misinterpret this gesture, she seated herself in one of the clinic's five bamboo chairs.

"Out!" said Miphon sharply, clapping his hands twice.

Reluctantly, curiosity unappeased, the woman left. Miphon pointed Drake to a bamboo chair, which creaked as the bloodstained pirate sat.

"Have you been fighting?" said Miphon.

"Nay, man," said Drake, looking around the clinic. His gaze lingered on a remarkable array of delicate steel instruments—hooks, blades, tweezers, spikes and probes. With luck, he could slip a couple into his pockets. Whale Mike might like them for his scrimshaw work. "I was testing my powers of flight when my wings fell off."

"How far did you fall?"

"Halfway from here to Narba."

"And you hit your head. What's the last thing you remember?"

"Why, the death and resurrection of the star-dragon Bel. A whore who turned into a horse as she came. Five dozen oysters dancing drunk in the streets of Narba. Why all these daft questions, man? I'm bleeding to death!"

"A little blood," said Miphon, "goes a long way. Tell me—what do you see?"

So saying, the green-eyed wizard held up three fingers.

"See?" said Drake. "Why, I see a blind rat mating with a seagull. Aye, and four blue lepers hauling a giant cockroach backward up a mountain."

"That's near enough," said Miphon.

And, turning away, the wizard began to wash his hands in a bowl of water. Drake smelt something strange. What? Oh—soap. He remembered his sister using it a couple of times. Swift and sly, he reached out, grabbed a couple of tiny cutlass-curved blades from a nearby bench and slipped them into a pocket.

Miphon, shaking the water off his hands, turned back to Drake and began examining his scalp.

"I'm the wizard Miphon," he said, easing Drake's hair this way and that as he explored the damage.

"I know that," said Drake. "We met on Stokos. Ow! That's sore! Hey—you really don't remember me?"

"In busy times," said Miphon, "I can see upward of a hundred people a day. How can I remember all of them?"

Drake felt insulted.

"But I was special!" he said. "You told me a tale about you being a mind-reading elf. You gave me a philtre to cure myself of love."

"Oh," said Miphon, pouring water from a ewer into a clean bowl. "Oh . . . I remember now." He balanced the bowl on the back of Drake's chair, the hard edge of it against the nape of Drake's neck. "Lean back. I've got to wash the blood out of your hair. Hmmm . . . I remember you all right. But the name . . . that escapes me."

"I'm Arabin lol Arabin," said Drake.

The lie came easily. It was a smart move. Who knows? This wizard could have converted to Gouda Muck's cult. He might be one of those who was hunting Drake, thinking him the son of the demon Hagon.

"Arabin lol Arabin," said Miphon. "I won't forget you when we meet again."

"We'll never meet again."

"It's a small world," said Miphon. "Hmmm . . . this looks good . . . the bleeding's more or less stopped."

"That's health for you," said Drake.

Miphon laid aside the bowl of blood-misted water. Taking a sharp blade, the wizard began to shave hairs on either side of the gash where Drake's scalp had been torn as his head hit the ground when the purple-skinned Oronoko threw him out of the kitchen.

"How much hair are you cutting away?" said Drake in alarm.

"Does it matter?" said Miphon.

"It matters much! Man, there's a beautiful red-breasted woman I want to make. I can hardly court her if you've cut me half bald."

"You're after the Kliedervaust woman?" said Miphon.

"That's her."

Miphon laughed.

"You won't get her," he said. "She's in the clutches of faith. She preaches the defiance of the flesh."

"And what do you think of that?"

"Flesh," said Miphon, "is that through which we live. No flesh, no life. Of course, flesh is but the medium in which our existence finds expression. The expression of existence is not to be confounded with the inspiration of that expression. Mere hedonism would exult the medium at the expense of the inspiration. So perhaps her doctrine is a necessary corrective for certain trends."

"Man," said Drake, "you make a right proper tangle out of simple language. What did you mean to say? That you agree with this talk of purity? Or that you don't?"

"That I both do and don't," said Miphon. "It is both wise and foolish. Something, perhaps, could be made of it in time."

"There speaks a wizard! Hey man—just how much hair are you cutting?"

"Just enough so I've clear skin to sew up this gash with cat-gut."

"Cat-gut!" said Drake, scandalized. "The gut of a cat? In me? Man, that's disgusting. Why not dog-gut?"

"Because the dog," said Miphon, "is a foul, polluted animal which has nothing to offer the healing arts." He took up a curved needle from which a length of dark thread trailed. "This thread is the cat-gut. Hold still, now. This will hurt."

And he began to sew up the gash in Drake's scalp. With cat-gut.

"Man," said Drake, doing his best to ignore the bright silver pain of the needle, "tell me. How long has this Zanya Kliedervaust been here?"

"I've been here ninety days myself," said Miphon, tying a knot. "She was here when I came. She preaches nightly to the troops."

"Surely she must have preached to every soldier here long, long ago."

"The garrison," said Miphon, guiding pain again into Drake's flesh, "rotates. These soldiers are from the Landguard of the Confederation of Wizards. They guard the castles ranged along Drangsturm; they patrol the shores; they hunt down the few stray monsters which escape our scrutiny and flee to the mountains north of the flame trench."

"They work . . . for wizards, then?"

"Yes."

"So you, as a wizard," said Drake, "do you command this island?"

"I've a commander's power on Burntos if I choose to use it," said Miphon. "I've a warrant from the Confederation to prove that power. But I've more sense to try that power except under the pressure of necessity."

"Man, power is for using. That's half the fun of having it."

Miphon made no reply to that, but finished off his sewing. Drake had got blood on his hands. Miphon sponged the blood away. Which was unnecessary, but . . . nice. The touch of his firm, competent hands was . . . strangely relaxing.

Having cleaned the hands, Miphon started removing bloodstains from Drake's sealskins.

"No need for that," said Drake, standing. "The job's done, aye. Done well. I'll be off now. Oh—but I'll need a bandage for my head first."

"For what do you need a bandage?" said Miphon. "Fresh air and sunlight, that's the thing. Whoever does the doctoring on your ship, get them to check your wound daily."

"How do you know of the ship?" said Drake.

"Do you think your vessel stands invisible?" said Miphon. "This island is well-watched, though you may not have noticed the watchers. Everyone on Burntos knew of your ship long, long before your rowing boat ever reached for the shore."

"Why so much effort spent watching?" said Drake.

"Because experience tells us it's necessary," said Miphon.

And, dipping a hand into the pocket where Drake had hidden the blades he had filched off the bench, Miphon recovered his cutlery.

"Man!" said Drake, wide-eyed with wonder. "How did those fancy little blades get in there? They must be magic, man! They must have flown through the air and slipped themselves inside there, for I swear I never touched them."

"I'd find it hard to believe you," said Miphon, "except that I did indeed see them fly through the air and hide themselves in your pocket."

"How did you manage to see that, when you were looking the other way at the time?"

"Being of elven descent," said Miphon dryly, "I have invisible eyes in the back of my head."

On leaving Miphon's clinic, Drake thought about going back to the kitchen. No! Not a good idea! He had no chance against Oronoko. Better to wait till evening came. Then Zanya would preach. He would watch. Look for an opportunity.

A little time, that's all I need. A little time alone with the woman. Man, when she knows I've been chosen as the next king on Stokos, she'll be hot to have me. Surely.

One thing was for certain: he was not leaving Burntos without Zanya. But for the moment . . .

Find the Walrus. Aye. He'll be wondering where I've got to.

The sun was well up. The island was baking. Oven-dry. Wet patches of mirage shimmered on the barren rock.

How do soldiers survive?

Drake tried to imagine a soldier's life. Day after day on this lifeless rock. The inhuman discipline of parades. Inescapable routines. Not much variety in the food, either, if what he'd seen in the kitchen was anything to go by.

He saw, in the distance, a few stray figures standing beside a long, low, isolated building. His comrades? Only one way to find out . . .

On closing the distance, Drake found his captain in conversation with two officers of the Landguard, who looked very smart indeed in their skyblue uniforms and their red leather open-weave sandals. Drake wondered what chance he had of stealing one of those uniforms. It would look real good on him, once the useless height had been cut out of it.

Slagger Mulps did not bother to greet Drake. He was talking money. His double-thumbed fists gesticulated as he emphasized his points.

"Where's the others?" said Drake.

Mulps did not condescend to notice him, but continued talking. His hands squeezed air, chopped it, shaped, thrusted and sliced. A dance of digital articulation, a counterpoint to his voice.

". . . must understand our funds are not unlimited. I'm working under strict limitations, as I'm only an agent for a foreign buyer; I've got scant discretionary powers. You've already heard my uppermost offer."

Man, friend Walrus is talking slick today! How came he by such slickness? Maybe he's a king in exile. Aye, Like King Tor. Like Menator, too. So many kings! A plague of kings . . .

"You must be getting a commission," said one of the officers. "If you really want to close the deal, perhaps you'll have to sacrifice a few percentage points of that commission. Because what you call your uppermost offer is in fact—and I'm sure you're aware of the fact—close to farcical. Our product is unique. You can't buy it elsewhere."

"Yes," said Mulps. "But demand is minimal. That colors the case somewhat, does it not?"

Drake, losing interest in this dickering, wandered round the windowless building. He found a huge iron-studded sliding door at its southern end. Strange. He kicked it. The door rattled slightly. Then shook with a thunderous crash, as if a giant had kicked back from within. Startled, Drake leapt back.

"Who's there?" he said.

No answer.

He continued his circumnavigation of the building. Right down at the northern end he found a slim doorway leading into the gloom.

Dare I? I'm Drake Douay. Of course I dare!

He went through the door, and found a narrow passage which twisted left, then right, then left again, before opening into a small room lit by a slim overhead lightshaft. Bucks Cat and Ish Ulpin were there, down on their hands and knees staring into what looked like a giant mousehole.

"Hi," said Drake. "What're you looking at?"

"A monster," said Bucks Cat.

"Let's see," said Drake, and knelt down in front of the hole, which was large enough for him to have crawled through had he wanted to.

He found himself looking into a long hall, dimly lit by overhead lightshafts. Something was in there. What? He saw a gleam of something cool white, like ivory. A tusk? A feeding spike! There was a Neversh in there. Drake's knees began to ache from kneeling on the stone, but he did not rise. He was fascinated.

"Amazing," he said. "How did they get it in there?"

"The Neversh flew to the island," said Ish Ulpin. "It found all meat fled within the stone. Seeking flesh, it went through the only door—then some hero closed the door and trapped it."

"But why would a Neversh go into this—this trap if there was no meat within."

"Oh, there was meat," said Ish Ulpin. "It's done like this. A few people stand by the large doorway to tempt the Neversh inside. Then they flee to this end of the building and escape through the bolthole which you're looking at."

"Man," said Drake, with a shudder, "they'd need to be heroes indeed to risk a face-to-face with a brute like that. I'm glad I'm not such a hero."

"Of course you're such a hero," said Ish Ulpin.

And he and Bucks Cat grabbed Drake. They forced him into the bolthole.

"Yaaa!" screamed Drake, struggling, bruising his shoulders on the walls of the giant mousehole.

The monster within stirred to life. Its wings beat, battering against the low stone roof. Its eight crocodile-sprawling feet tore screams of protest from rock floor. Suddenly, Ish Ulpin and Bucks Cat stopped pushing. Drake thrust himself back. And felt something snag his arm.

"It's got me!" he screamed.

The Neversh had spiked his right arm with the tip of one of its grapple-hooks.

"Help!" screamed Drake. "It's dragging me in!"

"We've got you!" yelled Bucks Cat, hauling on Drake's legs.

Drake felt his hands, greased with sweat, slide over the smooth stones of the mousehole as the Neversh dragged him toward his doom. Then agonizing pain ripped through his right arm. The grapple-hook had torn free. Pulled by Bucks Cat and Ish Ulpin, Drake shot out of the mousehole like a burst of water exploding out of a blowhole.

The three pirates collapsed in a heap on the floor. There was a hideous sound of ripping rock as the monster tried to tear its way through to the flesh which had just escaped. Drake got to his feet. He shambled through the dark, twisting exitway, colliding off first one wall then another.

A slash-sharp swash of sunlight. A giddy horizon. Swaying. The ground, buckling underfoot. Breath quick, heart quick. Quick to bursting. Glanced at the sun. White. Swaying. The sea was shuddering. The ground rocked underfoot.

"I can't come right!" he cried.

Tried to walk. Staggered, drunk, as the earth buckled. The ground split black in front of him. He screamed. The crack in the rock sprinted toward him. He jumped. Legs wide apart. The widening crack raced between his legs. Then slammed shut. Opened. Slammed. Opened. Slammed. Opened.

Drake jumped sideways. Tried to run. Fell. Saw Bucks Cat weaving from side to side, his black face shining with sweat and sunlight. Saw Ish Ulpin, the tall pale man floundering, grasping at air.

Am I mad?

The ground rocked again. Then steadied. Drake heard waves thrashing against the shore. Someone wailing. He got to his knees, breathed dust, coughed, sneezed. A distant shout. His torn right arm. Vivid red. Blood. Gore. Deep. Sweat dripped from his forehead in heavy drops. Running as free as blood.

"Man!" said Bucks Cat. "Oh man . . ."

Drake stood, slowly. There were gaping cracks in the building which held the Neversh. The monster was scrabbling fiercely within. Ish Ulpin clapped a hand on Drake's shoulder.

"You all right?" he said.

"I live," said Drake. "But, man, we'd better get out of here before that monster tries something else. It's powerful fierce, man!"

Bucks Cat hooted with laughter. And Ish Ulpin said, with unwonted gentleness:

"It wasn't the monster which shook the world. It was an earthquake."

"Earthquake?" said Drake.

"Aye," said Ish Ulpin. "Have you never been in an earthquake before?"

"This was my first," said Drake. "What makes these earthquake things?"

"War waged by demon-gods in the halls of hell," said Ish Ulpin. "That's what makes earthquakes, or so I've been told. The monster's a lesser danger—and we'll have no more trouble from it till we try to put it on our ship."

"How did you do this?" said the wizard Miphon, examining Drake's torn forearm.

"Man, I was stroking a tabby cat when the vicious little hussy scratched me."

"I suppose you pulled its tail," said Miphon, deadpan, clearing away some of the weltering blood with a moist sponge.

"Man," said Drake, in alarm, peering into the gaping gash, "there's the end of a tendon! I've cut a tendon! Man, I'm crippled for life!"

"Don't worry about that tendon there," said Miphon, touching the offending article with the tip of a probe. "That's surplus to requirements. We haven't used that for millions of years."

"Then when did we use it?"

"At an earlier stage in our evolution. Humans were fish once, then lizards."

"A likely story!" said Drake.

"More likely than some of those you tell," said Miphon. "I'll put some internal sutures in here."

"More cat-gut?"

"It's the only thing to use," said Miphon. "It'll dissolve within the wound when its job's done."

And he began to sew.

"I hope these stitches work better than your magic," said Drake.

"What magic is that?" said Miphon.

"Why, that magic philtre you sold me, to cure me of love when I first fell for the fair Zanya Kliedervaust."

"Ah, that," said Miphon. "I remember the philtre. But as for this business of selling it . . . as I remember, it was a gift freely given."

"Aye. Given free, since worthless. Man, that was no love-cure. That was an aphrodisiac! It set me lusting like an octopus."

"Did you use the philtre by moonlight, as directed?" said Miphon. "Did you kiss the ground to invoke her power?"

"Why, no, but—"

"True wizards never embellish magic with useless ceremony," said Miphon. "Every instruction must be followed if you wish for success."

"Oh," said Drake. "Now I understand. How about

some magic to help me out with my lady? I didn't do too well on our first encounter."

"How," said Miphon, swabbing the wound, "did you approach the lady?"

"I jumped on top of her," said Drake.

"That wasn't very nice!"

"Man, that's what women are made for."

"Have you asked a woman about that?"

"What would you know about it? You're a virgin."

"Whatever I am," said Miphon, "I can tell you this. Young Zanya has been through hard times."

"How would you know?"

"She speaks with me here on occasions," said Miphon. "I cannot tell you details, for that would be unethical. But I can tell you that. She is deeply suspicious of men and their motives. With good reason. If you would win her, then you must give her reason to trust you."

"How can I do that when she's crazy on faith?"

"Her faith," said Miphon, digging in with a needle, "is at least in part a source of reassurance. If you can give her such, then the faith may . . . it may, perhaps, accommodate the flesh."

"Give me a potion to make her love me," said Drake.

"There is," said Miphon, "no such potion. Magic is better at destruction than at building."

"Magic built the flame trench Drangsturm, did it not?" said Drake.

"It did indeed. But the flame trench is itself an instrument of destruction. All it creates is violence—a violence which divides the north of Argan from the terror-lands of the Deep South."

"Man," said Drake, "I've been thinking about that flame trench. That earthquake thing we had just now, could such rip Drangsturm into halves? Could it tear rock so wild that the Swarms found a way north?"

"Drangsturm is indeed vulnerable to earthquake," said Miphon gravely. "And, indeed, to other dangers. That is why the castles of the Confederation stand guard, with the Landguard to support them. But . . .

don't worry too much. Drangsturm has protected the north for the last four thousand years, ever since the end of the Long War."

"The Long War? I've heard rumors of such. Was it wizards and heroes, as they say?"

"It was before my time," said Miphon. "But there was indeed an Alliance of wizards and heroes. They fought the Swarms and threw them back to the Deep South."

"So . . . if the Swarms came north again, they could be beaten back."

"The Alliance," said Miphon, "had use of ancient weapons which were destroyed by their employment. None such remains to us—therefore, we could not be certain of a second victory."

"You talk of nonsense," said Drake. "There's no weapon you can only use once. A weapon lasts near enough to forever, aye, any swordsmith will tell you that."

"A burning arrow is a weapon, is it not?" said Miphon. "And how many times can you use a burning arrow?"

"Seventy-five thousand," said Drake, promptly.

"You've got a quick wit," said Miphon. "Your voice will serve you well in love and war, if you cultivate it. Remember that, when you court the lady Kliedervaust."

Evening. Mosquito dance. Standing on the stony beach by an open fire, Zanya Kliedervaust preached to a scattering of soldiers. The purple-skinned Oronoko squatted at her feet, a cudgel in his hands. There was, in consequence, no heckling. Drake hung back in the shadows, reluctant to risk the wrath of Oronoko. He was slightly weak from blood-loss, and definitely in no state for fighting.

She was talking of things he had heard before from Gouda Muck and Sully Yot. Talking of purity. Abstinence. Denial.

"How far away is the moon?" she said.

"Further than I can throw an apple," volunteered one of the soldiers.

Zanya took a few moments to make sense of that. Her Galish had improved, but it seemed she still found swift speech hard to follow.

"Yes," she said, at length. "It is further than we could throw an apple. But things lie hidden within the dark well within a stone's-throw. For dark hides. Dark conceals. Dark entangles. It is light which reveals. Light which clarifies. Light which makes possible. Fire is light. Light is fire.

"In darkness is secrecy. Secrecy is darkness. Which among you has not a secret which is shameful? Which amongst you could stand bare in truth like the purity of those higher fires, the sun and moon? Yield to the Flame, and the Flame will burn you clean, yea, and you too will stand naked to the eye of truth yet unashamed."

Thus she spoke.

But there was no fervor in her speech. She was tired. Weary from a long day in the kitchen. She had labored many days without a break. Each evening she had preached, mouthing the words so many times they had almost lost their meanings. She spoke by rote.

Drake saw she was so fatigued, so hollow, so worn by routine, that she herself had almost ceased to live. What lived in her was habit. She had become a puppet animated by the alien routines imposed upon her by Gouda Muck. The old man's words had replaced her will. It was not her voice which spoke, but his. She had become his creature.

Watching, listening, Drake had an unfamiliar intimation of evil. Muck had made Zanya into a weapon. A burning arrow. How many times can a burning arrow be used? She was destroying herself. Nothing on this island of barren rock and inhuman routine would nourish or cherish her. Muck had made her his voice and had sent her into the world to be ruined.

Drake felt sorry for her.

Creeping away into the dark, he made his plans. It was all very well for the wizard Miphon to suggest that he win Zanya by fair speech, but that was impossible. Oronoko would let him nowhere near the woman.

She would have to be kidnapped. For her own good, mind! Hauled aboard the *Walrus*. Then tamed at leisure. Taught to be a woman again. It might take some doing. But Drake Douay was equal to the task . . .

"What's she to you?" said Slagger Mulps. "You're in lust? You want her as your fancy woman, perhaps? Do you think I'll risk my ship for the whim of your cock?"

"Man, she's nothing to me," said Drake, hastily. "But she's lots to Muck. She's his disciple, don't you know. Man, we can use her as hostage. A pawn in the war for Stokos."

"Hmmm," said the Walrus, running his hand through his green beard as he thought. "Perhaps King Tor would like to lay hands on Muck's disciple."

"Oh, I don't think that's really a good idea," said Drake. "Man, he might rip her in half."

"Who cares if he does?" said Mulps. "She's nothing to you, is she? The boys can have fun with her first, before we hand her over. An'vory likes red meat. I've a taste for such myself, if it comes to that."

Atsimo Andranovory was indeed pleased when he heard about Drake's scheme to kidnap Zanya Kliedervaust.

"So the young pup's good for something after all," he growled.

"It's a great idea, man," said Bucks Cat, slapping Drake on the back.

"Aye," said Ish Ulpin, squeezing his shoulder. "We'll let you lead the rape pack when we get the wench aboard."

And Simp Fiche drooled.

Three days went by.

Drake endured agonies of horror, guilt and despair. His brilliant idea had gone wrong. But he should have known what would happen! He knew what pirates were like. Aye. And what would happen now? Why, Zanya would be likely ripped apart. And would welcome such death, having wished herself dead many times before.

He had planned for things to be so nice. Her and him, alone in the dark together. Him explaining things to her, reasonable like. Maybe a little force, if strictly necessary—but just by way of introduction, to show her what delights were available.

The reality . . .

The reality which threatened was like something out of nightmare. A long slow voyage of repeated rape, with death at the hands of King Tor at the end of it.

What should he do?

Warn Zanya? No—that would ruin his chances with the woman for a lifetime.

Talk to Mulps, perhaps? Explain that the woman was rightly his, was special, was—well, his true love. No. That would never work. He was only aboard the *Walrus* on sufferance. Mulps would scarcely take kindly to have Drake Douay dictate his behavior.

Then—

What if he betrayed Slagger Mulps? Narked to the soldiers, so an ambush was waiting when the raiding party came to kidnap Zanya? What then? The ship would be seized, Slagger Mulps and crew would be killed or enslaved, and Drake would have a lot of explaining to do if he ever got back to the Greaters.

Besides . . .

Whale Mike was his friend, was he not? Yes. The dumb yellow-faced earless monster was, when all was said and done, a true friend. Drake could scarcely sacrifice the ship—if only for the sake of Whale Mike. And Rolf Thelemite—he wasn't bad. You could even say a thing or two for Bucks Cat and Ish Ulpin, despite their murderous taste in practical jokes.

"The thing to do," said Drake to Drake, as he walked alone on the shores of Burntos, "would be to kidnap Zanya on my own. Aye. Then get her to the mainland in a boat."

Possible. But—where would they go? Where would they hide if Oronoko came hunting for them? If he killed his purple-skinned rival, how would the Landguard take that? How much of the mainland was under Landguard jurisdiction?

There were too many unknowns.

Besides—he had to go back to the Greaters. Otherwise he would never win King Tor's confidence. He would never get to marry Tor's ogre daughter, Hilda, or be crowned king of Stokos. He would never again see his brother Heth. Or Jon Arabin. Or any of his friends from the *Warwolf*.

"There has to be another way," said Drake.

On the afternoon of the third day, as the captive Neversh, weakened by lack of water, was dragged in chains to the ship, Drake realized what he had to do. He went to see the wizard Miphon.

"Man," said Drake, "you've a commander's powers on Burntos, isn't that so?"

"I said as much," said Miphon. "I meant as much."

"Then, man . . . I don't know how to put this. It's delicate, see. Some friends of mine . . . well, they've let high-spirits carry them away. You know how men talk, aye, wild-like, boasting of things round booze. Well, these friends . . . usually their crazy thinking wears off with the drink. But this time, it stuck. I'm . . . these are my friends, man. I don't want to betray them. But I thought maybe—maybe you could help them keep from trouble. By removing temptation. Subtle, like. Without saying anything about anyone informing or such."

"You can trust me," said Miphon. "Speak."

When Drake got back to the *Walrus*, the Neversh was being folded in thirds to make it fit into the treasure hold, which lay forward of the hold in which Whale Mike lived, cooked and slept. Ish Ulpin winked at Drake, and Bucks Cat slapped him on the back.

"Tonight's the night, eh?" said Bucks Cat.

"For sure," said Drake.

"You'll be coming with us, I suppose," said Ish Ulpin casually.

Drake's first thought was to answer "no." But he couldn't do that—it would arouse suspicion.

"Of course," he said, voice cool as a wet skinned squid hauled writhing from the blue-black depths of the sea.

So that was it. He was committed ashore on tonight's raiding expedition to capture Zanya Kliedervaust. What if the wizard Miphon had failed to exile Zanya and Oronoko, as he had promised? What if they were delayed in getting off the island? Worse—what if Miphon, despite his promises, had arranged for an ambush?

Tonight, man, perhaps tonight you die.

18

Miphon: a slender green-eyed travelling healer; a minor wizard of the order of Nin, who sometimes claims to be of elven descent.

It was night. The *Walrus* was ready to sail. Only one task remained: to kidnap Zanya Kliedervaust. The raiding party gathered on deck under a gloomy sky pitted by stars. Off to the south, some scanty cloud reflected the glowering red blaze of distant Drangsturm. The raiders were hot, fierce, excited.

"Action!" said Rolf Thelemite. "That's the thing! Blood and steel!"

"Don't be too keen to start anything," warned Praul Galana. "The odds are against us if it comes to a fight."

"Man," said Drake, "I'm in no state for fighting—or anything else. Better I stay on the ship."

His right arm, torn by a captive Neversh then sewn up by the wizard Miphon, was still in a sling. It ached incessantly; it had been keeping him awake at night.

"You're coming," said Slagger Mulps. "Get in the boat!"

"What boat?" said Drake, peering down at the darkened sea.

"It's down there," said Mulps. "At the end of the rope ladder."

"How do I climb down with only one arm?"

"Climb! Or I'll give you the problem of climbing with none!"

With difficulty, Drake descended the rope ladder to the raiding boat. Its crew was Slagger Mulps, Ish Ulpin, Bucks Cat, Rolf Thelemite, Praul Galana and Atsimo Andranovory.

"Who's been drinking?" said Drake, smelling alcohol.

"We're all stone-sober here," said Andranovory, his brewery breath washing over Drake's face as he spoke.

"Man, you're half-way pickled," said Drake in disgust. "This is a nice start! And where's Whale Mike? Eh?"

"What would we want with him?" said Ish Ulpin, as the boat got underway.

"He's muscle," said Drake, nursing his sore arm as best he could as dark-tongued waves nagged at the boat. "A monster like that—he must be something terrible in a fight."

"Let's not be calling our good friend a monster," said Slagger Mulps, a note of warning in his voice.

"Whatever we call him," said Drake, "he's built for battle."

"Oh yes," said Bucks Cat, with a chuckle. "Built beautiful. But soft as a sea slug. He never likes to kill. Not like some of us."

Silence, then, as the rowers pulled for the shore. Burntos, by night, was an ominous, almost featureless mass. Far off down the shore, a bonfire was burning. Praul Galana, having shaped words to his satisfaction, spoke:

"Whale Mike, he's a good cook and a better carpenter, aye, but he hates to hurt people. So he's not much good in a fight, not unless he's really stirred up. Anyway, there'll be no fighting tonight."

"Not unless our drunken friend starts some trouble for us," said Drake savagely.

"Who you calling drunk?" said Andranovory.

"Hush, An'vory," said Mulps. "Drake—keep your mouth shut. Your every word shows you shit-scared frightened."

"I'm not frightened," said Drake, trying to keep his voice steady. "But there's a right way to do things, aye. Like doing some thinking. Aye. And leaving our drunks behind."

"Yes," said Rolf Thelemite, "and keeping our voices down so we can't be heard more than twenty leagues away."

Drake realized then that his voice had been getting louder and louder as he spoke. He was about to explain the reasons for his anger further, then thought better of it and shut his mouth firmly.

"Ship oars," said Mulps.

Wet and dripping, the oars came into the boat. Pain jolted Drake's arm as the boat rocked as men jumped to the knee-deep water.

"Come, man," said Rolf Thelemite, helping Drake into the cold of the sea.

Drake trudged out of the water while the others hauled the boat onto the beach, where the sea's shuzzle and hiss, snake-sibilant, wracked shingle back. Onshore, the sullen shapes of massive buildings loomed dark against dark.

"Take her up," said Mulps.

And, boots sliding on the sea-wet stones, the men took the boat higher, scraping her underside against the shingle. They made so much noise about it that Drake wanted to scream. He controlled himself. Then could not help but say:

"Man, we'll be a long time getting the boat afloat if we have to leave in a hurry."

"Fear gives strength," said Rolf Thelemite. "If we run from war we'll shove it to sea so quick you'd think it flew."

By starlight they trooped in single file through the warm night, led by Praul Galana, who had been kept busy over the last couple of days locating Zanya's sleeping quarters and planning the best attack route.

What would the pirates do when they found Zanya gone? Would they suspect that Drake was responsible for thwarting their kidnap raid?

Man, maybe I should run.

It would be easy enough to slip away into the dark, that was for sure. But what then? He would be left stranded on Burntos, amongst strangers, hundreds of leagues from his hopes of a royal marriage and the throne of Stokos.

We've got to see this through, man. It's the only way.

From a building which must have been a bar came raucous sounds of singing; obviously soldiers were, in the time-honored fashion, relieving the tedium of garrison duty by getting drunk. Praul Galana halted the pirates beside a long, low, dark, silent building, not far from the bar.

"We're here," said Galana.

"What place is this?" said Rolf Thelemite.

"The kitchen," said Galana. "The red-skinned wench sleeps in a small room right at the end."

The door to the kitchen was locked, but the pirates broke it down. The noise was covered by the uproar from the bar. If Drake was any judge, then a brawl was in progress in that place of entertainment.

The raiders ventured into the bowel-black dark of the kitchen, picking their way between tables and benches. Inside, it was quiet; the noise from the bar was almost inaudible.

"Booze here," said Andranovory.

"Then leave it alone," said Mulps, shortly.

"As you will," said Andranovory.

"Here's the door," said Praul Galana.

The raiders gathered at the door to Zanya's quarters.

"Drake," said Slagger Mulps. "You go first."

"What?" said Drake. "Me with my torn arm and all? Man, that woman's a right handful. Let An'vory go. An'vory? Where are you? Boozing, is it?"

"Never you mind about An'vory," said Mulps. "in you go."

So saying, Mulps opened the door. Squealing, something flung itself forward.

"Ahyak Rovac!" screamed Rolf Thelemite.

There was a crash as Thelemite's blade, sweeping through the dark, chopped into a stack of dirty saucepans. Pirates swore, shouted and grappled with their enemy.

"It's a pig!" said Galana.

"Man," said Drake, sounding aggrieved, "you must've led us to the wrong door."

"There was only the one," said Galana.

While they were still arguing about it, Drake heard someone approaching.

"Hush!" he said.

"What?" said Andranovory.

"Gram grup!" said Mulps sharply.

Andranovory got the message, and was silent, as were the other pirates. Waiting. Breathing the dark. Listening. Hearing . . . footsteps outside. A voice talking quick and low. Someone answering. Trampling boots entering the kitchen. A sliver of wood breaking free with a twang as someone pried it away from the wreckage of the kitchen door.

The boots halted.

If Drake was any judge, at least half a dozen strangers had entered the kitchen. Demon's luck—they had no lantern! That was something to be thankful for.

"Epigrow manact agrama!" said a loud, curt voice.

Drake wanted to sneeze. He had to sneeze! He grabbed his nose, contorted his face, scrunched his chin down against his chest—and just managed to kill the sneeze.

"Lupopt elestag oxybund, morasuf aparsing," said the same harsh voice which had spoken previously.

Drake listened.

Did he imagine it? Or did he heard Mulps breathing? He was, surely, imagining it. He could scarcely hear his own breathing.

"We know you're in here, whoever you are," said the harsh voice, switching to the Galish Trading Tongue. "Surrender yourselves!"

Silence.

Then someone burped.

"Seize him!"

Boots clattered over the stone floor as half a dozen

soldiers homed in on the burp. There was a brief scuffle.

"Hey!" said Andranovory, slurring the word in a way which made it obvious he had been drinking.

As the soldiers hustled Andranovory away, the pirates followed as quiet as they could, slipping out into the night.

"Well," muttered Mulps, when they were in the clear: "That's An'vory done for."

"No!" protested Rolf Thelemite. "We can't leave a comrade!"

And, drawing his sword, Rolf Thelemite charged after Andranovory's captors, screaming a challenge as he went:

"Ahyak Rovac!"

Voices cried in alarm. Blade clashed against blade in the dark of the night.

"We're with you!" roared Praul Galana.

Slagger Mulps swore, then joined the fray himself.

Drake, ruled by his concern for his injured arm, backed off into the night. He bumped into someone, who grabbed his sore arm.

"Gaaa!" screamed Drake.

And won his freedom with a head-butt and a savage elbow blow. Then he backed off some more. He saw lanterns weaving through the night, drawn to the noise of combat. Then he heard the voice of Slagger Mulps raised above the confusion:

"With me, boys! Time to go!"

Feet pounded away into the night. Drake followed as best he could. Tripped. Fell. Rose. Blundered. Which way was which? He was disorientated. Lost. Some lanterns were coming his way. He scuttled away into the dark. Was brought up hard by a building. Sat down, half stunned.

More lanterns!

Help!

Drake eased himself along the side of the building until he found a doorway. He slipped inside. The building felt empty. He risked snapping his fingers, once. The crisp sound confirmed his impression of any empty, unfurnished building. He sat down in the shadows, and began to wait. Near dawn, light began to filter through gaping cracks in the roof and walls of the building Drake was sheltering in, and he understood the reason for its emptiness—it had been abandoned because of earthquake damage.

Shivering, he slipped outside.

A glance at the sea told him the *Walrus* was gone. He was marooned on Burntos! What now? Hide? Impossible. Swim for the shore? It was too far—particularly with his wounded arm. There was only one choice: to surrender.

Accordingly, Drake surrendered himself to the wizard Miphon, who took the matter lightly.

"While there was a brawl last night," said the wizard, "nobody was hurt. Your ship has escaped with all her crew, so there'll be no trials or other nonsense."

"What happens to me, then?"

"Why, you'll stay with me till you leave the island. I should by rights report to the Confederation regarding our earthquake damage. So . . . tomorrow will be as good a time as any. We'll leave Burntos then."

"Where going?" said Drake.

"Why, to Drangsturm, of course," said Miphon. "To the Castle of Controlling Power. That's where the Confederation's based."

"So that leaves me with a day to look around the island," said Drake, thinking he had better make the best possible use of this one last chance to hunt down Zanya Kliedervaust and make her his.

"Not so!" said Miphon. "It gives you a day to scrub out my clinic."

"Man," said Drake, "you can't make me work! I'm injured! I was wounded by that Neversh, you sewed up the wound yourself."

"You're fit enough for trouble," said Miphon, "so you're fit enough to work."

Drake was determined not to work—but the green-eyed wizard proved to have an unexpected amount of willpower. Much sweeping, cleaning, scrubbing and polishing later, night came. And, after night, the morrow.

After a lean breakfast of rice and fish, Drake and Miphon went and sought out the cutter which was going to take them to the mainland. She was commanded by a jowly, sunburnt boatman, and had a crew of three. The only passengers were Miphon, Drake, Zanya Kliedervaust and Prince Oronoko.

"Zanya!" said Drake, delighted to see his truly beloved once again. "You!"

"Who is he?" said Zanya, who was naturally suspicious of the rough-dressed fair-haired fellow who was gawking at her charms with such obvious lust. "What's he doing here?"

"You'd better ask him that yourself," said Miphon.

Oronoko, speaking softly in his native Frangoni, asked Zanya if the youth with the degenerate eyes was troubling her, and if she wanted him broken in half. Zanya, speaking in the same Frangoni, reminded Oronoko that the pure did not kill. Except, replied Oronoko, when confronted with the impure.

"Have you two begun to argue theology?" said Miphon, who had a fair command of Frangoni himself. "If so, get in the boat—we can't wait thrice seven years for your wills to come to agreement."

All embarked on the cutter, which set sail. As the frail vessel ghosted along, Drake listened to Zanya's incomprehensible argument with Oronoko, and watched some soldiers who were beginning to demolish an earthquake-damaged building. Unless he was mistaken, it was the same structure which had housed the captive Neversh before the unfortunate brute was loaded with chains and hauled aboard the *Walrus*.

He shuddered.

"Man," said Drake, to Miphon, "I've been thinking about this Neversh you let loose by way of trade. That's a mighty strange thing to do, isn't it?"

"Why so?" said Miphon.

"Well, I mean—wizards built Drangsturm to keep the Swarms south. Right? So why sell one of the monsters north? Surely that's as bad as breaching Drangsturm."

"If Drangsturm were breached," said Miphon, "then the Swarms would come north in their thousands. One single monster is little danger—for the Neversh, brute for brute, are weaker than dragons. Such sales give the Confederation profits. Also, they serve a wise purpose—they help remind the rest of the world what task we do here."

"Why should the world need reminding?" said Drake.

"Because," said Miphon, "since people are as they are, some refuse to believe that the Swarms exist at all. They think we fake nightmare through lies or rank exaggeration to preserve the wealth of the south of Argan for ourselves."

"I never thought such!" said Drake.

"I never said you did," said Miphon. "But there are those who believe the Confederation does not protect the north, but, instead, keeps the north in poverty by frightening honest men away from southern wealth. Ah . . . the fair lady Kliedervaust seems to have a question."

Zanya Kliedervaust did indeed have a question. Her argument with Oronoko concluded, she was ready to interrogate Drake Douay.

"Explain yourself," she said.

Drake cleared his throat noisily, hawked, then spat to the dark green sea. This was a very sticky situation. Zanya was a disciple of Gouda Muck. She believed that the infamous Drake Douay was the accursed son of Hagon. Beside her sat the formidable Oronoko, he of the purple skin and the violet eyes. And Drake was in no condition for fighting.

"My name," said Drake, "ah, that's not given lightly to strangers. But I've given it already to the wizard Miphon, aye, for I'm a friend to wizards and trust them well. So I'll give my name to you. It's Arabin. Or, to be exact, Arabin lol Arabin."

"There was a pirate named Arabin," said the jowly, sunburnt boatman who commanded the cutter. "I knew him well when I were of the Greaters. But he were black, not blond."

"Yes, well," said Drake, "that must be coincidence then. Though I've had affairs with pirates, aye, I'll not deny it."

"Affairs?" said Zanya, with an expression of disgust on her face. "Affairs of lust?"

"Nay, woman," said Drake. "Not thus but otherwise. I was a swordsmith of Stokos, where I trained under Oleg the Blademaster. He sent me to 'Marphos on a mission, aye."

"Androlmarphos," said Zanya, "is a seething brew of vices, a den of iniquity, a pit of poxed spirits and demented souls."

"Very likely," said Drake, "but I can't speak for that myself, since I never reached the place. The ship which bore me was taken by pirates."

"Yet you lived," said Zanya, her voice accusing. "You did not die in the defense of your ship against evil."

"I had no chance to die," said Drake. For I were below decks, helplessly seasick. Thus I was taken prisoner. Since then, I've slaved for the pirates as a cook's boy, working under pain of death. But now I've made my escape, and hope for gainful employment elsewhere."

Prince Oronoko addressed Zanya softly.

"We've met before, haven't we?" said Zanya.

"Tell me about it," said Drake.

"You were that demented fisherman's boy we dragged out of the sea near a horizon from Cam. That was before I'd first set foot on Stokos."

"Aye, that was me," said Drake.

"Then you came to me again," said Zanya, with undisguised anger in her voice.

"I did?" said Drake, all injured innocence.

"In the leper colony. You tried to rape me!"

This woman could obviously carry a grudge for a long time. Drake tried to think. How was he going to handle this one? He looked to the wizard Miphon for help—but that worthy was staring at a low-skimming seagull, as if in love with the thing.

"Man," said Drake, thinking quickly, "I jumped you, I'll not deny it. But I didn't get very far, did I? You punched me over something fearful."

"Failure excuses nothing," said Zanya.

"Man," said Drake, "then let the truth excuse me. It was my body which made the attempt, but not my will. For I wasn't truly myself. I was under the command of witchcraft. Someone worked the Black Arts on me."

Zanya turned to Miphon.

"Is this true?" she said.

"What?" said Miphon, jerking upright, startled, as if woken out of a dream.

"This—this pirate says it was witchcraft that made him try to rape me. Is that true?"

"That is hardly for me to say," said Miphon, blandly, "for I, as a wizard, know nothing of witchcraft."

Zanya snorted.

"Your excuse," she said to Drake, "lets you live. But don't presume that your excuse gives you permission to speak to me."

"I'll find the permission I want, in time," said Drake.

Fortunately, he said it in his native Ligin, which Zanya did not understand. She did not ask for a translation, but sat talking quietly with Oronoko as the cutter made its way south toward Drangsturm.

Near evening, after a long, hot day of idling calms and desultory breezes, the cutter landed her passengers at the western end of Drangsturm, where the awesome upthrust of the Castle of Controlling Power stood guard against the Swarms. Drake was dismayed to see that the flame trench did not run all the way to the sea. Instead, a buffer of basalt two hundred paces broad separated flame from sea.

"Man," said Drake, pointing at the bare rock, where only a low parapet protected north from south, "this is right daft, having a hole like this in our defense."

"The rocks of this fire dyke are so hot they'd explode if the cold sea touched them," explained Miphon. "Hence the plug of rock. It's a killing ground. Don't worry—little has crossed it in the last four thousand years."

And he led the way toward the nearest gate of the castle. That castle, its jumbled walls and towering spires flung upward as if at random, looked as if it had been fathered by earthquake and mothered by a bad-tempered volcano.

"Why stands the castle in such strange array?" said Drake.

"Because it was not built by human hand," said Miphon.

"How was it built then?"

"Wizards united their power to call from the ocean legion upon legion of squid and of octopus. Yea, even the might of the kraken was summoned to the building. Hence the intelligence you see in the stone is not that of mortal men."

"That's a strange way to build," said Drake.

"But a quick one," said Miphon. "The castle was built in a night. It had to be done by dark, since the creatures we worked with hate the light. That explains, you see, some of the flaws in the construction."

"Oh," said Drake.

Then stopped, pointing south.

"Look! A league south! Men!"

"Southsearchers, that's all," said Miphon. "They've started out on patrol. They march mostly by night since the Swarms sleep then. By day they shelter."

"Do the Southsearchers dare themselves that way?" said Drake, pointing westward, in the direction of Ling.

"Lands west do not concern us," said Miphon.

"Have you tried to explore those lands?"

"Why should we? There's no profit in exploration."

"Man," said Drake, "there might be cities out

there, aye, cities built of gold. Or lands of pearl diving, perhaps."

He was trying to find out whether his knowledge of the existence of Ling might have some value in the market place. His hopes were disappointed when Miphon laughed and said:

"Perhaps. But we're rich as it is, for all trade between the Inner Waters and the Drangsturm Gulf passes through the Confederation's hands. Come on, let's not stand here chattering."

"What trade is that you speak of?" said Drake.

"The trade in sponges, pearls, slaves, crocodile skin, whale oil, scrimshaw and keflo shell, amongst other things. The Galish kafilas take such north along the Salt Road, together with siege dust of wizard manufacture, and other things. And it is with the Galish that you yourself, in all probability, will soon be going."

"Soon?" said Drake.

"Depending," said Miphon, "on what the Confederation decides to do about your case."

"My case?" said Drake. "Man, what are you talking about?"

"You are, after all, a pirate," said Miphon, "or an associate of such. I bear you no will. As for the Confederation—well, we own no ships, and none of the sea reavers ventures this far south. Hence we suffer nothing from pirates. But, even so, the Confederation cannot lightly accept the presence of a lawless pirate in the heart of power."

"Man," said Drake, "I'm a very law-abiding boy! Famous for it! Man, I'm meek, mild, honest, upright, and sober as a sledgehammer. You'll get no trouble out of me."

He desperately wanted to win the trust of the wizards, so that he would be at liberty to use his wiles on Zanya Kliedervaust. But, shortly after passing through the nearest gate of the Castle of Controlling Power, Drake found himself taken in charge by some blue-uniformed Landguard troopers, and thrown into a prison cell to await the pleasure of the Confederation.